LILY RILEY

THE ASSASSIN AND THE LIBERTINE

LES DAMES DANGEREUSES

MYSTIC OWL

AN IMPRINT OF CITY OWL PRESS

This book is a work of fiction. Names, characters, places, and incidents either are products of the author's imagination or are used fictitiously. Any resemblance to actual events or locales or persons, living or dead, is entirely coincidental and not intended by the author.

THE ASSASSIN AND THE LIBERTINE
Les Dames Dangereuses, Book 1

MYSTIC OWL
A City Owl Press Imprint
www.cityowlpress.com

All Rights reserved. Except as permitted under the U.S. Copyright Act of 1976, no part of this publication may be reproduced, distributed, or transmitted in any form or by any means, or stored in a database or retrieval system, without the prior consent and permission of the publisher.

Copyright © 2021 by Lily Riley.

Cover Design by MiblArt. All stock photos licensed appropriately.

Edited by Heather McCorkle.

For information on subsidiary rights, please contact the publisher at info@cityowlpress.com.

Print Edition ISBN: 978-1-64898-089-3

Digital Edition ISBN: 978-1-64898-088-6

Printed in the United States of America

PRAISE FOR LILY RILEY

"Scandal, seduction, and supernatural secrets animate Riley's deliciously decadent debut and Les Dames Dangereuses series launch. Riley brings the heat as the erotically charged animosity between Daphne and Étienne...evolves into a genuine connection. This hits all the right notes." – *Publisher's Weekly*

For Mom.
I hope you're allowed to read romance novels in Heaven.

PROLOGUE

DAPHNE

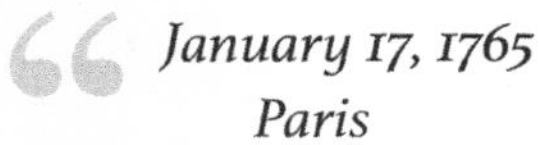

January 17, 1765
Paris

I WATCHED HIM, PATIENTLY, FROM BEHIND MY CARVED IVORY FAN. HE appeared to be a capable servant—unobtrusive, almost preternaturally aware of the needs of the duke's guests, and just on the attractive side of plain in his dark-gray livery. When he finally flicked his gaze to me, I lowered my lashes flirtatiously and drew my fan across my lips—an open invitation for a clandestine dalliance. The corner of his mouth twitched, and he nodded almost imperceptibly.

From the edge of the stifling ballroom, a gong sounded, announcing dinner. Gentlemen paired off with ladies, making their way into the dining room.

"Madame, shall we go in?"

The fat, thick-headed, wealthy lout at my elbow held out his arm. He'd been trying to monopolize my attentions all evening, despite my thinly concealed distaste. He reminded me of an overfed leech, pawing at me with his slimy, limp appendages and grinning with his yellow, toothy mouth. I covered my grimace with a wan smile.

"*Monsieur le Vicomte*," I answered. "Please, do go in and find your seat. I need a moment to refresh myself. I'll be along shortly."

The leech eyed me up and down, offering a prurient wink. Unable to suppress my disgust much longer, I turned from him before he could see my expression.

The smell of food wafted in through the open doors. I hadn't eaten all day, but truthfully, I was not hungry—for *dinner*.

I left the gilt opulence of the ballroom and made my way down a candlelit corridor, discreetly checking the rooms for errant party-goers and trysting courtiers. I required absolute solitude, and fortune appeared to be on my side tonight. The duke's Parisian town house was impressive—if a little dated with all its baroque enthusiasm—and seldom in use. Like some members of court, he lived almost year-round at Versailles. Years before, King Louis XIV's paranoia had set that precedent for the aristocracy. *If you wish to feel the warmth of the Sun King, you must remain within his orbit.*

How suffocating. I was almost glad my husband had fled to Italy in disgrace, despite him leaving me to the absent mercy of the wolves of Versailles. At least I was free to maintain my own residence—and more importantly, I was free of him. The thought of my vile, abusive husband soured my stomach.

It seemed that King Louis XV, the Beloved, had a more relaxed view of things. *But for how long,* I wondered. France was changing at the speed of infection. The king could not continue to ignore *la peste du sang* that was starting to seep through the streets of Paris. The blood plague was upon us, and I feared what was happening to the people of France.

Several doors down, I found what I was looking for—the duke's empty study. A few candles flickered inside, casting dancing shadows upon the gold brocade of the walls. Hopefully, young Giles had accepted my invitation and I wouldn't have to wait long.

I perched on the edge of the large desk, careful not to bend my panniers, and adjusted my navy skirts around me. The dark color was somewhat unfashionable this season, but I wasn't at Versailles and tonight I favored a gown that was a touch more utilitarian. The pastel palette of the court was hellacious for us more *active* members of the nobility. The stains could be murder.

Movement outside caught my eye, and I went to the window to observe. Snow had started to fall in soft, downy clumps. I watched the flakes drift gently onto the balcony terrace and smiled to myself. I flung the doors open, letting in a flurry of frigid air.

I almost didn't hear the soft click of the door closing behind me, but I'd been waiting.

Without turning, I spoke out to the snowy balcony.

"I'm so glad you came, darling Giles. I've been waiting all evening to get you alone."

Strong arms circled my waist, turning me to him and pulling me back inside the study. His eyes glittered fiercely, hungrily.

Without a word, he crushed his mouth to mine. His hands roamed my body, seeking the softness of skin beneath the silken layers of my gown.

"I don't have long," he grunted. He pushed me roughly against the wall, attempting to lift my heavy skirts.

"*Oui*, I know, *ma cher.* Neither do I." He'd found my legs beneath the copious underskirts and ran a cold hand up my thigh. I grabbed him by the shoulders and reversed our positions, pressing his body to the wall with my hips. He gasped in excitement and fumbled for the buttons of his breeches. I kissed him softly.

Dispassionately.

With him distracted, it was almost too easy for me to stab him through the heart.

He pushed me away—bewildered, pained—as smoke curled from the small wound in his chest. I slid the thin wooden stake out, wiped the blood on his livery, and tucked it back in my garter for my next assignment.

Only then did his fangs distend.

"*Putain de salope,*" he hissed. His skin turned a mottled gray, and he slumped to the floor.

I *tsked*. "Oh, Giles. How long did you think you could carry on like this—feeding your way through His Grace's housemaids? Six young girls are dead already, Giles. Six! Did you think we wouldn't notice a rotten little *sanguisuge* in our midst?"

He groaned in pain and glared at me. "You're with them, then. *The Order*. Didn't think they allowed women in."

"Yes, well, what a lesson for you to learn today. *We are everywhere*. Too bad you won't be able to share that news with your filthy parasite friends, eh?"

The dying footman rasped a laugh, coughing up a trickle of black blood that steamed in the cold room. "It won't matter if you're *everywhere*. It won't matter how many you are, how much money the aristocracy has, or how good the Order's spies are. None of it will save you from what's coming."

A chill went up my spine that had nothing to do with the snow blowing in through the open terrace doors.

"What's coming?" I demanded, leaning in.

"*La mort*."

His eyes dulled on a final exhale, and the young vampire Giles sagged against the wall. I dragged his body to the balcony and heaved it over, leaving it in the snow-dusted bushes for another agent to find and dispose of. I never asked anyone at the Order what they did with the bodies of all the vampires we dispatched. Truthfully, I couldn't bring myself to care.

After setting the room and my gown to rights, I exited the study and made my way to the dining room. I passed a note to a footman—a coded message for the Order that read *Assignment complete, target retrieval requested*—and sat next to the leech, who would no doubt boast about spending the entirety of the evening flirting with the *duchesse de Duras*, thus providing me with an unattractive, dimwitted, but unquestionable alibi.

The remainder of the evening passed as planned. Giles likely wouldn't be discovered missing until the morning, and even then, people would suspect he'd run off with one of the "missing" housemaids. Even though the job was done, a whisper of unease went through me at his dying words. I tried to dismiss it as a final attempt to frighten me or swear some kind of undead vengeance, but I didn't really believe that. Giles knew something.

Death. Death was coming.

ÉTIENNE

That Same Evening
Palace of Versailles

Just before her pleasure crested, my fangs lengthened and I nipped firmly at her thigh, drawing the blood I needed to survive. I'd waited too long to feed again, and the hunger clawed at my insides. I forced myself to take only what she could give without suffering. Fortunately, it was enough. *Barely.*

"*Très magnifique,*" she panted, reaching for me. "Now I understand what Yvette meant when she said you were a delightful beast."

The marquise giggled and sighed. I lifted my head from beneath her hideous orange skirts and grinned wolfishly at her, but the words had stung.

A delightful beast.

"What would the marquis say if he found you in bed with such a beast?"

The marquise snorted and stood from the chaise we'd been enjoying. She adjusted the bodice of her unfashionable gown and straightened the powdered mass of curls atop her head.

"He stupidly thinks I don't know about his penchant for the

servant girls. If I were interested in catching his eye, I'd just have to don some depressing brown wool and bow gracelessly before bringing him dinner."

The *marquise de Balay* was a dangerous conquest—she was fiercely intelligent, wealthy as sin, and—as a distant relation to the king—her witless husband enjoyed an impressive set of privileges at court. Her opinions formed his, and so if I needed help to sway the king's mind, I needed her manipulations at my disposal. The *marquise de Balay*, despite her unfortunate taste in clothing, was a powerful influence.

"He wouldn't be offended to find his wife *fraternizing* with a vampire?" I pressed.

She cut me a disdainful look and arched a supercilious brow. "Possibly. But you're not like the rest of them, are you? Your father was the former *vicomte de Noailles*. Even if he was disgraced, you come from noble blood. The rest of those plague bloodsuckers are all peasants, aren't they? Farmers. The *poor.* You're the king's appointed emissary and advisor on how to deal with the *sanguisuge* menace. You aren't really one of them," she sniffed.

She left off, *you aren't really one of us either,* but the words seemed to hang in the air, nonetheless.

Anger burned through me at her distaste toward my family and my kind. With a flare of disappointment, I realized she wouldn't be willing to join my cause. *Vampire rights* were a joke to the over-primped peacocks mincing through the halls of Versailles. She didn't see the tension stretching between the classes—the danger we were all in as the impoverished vampire populace grew. She, like the rest of the court, was blind to the true threats to France. Terror would not come from the battles fought on foreign soil. It would come from within.

And nobody would heed my warnings.

"Besides, the Order will certainly stop them," she offered casually. She was replacing her diamond chandelier earrings—fat, colorless stones that winked in the candlelight.

I stilled.

"What do you know of the Order? I always heard they were a myth." I laughed. I knew they were *not* a myth, but it surprised me to hear the marquise discuss them so openly.

She shrugged. "Only the gossip, I suppose. Surely you've heard?"

"I haven't." I *had.* They'd sent two assassins after me already—one disguised as a cut-purse and the other masquerading as a drunken brawler in one of my favorite taverns. I'd smelled the lies on their clothes before they'd had the chance to stake me. At least their blood had sustained me for a while. The intervening years of poverty between my father's disgrace and my royal appointment had taught me that much—*waste not, want not.*

The marquise waved her hand dismissively. "You know, they've finally gotten sensible about the plague and excommunicated the members of the Order from the lower classes. I mean, if it's only the weakest peasants that suffer the infection, it's right that the stronger elites should decide what to do about it. We have the intelligence, the funds, the breeding. Don't expect me to listen to some dirt farmer about how to save my noble soul."

She giggled venomously. My stomach churned with her snobbish blood. I swallowed my disgust and nodded.

"We should return to the party," I said. "I believe I'm wanted for a card game."

The marquise smiled, but it didn't quite reach her eyes.

"Thank you for the distraction," she said as she turned for the door. "It was rather...*animal.*"

Instead of following her back to the party, I summoned my carriage and returned to my château. Only when I was safely ensconced in my familial home did I allow myself the pleasure of venting my rage by smashing my fist through the wall.

She didn't care. None of them did. Despite my attempts to stop it—to prevent it from happening, nobody else could see what was coming. And many of them would pay with their lives.

1

DAPHNE

" *September 22, 1765*
Palace of Versailles

I HURRIED THROUGH THE HALL OF MIRRORS AS FAST AS I COULD, which was—unfortunately—not *at all* fast. It wasn't the formal court dress that hindered my progress—I could run from one end of Paris to the other in stays and panniers if I needed to. Nor was it the flintlock pistol, wooden stakes, and throwing knives strapped to my thighs. My stilted pace was all for the sake of propriety. My need to blend in with the other titled ladies of court was distinctly at odds with my real reason for attending the king's party tonight. Running through the palace was not exactly the kind of behavior one would expect from one of the most notable duchesses of the *tonne*.

Since I wanted to avoid unnecessary notice, *hurrying* was well out of the question, and the best I could manage was an ambitious glide—possibly an assertive shuffle. I regretted the decision to delay my arrival until after sunset. I should have given myself more time to make a proper appearance, circulate with the other members of court, and then ready myself to lay my deadly trap.

I paused in front of my reflection in the mirrored wall that led to the courtyard outside, frowning at the beads of sweat on my forehead. Darting a look at the stoic footmen in the room, I blotted my face with my handkerchief and opened my fan to cool myself.

Breathe, Daphne. It's almost over. Soon, there will be justice for Jeanne—and vengeance for Michel.

I caught the eye of one of the servants and raised my chin haughtily, as if to say, *Of course I wasn't sweating! Duchesses do not sweat. They glow with the pleasure and privilege of nobility*—even though none would dare make such a comment to me, particularly the footmen in the palace of Louis the Beloved.

As I made my way into the courtyard, a squeal erupted from behind a tower of champagne glasses.

"Daphne, *chérie*! You're finally here! I've been waiting for over an hour already."

I smiled at the mass of swirling blue silk careening toward me. My cousin, Charlotte, did not have the same issues moving in haste, though she had never been one to care much for propriety.

She kissed my cheeks, and I embraced her tightly. After my brother, Michel, was murdered, Charlotte was my only remaining blood relative. She'd stayed with me for a time after his death, fussing over me in a way that helped to distract me from the abyss of my grief. She had become like a sister to me.

"*Bonsoir*, Charlotte! I see you have swindled your husband for another new gown."

"That's not all," Charlotte giggled, gesturing gracefully at the diamond choker around her neck.

I furrowed my brow. "Oh no! What's Philippe done now?"

Charlotte snorted with laughter, attracting the attention of several courtiers. Clearly, she'd had one too many glasses of champagne while waiting for my arrival.

"It's an 'I miss you' gift he brought back from Venice. It's beautiful, no?"

She twirled around, stumbling slightly. My arm shot out swiftly to steady her.

"Why, *Duchesse de Duras*, what *exceptional* reflexes you have," came a silky voice at my ear. I dropped Charlotte's arm and whirled around. The man seemed to have materialized from a pool of darkness at the edge of the garden. Despite the unseasonable warmth of the evening, I shivered.

He was clad in a rich, emerald-green coat that made his striking hazel eyes appear strangely golden—almost wolf-like. They burned with heated intensity beneath long, feathery lashes. His sharp cheekbones, chiseled jaw, and elegant patrician nose looked like they'd inspired features of Michelangelo's *David*, but his full lips hinted at something much less divine and far more sinful. Unlike the other nobles, he wore no wig but had powdered his own dark locks in a soft gray and had tied them back at the nape of his neck with a ribbon. Beneath the well-cut coat, expertly tied cravat, and indecently tight breeches, I knew he was a powerfully built man. His laid-back elegance and rakish charm did little to disguise the coiled tension and corded muscle of a predator.

I schooled my features in a mask of bland entitlement to cover my apprehension.

I'd been shadowing him whenever he turned up at court, usually when he was waiting for his weekly audiences with the king. Most of the *dames* and *demoiselles* at Versailles refused to acknowledge him publicly, but their lustful gazes followed his every move. I supposed I could admit—entirely dispassionately, of course—that he was attractive in an obvious sort of way. It didn't change the fact that beneath the seductive exterior lurked a bloodsucking villain—a selfish parasite of sheer malevolence. In fact, it made his allure that much more disturbing.

He bowed stiffly and smiled, his eyes never leaving mine. Despite my outward detachment, my heart pounded. Tonight was the night I'd been waiting for—the assignment that I hoped would further my position within the Order. I'd had to work twice as hard as the male agents—first, to prove I was worthy to join the Order in the first place, and then to be taken seriously enough to earn assignments that were more than just gossip-collecting intelligence work. Tonight, I'd banish any lingering doubts for good.

Realizing I'd yet to formally acknowledge the man before me, I inclined my head. "I don't believe we've been introduced, monsieur."

His strange eyes glittered, assessing. "Oh, but I'm sure we have, madame. You do not remember? It was perhaps a year ago, but I remember you, of course." One corner of his mouth kicked up in a suggestive grin.

I did not return his smile.

"Étienne de Noailles, vampire emissary to His Majesty," he said, executing another bow.

He left out *disgraced former vicomte*, *legendary rake*, *outspoken bourgeoisie sympathizer*, and—if my sources within the Order were correct—*cold-blooded murderer of Jeanne Antoinette, Madame de Pompadour*.

"Monsieur de Noailles," I returned. A tense moment passed between us, like a bowstring pulled taut.

Then, unfazed by my cold address, he turned to greet Charlotte. The flirtatious greeting he issued my cousin was nauseating in its effusiveness. I watched him carefully, trying to decide if he really was as dangerous as the Order affirmed or if he was simply the rutting beast the women of court believed, driven entirely by his libido. Either way, his very presence unsettled me.

"*Comtesse de Brionne*, you look resplendent this evening! Did you know that sapphire blue is my second favorite color?"

"And what, *Monsieur l'Émissaire*, is your first favorite color?" Charlotte tittered.

"Perhaps it is a mystery," he said with a wink. "Or perhaps it is the lovely pink of your blush."

I suppressed a gag at Charlotte's breathy giggle and playful slap. I had strict orders to dispense with Noailles covertly, so I couldn't just stake him here in the middle of the party—despite being sorely tempted. I'd lure him away from everyone—definitely away from Charlotte. The hedge maze in the back of the grounds was the perfect spot.

In the corner of my eye, I caught Charlotte's husband, Philippe, *comte de Brionne*, beckoning me over to a large potted palm. He'd helped convince the Order to train me as an agent—their first and only woman, I might add—in exchange for my permission to let him court Charlotte. The arrangement suited all three of us. Philippe was tall and plain, but he had always been friendly to me and kind to Charlotte. At any rate, he was less of a scoundrel than my own villainous husband, which meant Charlotte would be protected from the things I'd already had to endure. If I could shield her, at least, I might be able to convince myself that my marriage to the *duc de Duras* had been worth something.

I frowned at my melancholy memories and then at Charlotte's outrageous flirtation with Noailles. Not bothering to make my excuses, I turned on my heel and made for Philippe.

"An 'I miss you' gift of diamonds? Really, Philippe?" I teased.

Philippe winced. "The Order is sending me to London for another three months. I haven't told her yet. I meant to tell her when I gave her the necklace, but she assumed it was for my last trip to Venice."

He pulled me back behind the large palms, safely obscuring us from the view of the other guests.

I looked back at Charlotte and Noailles, still engrossed in each other's company. "Perhaps she needs some looking after—or your company, at least. You could take her with you."

Philippe shook his head. "No. It will be difficult enough for me, and soon it will be nearly impossible. The king is considering closing the borders to stop the spread of the blood plague."

"Close the borders! Around all of France?"

He motioned for me to keep my voice down and looked around.

"Be silent, Daphne. Very few at court know, and the king harbors no delusions that the act will go over well."

"But the plague is already here!" I argued. "What good will closing the borders do? And how will he enforce it with most of the army and resources depleted by his petty foreign skirmishes?"

Philippe shrugged. "The king is—shall we say—concerned. The latest reports indicate that it's more than just grubbing peasants being infected. The plague is starting to sweep through the bourgeoisie. Vampire numbers keep growing, Daphne, and no one knows what to do about it."

"Other than the Order," I said dutifully. The Order—a long-shadowed assembly of powerful individuals (some say descended from Templar Knights) had been convening on the matter since the first cases of plague had appeared in France a few years ago. They'd taken a stand against the virulent disease, determined to protect the people of France at any cost.

"Yes, naturally." Philippe nodded. "The emissary isn't really helping matters either. Instead of trying to find ways to safeguard the uninfected, he keeps insisting that we address the needs of the *sanguisuges* first. As if *vampire rights* would save the rest of us from such damnation. It'll be better for all of us when his influence has been tempered." At his last words, he eyed me meaningfully.

The news was grim. I looked toward the hedge maze, trying to find my focus.

"I'm sorry to tell you all of this tonight. I know you've other important things on your mind," Philippe said, taking my hand and holding it between his. I flinched and pulled away.

He frowned behind a pink wash of embarrassment.

"I'm sorry. I didn't mean— It's just that ever since Henri, you know..." I faltered.

He held up his hand to stay my explanation. "Please. Don't think on it. We all knew what kind of a man Henri was when you married him. For that matter, we all knew you were fragile—in a delicate position—"

My cheeks reddened with the unintended insult, but he blustered on. "And, of course, I don't fault you for that. I only wish you would've let me—us—help you more. But I suppose now his absence is something of a blessing, is it not?"

"From the Depraved Duke to the Departed Duke, even when he's gone his scandal blackens me," I sighed.

Philippe stirred the gravel with the tip of his shoe and coughed uncomfortably.

"Do you know how you're going to do it tonight?" His icy blue eyes were fixed rigidly upon Noailles, who was whispering something in Charlotte's ear. A muscle ticked in Philippe's jaw.

I exhaled uneasily. "Yes. I've got it all worked out."

Philippe looked skeptical. "This isn't like dispatching some infected peasant, you know. Noailles is older than most of the other infected in Paris, and you mustn't underestimate his cunning. He is *dangerous*, darling. You know I adore you, but I just don't think you're up to this kind of assignment." He made a peculiar noise of frustration, and I almost laughed. He glared.

"I am ready. I'm certainly more prepared than anyone else," I argued.

"Perhaps, but you just don't have the same physical capabilities as the other men. You lack their edge. Now, don't get upset, Daphne. I'm not saying you don't possess other exceptional qualities. I mean, you're certainly the best intelligence gatherer we have. It's only that I want you safe. The Order should have assigned another agent. I hate that you're mixed up in all of this, and I don't mind telling you I don't fancy you being alone with him."

"Jeanne wasn't just the king's mistress, Philippe," I whispered, ignoring the irritation I felt at his slights. "She was a friend. When I heard that she'd been attacked and left to die, I couldn't help but think of my brother, Michel. If Noailles is the bastard that killed her, then I'll happily dust him."

At that moment, Noailles looked directly at me and our eyes locked across the courtyard. I wondered if he'd heard our whispered conversation. I cursed my carelessness. I knew the creatures had supernatural hearing and sight as well as accelerated reflexes. Something in his golden eyes made every nerve in my body crackle with energy. His otherworldly beauty was too much for something straight from the depths of hell. Had Jeanne felt the same way? Entranced by the hypnotic eroticism of a predator? Had she left the king's bed one night to steal away with the irresistible libertine, only to be ruthlessly savaged while the rogue took his pleasure?

I closed my eyes against that disturbing vision and took a glass of champagne from a passing footman. Draining it in one swallow, I forced myself to face him, but he was gone.

Charlotte approached and threw her arms around Philippe's neck. "*Mon cher*, everyone loves my new bauble! You are truly the best husband in France. Perhaps in all the world," she said. She swayed a bit as she spoke.

"Charlotte, darling, what did Monsieur de Noailles want?" Philippe asked with a touch of irritation.

She waved her hand airily. "Nothing of consequence, really. He mostly wanted to know about Daphne. I didn't tell him anything worthwhile, of course."

Philippe and I exchanged a look.

"You know, I think perhaps the good emissary fancies you. You should give him a whirl! All the ladies at court say that he's the most accomplished lover they've ever had," Charlotte whispered, though none too quietly.

Philippe sputtered a bit and wrapped a possessive hand around Charlotte's arm.

"Well," he huffed. "I believe, on that note, we'll take our leave. Good night, Daphne, and good luck." He ushered his wife back through the palace, casting a meaningful glance at me.

"Come for tea tomorrow, *chérie*!" Charlotte called. I smiled and waved at the retreating pair.

"Your cousin is a charming creature."

I jumped at the vampire's voice near my ear again. Instinct had my fist at his throat before I could stop myself. He easily blocked the strike, grabbing my hand and using it to pull me in close to him. His iron grip didn't loosen when I tried to pull away, so I clenched my other hand and punched him in the stomach, only to connect with a wall of hard, tense muscle. He barely flinched—merely arched one dark brow and *tsked*.

"I think, *ma chère duchesse*, we have a few things we need to discuss."

2

ÉTIENNE

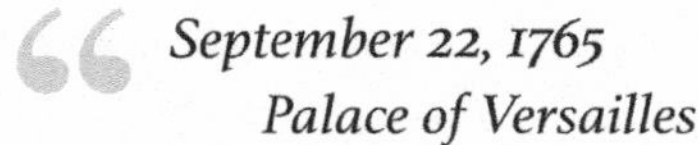

September 22, 1765
Palace of Versailles

SHE WAS MUCH STRONGER THAN SHE APPEARED. NO MATCH FOR THE supernatural strength the plague had bestowed on me, certainly, but still, much stronger than I expected. While I didn't put much stock in the usefulness of the women of the court beyond slaking certain appetites and exerting occasional influence upon their more dim-witted husbands, I could at least acknowledge when some ornamental ninny possessed something outside the ordinary. I'd seen the duchess watching me over the last several months but hadn't considered her a proper threat until recently. I realized now, clutching her arm, I had miscalculated—an oversight I soundly regretted. As my father had often warned, *Never underestimate a woman.*

Especially one sent to assassinate you.

I had to hand it to the Order—of all the ways they'd tried to deliver me unto Death, this was the most...*enticing.*

Her soft peaches-and-cream complexion, wide violet eyes, and pert rosebud lips set in a furious pout gave her the appearance of a wrathful angel boiling over with self-righteousness. She was unable to free herself from my grip, so I allowed myself the luxury of an intimate perusal of her full form—partly because it unsettled her, but partly because I found her *fascinating.* My gaze raked lazily over her, from the top of her powdered curls, down the graceful column of her neck, to her luscious breasts straining at the top of her neckline. I tracked down the crimson silk of her bodice to her trim waist, ensconced in those unseen stays, and wondered what her undergarments might look like. Would they be silk? Would they be adorned with ribbons, rosettes, or lace? Would they match this daring, provocative gown? I hardened at the thought.

"If you wish to speak with me, monsieur," she spat, "then perhaps you might release my arm so that we can converse properly."

"Perhaps I don't want to release you," I murmured in her ear. "Perhaps I don't feel like being staked tonight, despite your *orders.*" I breathed in her scent—orange blossom and vanilla. I wondered what she'd taste like.

I saw her eyes widen momentarily. So, now she knew that I knew her allegiance to the Order. When the moment of shock wore off, she huffed in irritation and gritted her teeth.

"Then go on and break it."

I stepped back, stunned. She hadn't offered it as a careless challenge. Her expression was determined, not daring.

"I beg your pardon?" I relaxed my grip on her arm but did not let her go. A quick glance across the courtyard told me we were beginning to attract attention. The disappointed moue of the *marquise de Balay* told me that people would be gossiping already.

The beast has found his next diversion.

Cursing silently, I tugged her into the king's ridiculous hedge maze, away from the prying eyes and wagging tongues of the idiotic aristocracy. After so many clandestine trysts out here, I knew the ins and outs of the garden labyrinth almost as well as my own château.

She practically growled at me in response, exciting something embarrassingly primal in my blood. I was trying to sort out whether I wanted to feed on her or fuck her. *Probably both, provided she doesn't plunge a stake into my heart.*

"Break it, then," she repeated, steel in her gaze. She struggled, and I tightened my hold on her.

She hissed at me in disgust and tried to pull away again. "If you know that I'm with the Order, monsieur, then you'll know why they sent me. You may break my arm to escape death at my hands tonight, but I assure you, I have had worse and it will only buy you a few hours reprieve."

I enjoyed that the spoiled little minx had spirit, but her comment ignited a spark of dread and anger. *She's had worse than a broken arm? She is a beautiful woman—and a duchess, for God's sake.*

Infuriated, she continued. "Allow me to tell you how this will go. You will break my arm, I shall scream, the guards will come running, and even with your monstrous strength and speed, they will catch up to you—probably in the daylight hours when you need your rest. And because you'll have brutally injured the *duchesse de Duras*—when you are *not*, in fact, her husband—our beloved king will have your head cut off, and my task will be accomplished regardless of the function of one arm. So, either let me go or break my arm. It matters little which."

I tugged her farther into the maze, impressed by her vivid imagination and the speed at which her mind worked. Yet again, her words gave me pause.

"*When I am not, in fact, your husband*—what do you mean by that, madame?"

"None of your damn business, you brute!" Her cheeks flamed near the color of her gown. In her fury, she'd obviously admitted more than she would have liked. She kicked at my shin, but I sidestepped it. I twisted her arm behind her back and pushed her forward. She let fly a string of curses that I hadn't heard many ladies use. With her free hand, she produced a wooden stake from one of her pockets, which I knocked away. She uttered a muffled scream of frustration.

"Let me go, you oversexed bloodsucker!"

I couldn't help but laugh at the insult. *This is too much fun.*

Finally, we neared a stone bench at the center of the maze. Few other revelers would make it in this far, which guaranteed us a modicum of privacy.

"I'll offer you a trade, then," I said. "I'll return your arm to you in exchange for the opportunity to *enlighten* you."

She narrowed her eyes, and her lips twisted in derision. "If you think to *enlighten* me carnally, know that I would rather fuck Lucifer himself than willingly let you defile me."

My cock twitched at her profanity, and I chuckled again. "What a wicked mind and sharp tongue you have, madame. But no, rest assured I prefer my bedmates' dispositions to be much more amiable and, more importantly, willing. No, *ma chère duchesse*, I mean only to enlighten you with the truth. With several truths, in fact."

"And you'll let me go unharmed? If I merely listen to you?" Suspicion darkened her tone.

"Of course. But you'll have to promise the same. We'll both leave this meeting alive—well, alive or undead."

"You'll just be postponing the inevitable," she sneered.

"Perhaps, but if that is the case, you have nothing to lose," I pointed out.

She considered this. Testing my grip on her arm once more as if to confirm her predicament, she groaned in irritation and relented. "Very well. You have my word. I will hear you out."

"And?"

"And I will not attempt to kill you tonight. I cannot promise the same for tomorrow."

I nodded, satisfied, and released my hold on her arm. She

pulled away and sat on the stone bench, rubbing her hand. When I was sure she wasn't going to stake me or run, I sat on the opposite end of the bench and faced her.

"I wouldn't have broken it, you know," I said. "I do *not* hurt women."

She scoffed at me—her disbelief needling me more than it should have. *Irritating harpy*.

"...unless they ask me to," I purred. She attempted that imperious glare again, but it faded with her impatience.

"Plead your case, Noailles," she demanded.

"Étienne."

"Your Christian name will not soften me to you," she chided. "But in the spirit of *temporary* truce, you may address me as Daphne."

Daphne. The beautiful nymph who begged to be turned into a laurel tree rather than love the sun god, Apollo. A fitting myth of one woman's pride in the face of love.

"It suits you," I chortled.

She tapped her foot expectantly. I sighed.

"I did not kill Madame de Pompadour," I said. "I'm sure that's what the Order has told you and I'm sure that's why you're here tonight, but it isn't true."

"And I'll just take your word for it, shall I? You'll have to do better than that if you are to convince me."

"Were you at court that day? The day they found her body?" I asked.

She shook her head and glared at me accusingly. "No, but I heard the report and the stories. Her throat had been bitten, almost all of her blood drained. You are the only vampire allowed inside the palace. There are guards posted everywhere. If any other *sanguisuge* had come in, they would have been found and executed."

At her use of the elitist slur for the vampire peasants, I could not stifle my disgust. I whirled on her, enraged. My fangs lengthened and my eyes darkened. A predator ready to strike.

"Take care with your words, Duchess."

She leaned back, eyes wide.

"Do you know why there are so many vampires in Paris?"

"The plague," she said. "Most say it came over from the East. There is no treatment or cure. It spread through the city because of the deplorable conditions the peasants live in." She spoke slowly —guardedly.

Waiting for me to attack her, I suspected. Most of the nobles thought vampires were little better than slavering dogs, unable to master their baser instincts. *The fools.* I leaned into her, forcing her back against the barrier of greenery.

"Wrong. Oh yes, it's true enough that it came from the East. From somewhere around the Carpathian Mountains, in fact. And it's true that there are no treatments and no cure. But it didn't spread because of the *filthy peasants* and their *deplorable* homes. It spread because they are deliberately infecting themselves."

"What utter nonsense! No one would willingly choose such a life."

I stared into her lovely violet eyes, so blind to the struggles of a country—a world—outside Versailles. Frustration clawed at me, loosening the tether of my self-control.

"You might if you were starving! If you had too many mouths to feed and not enough bread because of the grain blight and your beloved king had nothing to offer you but empty promises. No help, no charity, just taxes to pay for his foreign wars and the champagne at his garden parties, while he remains safely ensconced in his walled palace of decadence. How fortunate you are, Duchess, that you've never had to put yourself in a position risking your very soul for a full belly."

"You know nothing of my life," she hissed, her eyes suddenly wild with emotion.

I seethed in silence for a moment, too afraid I'd given away my own secrets—my family's secrets. Anger, desperation, and a sense of solitary forlornness flowed through me. I was fighting a losing battle with the king and the court, and this damned woman represented every part of my struggle—the ignorance, the entitlement, and every backward aristocratic ideal. The beauty, the glitter, and the wealth were everything I'd once been promised that had been ripped away from me, only to be dangled in front of my face like some kind of poisoned apple when the king needed a vampire to control.

"I can't believe you," she breathed. "That cannot be true. I know they are struggling because of the grain blight, but surely they can find other ways to—"

"To eat? Yes, they have found another way. Many of them have reasoned that it is easier, *more economical*, to sustain themselves on blood instead of bread. And I'll tell you something else, Duchess—they have not forgotten who has forced their fangs. A day of reckoning is on the horizon for Louis, for all of us. And damned if we don't deserve it when it comes."

Daphne gasped. "You speak of treason!"

Defeat weighed down my shoulders as I shook my head. My fangs retracted. "I speak the truth."

Unnerved by my emotional outburst and melancholy tone, she shifted uncomfortably on the bench and toyed with a ruffle on her skirt. After a moment, she recovered.

"And is this why you killed Jeanne? To visit some kind of twisted revenge on the king who has supposedly condemned your kind?" She shot to her feet with the allegation, but I saw the beginnings of doubt clouding her violet eyes.

I moved toward her slowly, stalking her. To her credit, she didn't back away or flinch. She stood her ground, staring up at me defiantly. I heard her pulse quicken and smelled the anticipation in her blood. *Exquisite.*

"Madame de Pompadour's throat was not bitten, Daphne," I said softly. "It was ripped out."

"What?" she uttered, horrified.

"I saw her body when they took her away that night. Her head had almost been severed."

Daphne paled. "But why would you— You could have—"

I rolled my eyes, my temper ebbing. "In theory, yes, I could have. I possess the physical strength it would take to do such a thing to a body, but as I told you, I do *not* hurt women. I only drink from them with their permission—and almost never from the throat."

She stared at me in confusion. "Then, where...?"

"There are so many more delicious places where the blood flows. Would you like me to show you?" I offered, my voice a low rumble of desire.

I grinned lasciviously at her, loving the sound of her gasp. I was inches away from her, mesmerized by the blush blooming across her chest and cheeks. Suddenly, I was ravenous with hunger—but not for blood. Her lips parted on an intake of breath, and my cock hardened to granite. *Damn it, man. Get ahold of yourself.*

I stepped back. Daphne blinked and straightened, and I felt a rush of pleasure at the thought that she, too, had been stirred by our encounter. That pleasure was swiftly followed by a jolt of panic —in the space of a few minutes, this woman had obliterated my carefully crafted sense of self-control. I'd have to be on my guard in the future. Clearly, she was much more dangerous than I'd anticipated.

She glowered at me.

"Are you so sure I'm to blame for Jeanne's death? Why do you think Louis has not ordered my arrest, then? If everyone is so certain I killed his beloved mistress, why is it left to the Order to be responsible for my punishment?"

She turned from me, and I knew I had her.

"Assuming you're telling the truth—which I'm still not certain of—you must have some idea who killed Jeanne."

"I'm at a loss, I'm afraid," I admitted. "But that's why I have a proposal for you tonight, Duchess."

She folded her arms in front of her chest, likely to signal her displeasure, but it merely served to squeeze her breasts tighter against her bodice. I forced myself to meet her eyes.

"You are charged with killing the murderer of Madame de Pompadour, no? I am in agreement because *of course* I didn't do it. Furthermore, I don't believe it was any vampire. I don't want the Order to send some other assassin after me, so it's imperative I clear my name before they do. Ergo, I propose you and I work together to find the killer and bring the bastard to justice."

"Absolutely not," she scoffed. "Perhaps you are telling the truth. If that's the case, I'll discover the murderer myself and deal with him as the Order commands."

"And how will you eliminate the possibility of vampire involvement? Just stroll through the streets of Paris and knock on the nearest coffin for questioning?"

"Why not? I am the *duchesse de Duras*," she said with a haughty sniff. "The title is good for something."

"No one will talk to you, Duchess. You represent the cause of their misery. You'll be lucky if you return to Versailles unmolested and unbitten."

She frowned, uncertainty creeping into her lovely visage again.

"If only you had some sort of intermediary who could help you —an emissary, if you will! Someone who had connections all throughout the city, in both high places and low. Someone else with a stake—no pun intended—in the truth. But where would you find such a humble, handsome ally?"

A look of sheer loathing twisted Daphne's face, and I preened.

"If I agree to a temporary alliance with you, it's just that: *temporary*. We will not become friends or lovers or anything more than a means to an end—the end, in this case, being the truth. And if I find out that you really are responsible for what happened to Jeanne, I will take great pleasure in cutting out your heart and feeding it to my dogs."

I arched a brow at the violent rage simmering beneath her soft curves.

"And they say that *I'm* the monster!"

3

DAPHNE

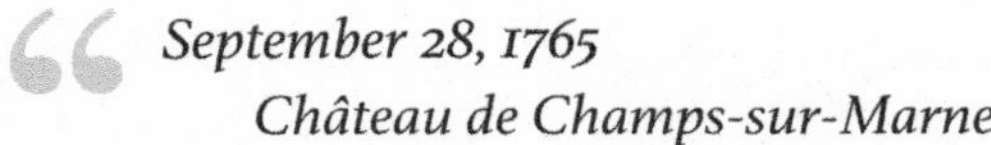

September 28, 1765
Château de Champs-sur-Marne

I HAD MADE A DEAL WITH THE DEVIL. *DAMN HIM*.

Monsieur de Noailles—or, as he preferred, *Étienne*—swore he didn't kill Jeanne. Did I believe him? I hadn't decided. It was true that Étienne was a vampire and, in my estimation, a worthless cad but I felt I owed it to Jeanne to be absolutely certain about his guilt as her murderer. He had, after all, alleged some rather shocking things that I felt compelled to disprove.

Tonight I hoped to do just that.

"Daphne, must we keep drinking this filth?" Charlotte whined, interrupting my thoughts. She wrinkled her nose at her teacup.

"Filth? I'll have you know this is one of the finest teas from China."

"Yes, it's fine and all, but couldn't we have something a bit more fortifying? Some champagne, perhaps, or even a glass of sherry? I mean, what's the good of being married to the Depraved Duke if you can't enjoy a little debauchery yourself once in a while," she said.

"It's ten o'clock in the morning, *chérie*. Doesn't Philippe object to you drinking this early?" I laughed.

She narrowed her gaze at me. "We agreed we weren't going to discuss Philippe, remember? Otherwise, I shall have to plead with you to respond to his messages, and we were having *such* a good time by ourselves."

I winced at her veiled chiding. I'd been avoiding Philippe and the numerous missives he'd sent on behalf of the Order. I knew they'd be furious with me for failing my assignment, but I needed to know if there was even a remote possibility of Étienne speaking the truth—not just about Jeanne but about the unfortunate people of Paris. Thinking of them offering themselves up to the horrible blood-drinking plague just because they had no alternative turned my stomach. It couldn't be true, could it?

"Incidentally," she carried on, oblivious to my wandering worries, "what he doesn't know won't hurt him, and I pay my servants assiduously to ensure that he *doesn't* know." She lifted her periwinkle-colored skirts and slipped a flask from her garter. She poured a healthy measure of brandy into her teacup and, with a saucy wink, into mine as well.

"Is he horribly cross with me?" I asked her.

Charlotte raised her eyes heavenward. "Philippe is cross about everything these days. The war, the grain blight, our estate, *les sanguisuges*—"

"Oh, don't call them that," I admonished, thinking back to my words with Étienne. I'd felt a curious sort of shame at his reprimand.

Charlotte's eyebrows rose with interest, and her mouth split into a wide grin. "Ah! So, you've been entertaining our handsome royal emissary, have you? Lucky thing! If I were the type of woman to have a lover, he would *definitely* be at the top of my list. That naughty smile, that muscled body..." She opened her fan and cooled the blush reddening her face. "You must tell me everything, darling. What's it like with a vampire? Is he—you know

—*well-graced*? Do his fangs get in the way when he's licking your—"

I nearly choked on my brandy. "Charlotte, I am *not* 'entertaining' him. We had a conversation at the ball the other night, and that's it."

"Daphne, when he approached us, you were so rude to him I find it hard to believe you're not secretly in love with him. I don't blame you, of course. You deserve a little fun, especially after everything with Henri." Her tone was light, but her eyes were full of sympathy.

I shook my head. "No, *chérie*. I'm afraid that the romantic part of me is simply gone."

"So is he," she added with levity.

The room started to close in on me, and I forced a wry laugh. "Étienne isn't my type anyway! He is, perhaps, *too* handsome, and he struts around like he knows it. I hear he's had so many women—well, one mistress wouldn't be enough to slake his appetite. Henri was just like that. One wife and one mistress were never enough. He had to screw half of Paris with that pathetic little worm of his. If I were to involve myself with another man—which is unlikely, so don't get any of your matchmaking ideas—he would be sweet, soulful, and sensitive."

"And hung like an ox," Charlotte added.

I dissolved in a fit of laughter and threw a cushion at her. She dodged it and drained her teacup. My lady's maid, Eve, came forward to refill it. Charlotte shook her head but placed a hand on her arm before she could leave.

"Eve, darling, do you hear anything from the other servants about the emissary's household? What do we know of him?"

Eve shifted, casting her eyes in my direction. "Madame?"

"Come now, surely you'd be obliged to report anything that might have some bearing on Daphne taking him as a lover," Charlotte pressed.

"Charlotte," I warned.

"Any unnatural proclivities? Any madness or cruelty poisoning his mind and his household?"

An awkward silence settled over the room. Charlotte's light manner belied her penetrating gaze, and Eve finally looked at me thoughtfully.

"*Non, vraiment.* I don't know any dark secrets—he is a good master. I heard that much from my *maman*, who knew the cook in the *vicomte*'s employ."

Charlotte seized upon this like a cat on a mouse. "The former *vicomte*, you mean? The emissary's father?"

Eve nodded.

"Why does the cook no longer work for the family?" Charlotte continued, then slapped her forehead. "Ah! I guess the emissary does not need to employ a cook. He let her go, I suppose."

"*Mais non!* That was not the case. When monsieur returned to Paris, he offered the staff a choice. They could stay and work for him, or leave with full references and a small stipend."

"Why would they leave if they didn't have to?" Charlotte asked.

Eve's brows shot up. "Madame, he is a vampire! Most self-respecting servants would not want to serve such a master."

"But the *vicomte* had already lost his title by then. Isn't that more of a disgrace than succumbing to the blood plague?" I asked in astonishment.

Eve raised a shoulder. "The *vicomte* was beloved by his servants. The emissary did not expect that loyalty to extend to him after he was turned."

I nodded, lost in thought. "*Merci*, Eve. As always, I am grateful for your candor. Go on and take your tea, *chérie*. Charlotte and I will be fine alone."

She turned to go, just as Charlotte called after her. "Eve, one more question before you depart. How many of the servants stayed on?"

"All but one or two, I believe," Eve said. She curtsied and, at my nod, left the room.

Charlotte turned a self-satisfied smile on me. "You see? I am *always* right, *chérie*. Now you can be assured that he isn't some kind of rotten scoundrel. Well, perhaps a bit of a scoundrel, but only in the best way."

"I fail to see how you've come to that conclusion," I argued.

"He had the grace to offer an out to his father's employees, but they all chose to remain with him. He cannot be a monster."

Not a monster, only a possible murderer, I thought.

"That doesn't mean anything. I understand employment is scarce, Charlotte, and lots of people are hungry. The servants probably didn't want to leave a sure thing for some unknown misery."

Charlotte rolled her eyes.

I sighed. "Besides, you don't know how much a person will endure in order to keep a roof over her head."

Charlotte's eyes snapped to mine, but her expression was soft as she considered my meaning. "Your servants stay for you, *chérie*. You bore the brunt of Henri's temper and shielded them from the worst of his torments. They aren't likely to forget it," she said quietly.

I finished the tea and brandy in my cup, briefly thinking about another stiff drink to hold back the sickening memories. Before I could sink into despair, Charlotte slapped her fan against my knee with a cheerful giggle.

"Well, *ma chère amie*, I should be on my way. I promised Lisette I'd look in on her since she turned her ankle. She says it was during her dancing lessons, but the rumor is that she tripped over her lover's breeches when the *comte* came home early. I shall let you know what I uncover!"

She kissed my cheeks and made for the door. For all her inappropriate behavior, Charlotte had a soft heart and a comforting nature. She was unfailingly devoted to Philippe and to me. Her loyalty inspired me to be honest with Philippe, but I needed to find the truth of the matter before I addressed him.

Later that evening, I dressed without Eve's help—I didn't need her worrying over my inappropriate attire. I needed freedom and a degree of anonymity tonight, so I'd donned some of Henri's old clothes—the ones he'd used to wear when he sought what he called *companionship* with the unfortunate prostitutes in the direst circumstances. *The ones who would not fight back against his demands,* I thought bitterly.

I donned the plain woolen breeches and hose, simple linen shirt, dingy brown waistcoat, thick black overcoat, and tattered tricorne hat. I'd taken care to bind my breasts beneath the shirt and hoped that no one would notice the ill-fitting wig, but as I surveyed my appearance in the mirror, I reasoned it would probably be acceptable given the late hour. In darkness, or even dim lighting, I would pass for a man.

In the pockets of my coat, I stashed a dagger, several small wooden stakes, my flintlock pistol, and a vial of holy water. While the holy water wouldn't do much good against vampires, the Order had instructed its agents to carry it for other potential supernatural threats. Since vampires were a reality now, the door to the impossible had been flung open. Monsters, ghouls, demons—it seemed only natural that other unholy creatures lurked in the shadows.

A soft knock at my door made me jump.

"Madame."

Eve poked her head in and blanched when she saw me. I offered her a sheepish grin. "It's necessary, Eve. Trust me."

"Of course, madame. Monsieur de Noailles has arrived. He's waiting for you downstairs."

"*Merci.*" I tucked an errant curl beneath my wig and took a steadying breath.

"Are you… Madame, are you sure you will be safe? Perhaps you should take one of the footmen—or Gaston—with you tonight," Eve whispered. She twisted her fingers in her skirts.

"*Non, chérie,*" I replied. "Grim business tonight. I'll be fine. I promise."

I smiled encouragingly at her, but she looked at me skeptically before nodding and hurrying back down the hall. Making my way downstairs, I paused by the table in the hall to put an apple in my coat pocket as well. I'd declined dinner, too anxious to have much of an appetite, and now my stomach churned with hunger and nerves.

"Midnight snack?" Étienne's voice carried up the grand staircase from the front hall.

I cursed him softly, but his mouth quirked up in a smile and I knew he'd heard. He was dressed simply, and it seemed at odds with his ethereal beauty. He hadn't powdered his hair but had tied back the thick waves in a simple ribbon. In the candlelight, his locks shimmered like a raven's wing in the sun. Alarmingly, my fingers suddenly itched to touch them.

"I apologize if you've been kept waiting," I grumbled. "Have you been offered refreshment?"

The words flowed out of me reflexively, but it was impossible for me to keep the irritation from my voice. It wouldn't do for the *duchesse de Duras* to have an inhospitable household, even if she'd rather tear down her beloved château brick by brick than have a lecherous vampire ruining its serenity.

"No, Duchess, but I doubt your household was prepared to offer me *refreshment*," he drawled. "Unless you'd care to do so yourself?"

Realizing my mistake, I felt my face burn in embarrassment. *Damn it, Daphne, you imbecile.*

"I meant water or wine. Perhaps a glass of something stronger. I have seen you drink, *Monsieur le Vicomte*," I said airily, trying to regain the upper hand.

He winced at my use of his lost title and turned his back to me, marching toward the front door. "I am no longer *Monsieur le Vicomte*, Duchess, and you would do well to remember that. You will call me Étienne. And no, I do not require refreshment. We must be on our way—my man at the graveyard will not wait for us indefinitely," he said, ushering us outside.

I nodded. "I—"

He turned, an impatient look etched on his handsome face.

"I'm sorry," I said. Flustered, my voice faltered. "For using your former title. I hope I did not offend."

He raised a brow at me. A slow smile spread across his lips. *The smug bastard.*

"What I meant to say was that while I do not mind offending you in many other, justifiable ways, that particular barb was not meant as offense. Just a force of habit. I'm not used to interacting with people who don't hold a title, you see," I said with acid-laced sweetness.

The pompous grin on his face didn't waver an inch, but he bowed politely and helped me into his carriage. I sat as far away from him as possible and stared resolutely out the window. How did he manage to come out on top of every interaction we had? Probably some kind of infuriating supernatural trick. It soured my mood even further, which I would've thought impossible considering we were on our way to the graveyard to dig up the body of my friend.

"Are you certain this is truly necessary?"

"*Mais oui, ma chère duchesse.*" His low voice was like velvet across my skin. Goose bumps rose on my flesh.

"You do not believe me," he stated matter-of-factly. "But you will. I will prove it to you, and to do that, you must first see Madame de Pompadour for yourself."

I shut my eyes and leaned back against the plush seat. The carriage pitched roughly over a hole in the road.

"It will be difficult," he continued. "I know she was your friend, but this is essential. We must begin our investigation in the right place, however gruesome it may be."

"I do not faint at the sight of blood, Étienne. I will do what must be done in order to bring justice to Jeanne's killer." I stared hard at him—at least, I thought it was him. In the gloom of the carriage, it was hard to tell.

"Is it that you are uncommonly brave, madame? Or is it that you are used to such brutality?"

"Perhaps it is both," I replied. He didn't respond, but I had the distinct impression he was studying me. I felt at a disadvantage yet again.

We rode on in silence, until about a quarter of an hour had passed and the carriage slowed.

"We've arrived," he said. He'd moved in close to my ear, and I caught his scent. Surprisingly, he did not smell of blood and death. He smelled of soap, cedar, and peppermint—putting me in mind of winter gardens and snow-covered pine trees.

"I'm well aware you find my company distasteful, madame, but for your own safety, I must insist you stay close to me. Your disguise may fool drunkards and blind men, but anyone with two functional eyes and a brain will quickly recognize your—ahem—*charms*. Keep your hat low, your head down, your hands in your pockets, and let me do the talking."

As he spoke, his breath on my ear encouraged a blush that I felt creep all over my body. My nipples hardened beneath the painful linen bindings. Disgusted with him and with my body's instinctive response, I pushed him away and surged forward, nearly tripping on my way down from the carriage. With supernatural speed, he seized my coat to keep me from toppling into the street.

"Careful, Duchess," he taunted, his golden eyes flashing. "We wouldn't want the Order to lose one of their talented hunters."

Chagrined, I followed him into the graveyard. Perhaps in another time, in another place, I would have delivered some kind of dressing down, but I found myself flustered by his presence, uncomfortable with my sudden ineptitude, and queasy at the thought of disturbing the resting place of my former friend. *Forgive me, Jeanne.*

Étienne led us farther into the cemetery toward the only source of light—a dim lantern near a copse of trees. I'd been here back in the spring when they'd buried her, and it had been beautiful, surrounded by flowers and greenery, flecked with dappled sunlight. Tonight, however, the clearing felt alien and malevolent. I tugged my coat close to me and fingered the pearl handle of my dagger. Its smooth warmth comforted me.

Étienne greeted his man, the grave digger, who stood next to a pile of newly turned earth and poor Jeanne's waiting casket.

"Give us some privacy, will you?" Étienne commanded. He flipped the lanky grave digger a coin. The man nodded and walked some distance away.

Étienne bent to pry the lid to the casket open, and I braced myself. *God, help me. Please don't let it be like last time—like Michel.*

Étienne looked to me, waiting for my signal. I nodded, and he pulled the lid away, letting it crash to the ground at my feet. I held my breath and opened my eyes. I was ill-prepared for the sight.

Oh God, Jeanne Antoinette! What have they done to you?

4

ÉTIENNE

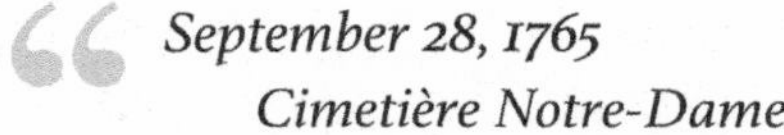

September 28, 1765
Cimetière Notre-Dame

Belatedly, I wondered if I should have brought some smelling salts. I knew this would be unpleasant for Daphne, but even I found my stomach souring at the grotesque scene before us. Having witnessed more than my fair share of deathly horrors, it still pained me to see a beautiful woman struck down in the prime of her life by something so unbearably savage.

I peered at my companion, ready to catch her if she swooned. Her breath came in shallow gasps and her pupils had dilated considerably, but she seemed steady enough. Assured that she wasn't about to keel over and fall into the open grave, I turned my attention to Madame de Pompadour's decaying body.

She was farther gone from the last time I'd seen her, but her wounds remained pristine. I leaned in to inspect them. They weren't like anything I'd ever seen—they were certainly unlike any vampire bite I'd known.

"It looks like..." Daphne's whisper sounded unsettled. "It almost looks like she's been attacked by a wild animal—a wolf, perhaps.

The edges of the wound are jagged and rough, as though the flesh has been ripped away. It would suggest fangs in the upper and lower jaw as opposed to the neat insertion of a single pair of canines common in vampire bites."

I stared at her, unable to mask my astonishment. She was studying the body as intently as possible, though a sheen of sweat had broken out across her worryingly pale brow. Her voice shook as she continued.

"Étienne, her ring."

"She isn't wearing a ring, Daphne," I said, gently prodding the casket to feel for some misplaced jewelry.

"Exactly. Where is her ring? Most of her jewels were given back to the king after her death, all except for one ring that she never removed. It was a large pink pearl surrounded by diamonds—the first gift that Louis ever gave her. It was very precious to her, but I do not see it. Do you think grave robbers could have claimed it?" She wavered a bit on her feet. I needed more time to look around, but I wasn't sure how long Daphne's strength would hold out.

"Steady, Duchess," I urged. "If you swoon now, I'll be forced to lay hands on you and carry you home."

That startled her enough. She snapped her eyes to mine and choked on an incensed huff.

"I am not going to swoon," she bit out.

"Too bad. I was rather looking forward to carrying you back."

I searched the rest of the coffin—no ring. She was right. It could have disappeared at any time, but I doubted grave robbers. They would have taken the simple burial shift—it was silk, after all—as well as the ribbons tying back the dead woman's hair. Daphne clearly suspected the killer had taken the ring, and though I was loath to admit it, I agreed with her.

I'd hoped to find something else that would point toward a suspect, but other than convincing Daphne I hadn't killed the king's mistress, I was no better off than when we'd started this morbid little adventure. I scanned the body from head to toe, looking for clues.

Something nagged at me—some peculiarity that I couldn't quite place. Closing my eyes, I inhaled deeply, allowing my heightened sense of smell to paint parts of the scene I could not see. I smelled death, of course, and rot. I smelled the decay before me but also something else. There was a bitter musk in the air that I'd never encountered. It wasn't quite an animal, I didn't think, but—

I leaned down next to the gaping wound in Jeanne's neck and breathed. Yes, this was where it was coming from. It must have been the scent of the killer. Bitter, sour, smoky, almost sulfuric. *Fantastic.* Now all I needed to do was walk around, sniffing everyone in Paris until I found the same odor. *No problem at all.*

Daphne was motionless, staring at me with revulsion.

"I think I know what the killer smells like," I explained. "There is something odd about her neck—the way it smells, even in death."

She nodded and crossed herself. I went to bring the grave digger back to put Jeanne in the ground again and caught Daphne wiping a tear from her cheek. At my notice, she dropped her hand and straightened, her gaze turning instantly icy. My dead heart gave a curious little squeeze, and I led her away.

When we reached the shadowy comfort of my carriage, I handed her my gold flask. She considered me a moment, her face inscrutable. I shrugged and started to pull away, but she finally reached for the flask. Without asking about its contents, she took a long pull on it. When she saw my surprised expression, she gave a tired half shrug.

"I figured it was either blood or brandy, but you don't seem the type to carry around an expensive flask full of blood."

"I am fortunate enough to find willing sources when I require them," I admitted, taking a drink of the sweet brandy. I imagined I could taste her lips on the flask, and heat spread through me.

She leaned back and closed her eyes, allowing me the time to drink in her lithe body, wrapped in those ridiculous masculine clothes. Who would've thought that a woman wearing breeches could be so *erotic*? The way they clung to her shapely legs and followed every sinful curve of her bottom—

"We should take you home," I said. I needed distance from her to clear my head and think. "I imagine your husband will be worried."

She barked a laugh and snatched the flask from me again, drinking deeply.

"I didn't realize you had such a scathing sense of humor," she seethed.

When she recognized the confusion in my face, she was taken aback.

"My apologies, Duchess. Has he passed on?"

"You mean you really don't know? How can that be? You worked out I was with the Order, but you managed to avoid the gossip about my marriage? It's all anyone's talked about for the last two years."

Frustration rose. "My presence at court is not the same as it once was. I am seldom privy to the gossip of the *tonne*. When I am around the ladies of the nobility, we usually aren't engaging in idle conversation."

I'd said it to shock her, but the night had taken its toll on her caustic façade. She had dimmed, somehow—softened beneath the weight of her own sadness.

"You are right, of course. Forgive my offense yet again. People do not often speak to me about my husband, preferring instead to delight in the scandalous rumors. No, Étienne. My husband does not worry for my safe return, and he does not wait for me at home." She trailed off, a thousand miles away. Her manner made me uncomfortable, as if teasing her now would be like kicking a puppy. I tried for my courtly charm.

"Then he is either dead or a fool," I said, taking the brandy from her for another drink.

A guarded smile broke upon her lips, like sunlight through storm clouds. *If only she weren't the* duchesse de Duras. *Hang that. If only I weren't a vampire.* I noticed that the brandy had restored some color to her cheeks, and I imagined her warming all over—warming to me. *Damn it.* I hungered again. I would need to find a woman tomorrow—or tonight, if possible.

"*Alors,*" she said, stretching her legs out in front of her and eagerly changing the subject. "Where does our investigation take us now, Étienne? I am disturbed by the absence of the ring. I think we should try to eliminate the possibility that someone stole it between the palace and the cemetery for a quick sale."

"Sounds reasonable."

"As an underworld emissary to His Majesty, I don't suppose you'd know where to find a reputable fence for disreputably acquired jewelry?"

"I could certainly make some inquiries," I offered.

"*Bon,*" she said. "Shall we go, then?"

"Go where?"

She waved a hand dismissively. "To make the inquiries."

"I will do that on my own. I can't have you running amok in the streets of Paris, inciting some kind of scandal that I'll be responsible for," I chastened. "For now, you must be patient. I'll have my driver take you home." I knocked on the roof of the carriage, signaling our departure.

"I assure you, I've weathered far worse scandals than you could possibly imagine, and I don't have a lot of time. My report to the Order is already long overdue and I need to give them a good reason why I haven't killed you yet. I would think haste would be a top priority for you as well, monsieur. As soon as your name is cleared, you're free to go back to your debauchery with your former impunity."

Her disdainful impression of me, like so many of the Versailles courtiers, stung more than it should have. She was right about one thing though: time was of the essence. Despite my irritation, I still didn't want her out in the seedy underbelly of the city where the whispers of revolution were stirring. The vampires were becoming increasingly hostile to humans from every class—especially the aristocracy. My attempts to negotiate with Louis had slowed to the point of failure, and there was a palpable restlessness across the city. I could protect Daphne from bodily harm, of course, but I knew I wouldn't be able to protect her from her world crashing down around her. To expose her to such brutal reality after forcing her to dig up her ghoulishly murdered friend all in one night seemed cruel, even for me.

"You're right, Duchess, but I need some time to find out if my contacts are still in Paris. You should go home tonight. Send your report to the Order. I'd be obliged if you told them that you didn't think I was a murderer, but somehow I doubt it will make much of a difference in their minds."

"What do you mean by that?"

"You are not the first to make an attempt on my life on their behalf."

She stared at me in surprise. "What else have they convicted you of? They do not kill arbitrarily. There is always a good reason. Protection of the king and country. Justice for those wronged," she defended.

I laughed bitterly. "They further their own aims, just like every other governing body. The Order protects its own power and its own interests, operating in shadow and serving as judge, jury, and executioner. It isn't right that so few should hold such sway over the lives and deaths of others—especially those who have no way to defend against their judgment. We already have a king, after all."

"What would you have, then? Anarchy in the streets? People left with no law and no moral guidance? Of course that's what you dream of—a city overrun with vice and depravity. You and your creatures of the night," she spat. "Your only aim is to bring your stain of darkness to the world around you. Well, you'll have to excuse me, but I for one do not wish to live in your realm of blood and filth and fear. I choose the light, Étienne, and I will always fight for it."

Rage ripped through me at her contempt, and I leaped forward, pinning her back against the seat.

"You know nothing of my world," I hissed through my lengthening fangs. "And your privilege blinds you to the reality of light and dark."

Her heart beat a tattoo of fear and excitement in her chest—something I'd no doubt she'd deny.

"Release me," she said through gritted teeth. "I'm not going to stay here and allow you to insult me further."

I crowded in closer, the anger in my blood suddenly giving way to white-hot lust. I could see the rise and fall of her bound breasts beneath the coarse linen shirt. Her fragrance of orange blossom and vanilla surrounded me, and I was suddenly desperate to taste her. My hardening cock pressed against my breeches.

Time stood still—neither of us seemed willing to concede and back down. The delicate flare of her nostrils, the defiant tilt of her chin, and the wild look in her eyes nearly unmanned me. I briefly considered tearing those damn breeches from her, bending her over the seat, and claiming her, but I reminded myself that I wasn't the animal she took me for.

The rasp of gravel beneath the carriage wheels signaled arrival at her impressive château, saving us both from God only knew what.

I sat back in my seat and let her descend on her own. As she climbed the stairs into her grand house, I called out to her.

"If we are to work together, Duchess, I suggest you keep an open mind. In the world beyond Versailles, your pride will be your undoing."

And you will be mine.

5

DAPHNE

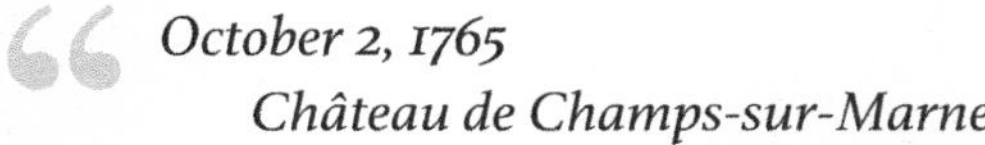

October 2, 1765
Château de Champs-sur-Marne

"Daphne, are you even listening to me?" Philippe complained. He seemed more ruffled than usual.

Truthfully, I was not. My mind had wandered back to the same place it had been for the last four days—Étienne's carriage. I'd tossed and turned for the last three nights, poring over his words. Had the Order really tried to kill him before? Why would they? What had he done?

Was he right about me?

He'd been right about Jeanne. I'd seen it for myself. The vicious tears in the flesh of her throat—no vampire would have done that. I'd seen real vampire bites firsthand. *My poor Michel.* I shut my eyes against the painful memories.

Philippe crossed the room and kneeled before me. Concern marred his face. "Daphne, please. Talk to me. You've got to tell me what's going on. I can't keep the Order at bay much longer. Why haven't you killed Noailles yet?"

"I do not believe he is Jeanne's killer," I finally said.

Philippe rocked back on his heels and stood. "Why not? You read the report. She was bitten. Her blood was drained."

"Who wrote the report?"

Philippe lifted one shoulder. "Another agent. I don't know who."

"Well, whoever it was either wasn't present and was putting it together from rumors, or is deliberately trying to accuse the emissary. That report is all wrong, Philippe. Her blood was not simply drained. Her throat was ripped open. She likely bled out. The wound was no vampire bite—it was too savage. Inhuman, even. It looked like some kind of animal attack."

He narrowed his eyes. "How do you know? Did *he* tell you that?"

I'd been debating telling Philippe the entirety of the situation. I knew he wouldn't approve, but up until now, I hadn't told anyone, and I needed someone I could trust within the Order. I faced him, mustering my courage.

"We exhumed her body. I inspected her myself. Étienne professes his innocence, Philippe, and I am starting to believe him."

He took the news like a physical blow. Eyes bulging, he gaped at me. "Daphne," he breathed. "That is—it's blasphemous! How could you?"

"Perhaps it is, but I wanted the truth, and now I have it. Well, part of it anyway," I said, resigned.

Disappointment flowed off Philippe in waves, and I found myself caught up in the tide. He stared at me in stunned silence.

"So, it's *Étienne* now, is it?" he asked, shaking his head. "If you don't believe he is guilty, why haven't you informed the Order?"

"I don't think they'll listen to me. They might listen to you though," I hedged.

Philippe sighed deeply. "Have you any other evidence of his innocence?"

"Not yet," I admitted. "But I hope to soon."

"Darling, you know I can't just go to them armed with your unsubstantiated suspicions. You know what they'll say. They'll say he has bewitched you, just like he bewitches every other woman—

that you think his handsome face and his charm excuse the horrible things he has done. They'll say you've been compromised by your emotions, and I'll have nothing to show them to prove otherwise."

"I'll get proof," I insisted. Philippe cast me a doubtful look. "One other thing—he mentioned that the Order had sent agents to assassinate him before. What do you know of that?"

Philippe shrugged. "Nothing, really."

"What else is he accused of?" I pressed.

Philippe looked at me like I'd gone mad. "Well, murder, for one! And treasonous slander. And adultery!"

Suspicious, I approached Philippe and stared hard into his eyes.

"Adultery is the currency of Versailles, Philippe," I said. "That doesn't warrant a death threat from the Order. What has he done? Is it his politics? Does it have something to do with his title?"

"How should I know?" he blustered.

"You've been with the Order for eight years," I pushed. "You were with them before the blood plague came to Paris. You're one of their most trusted members."

Philippe's eyes flashed and his temper flared. "Not even I know everything, Daphne. Besides, why do you care? He's a *vampire*, just like the ones that killed your brother. Or have you forgotten? Do you need to be reminded of the fact that it was but five short years ago that Michel was found murdered—*drained*—right outside your family's home?" He threw his hands up and began to pace the room.

Pain at the memory rendered me speechless. But Phillipe wasn't done.

"You were *this close* to poverty, Daphne, when the title and lands passed to a distant relation with no provision for you. The only thing that saved you was an ill-advised marriage to a wealthy, titled man no better than the monsters who took your brother from you! And here you are! Throwing yourself in with their kind. I simply don't understand it."

The utter ass—bringing up my past in such a callous, judgmental manner and then refusing to help me.

"I have not thrown myself in with their kind!" I snarled, outraged at his scorn. "And I don't know why you don't understand my hesitation. Does the truth matter so little to you?"

"Does it matter that much to you?" he countered. "He's just some vampire!"

I gritted my teeth, trying to force down my rising temper. I recognized we were at an impasse, and alienating Phillipe seemed unproductive and unwise, even if he deserved a very thorough chastening. Despite the fact that I held a title above his in society, he was still senior to me in the Order and enjoyed all the undeserved privileges of the patriarchy.

I went to the front window and stared out at the drizzly, pewter afternoon.

He stopped pacing, then blew out a breath. "I'm sorry, Daphne. You know I'd do anything to help you, but with the Noailles assignment, I don't know if I can."

"Well, if I am on my own, then, so be it," I replied in a wooden tone.

He made a noise of exasperation in his throat. "Even if I could, I doubt they'd listen to me any more than they would you. Noailles is on their list, and I'm sure they have their reasons beyond Jeanne's death. I'm sorry, Daphne, but I can't protect you from the Order anymore. You wanted in—now you've got to figure your way of this mess. Find your proof, or find yourself facing their judgment."

With that, he picked up his hat and walked out of the room.

Frustrated, I stormed upstairs, my ire growing with every step. Certainly, he could refuse to help me, but how dare he shame me for Michel's death and for my marriage to Henri! I did what I had had to do to survive. I paced my bedchamber, punched my pillows, and threw a book across the room. The idea that the Order would suggest I'd developed feelings for Étienne enraged me even further. Of course I didn't care for the rogue! I cared about the truth—and so far, Étienne had been more honest with me than Philippe had. That was what mattered in all of this: *the truth*.

With renewed resolve, I went to my desk and drafted a missive to the vampire. It was time we continued our investigation.

When I dressed that evening, I donned one of Eve's simple gray dresses and pinned my dark-blonde curls beneath a cap. I wrapped my shoulders in a brown wool shawl and strapped my flintlock to my thigh. I kept my dagger and a thin wooden stake in my pockets, though I hoped I wouldn't need them tonight. I wasn't sure where Étienne was taking me, but I knew it wouldn't be anywhere near the world of Versailles.

He had responded promptly to my message, stating that he would be around after sundown to collect me. His terse response irked me. I wondered if he was still angry with me over our argument in the carriage. I hoped not. I only had the energy to deal with one intractable ass today, and I'd already gotten my fill from Philippe.

Eve knocked at my door and informed me that Monsieur de Noailles had arrived. I braced myself for his broody temperament and went down to greet him.

He sat in the front parlor, staring fixedly into the fireplace. He was dressed in plain but well-tailored clothes, his hat resting idly on one knee. The warm firelight flickered across his sculpted features, casting him in a glow of amber heat. It struck me that he looked like one of Louis's golden statues come to life. I had the strange urge to reach out and run my fingertips across his lips to see if they really were as soft as the gossips said.

"If you're going to stand back there all night staring at me, Duchess, perhaps you could make yourself useful and pour me a drink while you're at it," he said, his focus never leaving the flames.

I stiffened at his rudeness. "I can, if you require one. I was waiting for you to stand so that we may go."

"Go where?" he asked. "It is you who summoned me."

Still, he did not look at me. He seemed...strange, distant.

"Monsieur, are you well?"

He smiled cruelly and his tone dripped with sarcasm. "But of course, madame. Why shouldn't I be well?"

"I'm sure I do not know, but you seem...not yourself tonight. I was under the impression that you had a lead for us to follow. Possibly related to Jeanne's missing ring?" I prodded.

I came farther into the room, and he finally looked up at me. I gasped when I saw his eyes—the honeyed hazel of his irises had changed to a deep blood red.

Instinctively, I stepped back. "What happened to your eyes, Étienne? Are you ill?"

He laughed acidly. "I am dead, Duchess! But do you mean, ill besides being a vampire?"

He stood suddenly, his movements erratic and supernaturally quick. He stalked toward me and backed me up against the wall. Caged between his hard, muscular arms, I took in the rest of his appearance—the stubble on his sallow-skinned jaw, the tendrils of dark hair escaping his queue, the shadows in the hollows of his cheeks and beneath his eyes. He looked like he hadn't slept in days.

He closed his eyes and buried his face in the crook of my neck. I froze like a rabbit before a fox. He wouldn't bite me, would he? What was wrong with him? I reached for the wooden stake in my pocket.

He inhaled deeply and growled. Panic started to build inside me. My heart thundered in my chest. *No, no, no. Please, no.*

Come back to your senses, Étienne.

"Shh," he whispered against my skin. "Calm your racing heart, little nymph."

I felt a hot, wet caress and realized he'd licked my neck. Unbidden desire ignited in my blood, warring with fear and shame.

"Étienne," I breathed. *I should stop him.*

Soft kisses danced up the column of my neck and a firm hand stroked my back. *When has it ever felt this good to be touched?* I wondered.

Never.

Something isn't right. He isn't well. You must stop this, Daphne.

"Étienne," I stammered, tears pricking at my eyes. "You are not yourself. Allow me to call a doctor for you."

"But I am myself, Duchess," he drawled, dragging his lips up to my ear. "I don't need a doctor. You have everything I need."

He pressed his hips into me, and I felt the hard length of his arousal against my stomach. My knees nearly buckled, and I grew wet with reflexive desire. *No! We mustn't!*

"Yes," he moaned, sucking on my earlobe and raining kisses across my jaw. "I can smell your passion, little nymph. I want you. Feel how desperately I want you. How I need—"

He stopped abruptly, pulling back. His eyes paled to hazel again, and he stared at me in bewilderment.

"Daphne?" he questioned. His feeble voice sounded miles away. "What are you doing here?"

His unfocused gaze shifted to his surroundings, and he blinked in confusion. As quickly as he'd returned to me, he vanished again—the blood-colored irises were back. He took a step in my direction, then stumbled and fell to his knees.

"Help me," he wheezed. "I need..." He trailed off, falling to the ground. Curling his knees to his chest, he gagged, vomiting black blood and bile across the carpet.

Angrily, I dashed the tears from my face. Warily, as if I was approaching a wounded animal, I leaned forward and pulled him up, gently shaking him.

"What do you need? What happened? What, Étienne?"

One of the footmen heard the commotion and came running into the parlor. He helped me attempt to rouse him, but it was no use.

Étienne slipped into unconsciousness.

6

ÉTIENNE

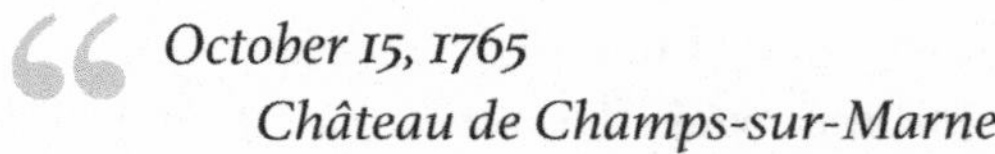

October 15, 1765
Château de Champs-sur-Marne

IT WAS BETTER THAN THE DREAMS I WAS USED TO. SOFT PINK LIPS parted in ecstasy—heavy-lidded violet eyes glazed with desire—my throbbing cock sliding into warm, wet silk. Attempting to hold on to the blissful vision, I kept my eyes closed and snaked a hand beneath the sheets, intent on alleviating my growing need. A rough moan escaped my lips when I grasped my erection.

"I see you're awake."

My eyes flew open and I jerked upright—*mistake*. Blinding pain rioted through my brain. I clutched my head and fell back on the bed with a curse.

"*Merde,*" came the voice again. "Don't try to get up yet. The doctor said you would be weak for some time."

I took stock of my surroundings, and the confusion only made my head ache more.

"Daphne?" I rasped. My parched throat felt like sand.

"I'm here, Étienne," she said. "What do you remember?"

Things were fuzzy. I tried to piece together my remaining memories, but everything seemed unclear. "Where am I?"

I closed my eyes to block out the pain. I was in a bed somewhere. The room was dark and cool and smelled like damp earth and stone.

"You're in my wine cellar," she said. She came to the side of the bed and tipped a glass of water to my lips. I drank deeply.

"Should that mean something to me?" I grumped, wiping my mouth with the back of my hand. I felt several days' growth of beard. "I don't remember much right now, so I'd be much obliged if you filled in some of the blanks."

She busied herself at a small table by my bedside and returned with a shallow porcelain bowl filled with—*it couldn't be.*

"Whose blood is that?" I asked, surprisingly concerned given my weakened state.

Daphne's pale cheeks and tight lips expressed her disapproval without words.

"I haven't murdered anyone on your account, if that's what you're asking," she said tartly.

Questions formed in my brain, but the smell of the blood made me ravenous. I didn't know how long it had been since I'd fed, but considering I felt like I'd been run over by a stampede of horses, I assumed it had been awhile. Normally I preferred to drink from the thigh veins of women in the throes of passion, but I supposed beggars couldn't be choosers.

"It's warm," I remarked, taking the bowl from her.

She sniffed haughtily. "Well, of course it is. My cook kept it at the proper temperature. I assume you don't eat it—drink it—cold."

My fangs distended, and I drank from the bowl voraciously.

Never had I tasted anything so delicious. *Good God.* Rather than quenching my burning thirst and alleviating the painful hunger, I felt a bigger, more desperate need—lust. The desire for sexual release and more blood—no, more of *this* blood.

It must be because I haven't fed in so long, I thought, unsettled.

Already, I felt strength returning to my muscles. The ache in my head began to ebb.

Daphne took the empty bowl from me and set it back on the table. She crossed to one of the dusty crates, grabbed a bottle of wine, and uncorked it with practiced efficiency. She let out a shuddering breath and raised the bottle to her lips for a long swallow. She tilted the bottle in my direction, offering me a swig. I declined.

"Daphne, are you all right?"

With the sharpness of my supernatural senses coming back to me, I finally noticed her disheveled appearance. She wore a plain day dress of navy cotton that had smudges of dust and blood on it. Her eyes were red rimmed, and several blonde curls escaped her lace cap. She'd been watching over me.

She cast me a withering look and chugged from the wine bottle again. When she was down a quarter of the bottle, her shoulders relaxed a bit and she came back to sit in the bedside chair.

Clearing her throat, she pointed at me accusingly. "Now that you're not dead—or undead—re-dead?—you have quite a lot to answer for, monsieur."

"I'm listening," I grumbled. Not like I had any choice in the matter. I was still too weak to leave, and belatedly I realized I was naked beneath the covers.

She got up and strode anxiously around the room, like some kind of wildcat in a cage. I wondered how long it had been since she'd slept. She put the bottle to her lips again but merely sipped at it this time. "This is a fine Bordeaux."

Distracted, she offered me the bottle again. She obviously didn't want to drink alone. I took it from her and poured some into my empty water glass.

"*Santé,*" I toasted. It really was a fine Bordeaux.

Heaving a great sigh, she sat once more.

"I have broken so many oaths these last few weeks, I fear the punishments awaiting me—in this life and the next." She scrubbed one hand across her face, trying to wipe away some of her fatigue.

"Did you ever know my brother, Michel? Before he died, he was... He would have enjoyed your company, I think."

I shook my head. "No, I did not have the privilege. I returned to Paris some time after he died."

"After he was murdered," she corrected. She sipped her wine. "He was the *duc de Lorraine* for such a short time. Less than a year. He inherited the title after both of our parents died from consumption. He had such plans, Étienne. He was on his way to becoming a remarkable man and a dutiful steward of my family's title. His only worry was about siring an heir. He was never inclined to enjoy the company of women, even during his teenage years when all men are predisposed to—what is the phrase?—*sow their oats*. Not Michel. He was content with his books and his music and was dedicated to his duties. It never bothered me that he desired other men. I loved him so much—I didn't care. I only wanted his happiness. Things were simpler then, when we thought we had a lifetime ahead of us. But Fate—she always has other plans for us, no?"

"Truer words were never spoken, Duchess." Unease threaded through me. I worried where her recollection was going and why she seemed compelled to share it with me now.

"Michel knew his duty. He did plan to marry and produce heirs. His predilections are not uncommon—he knew he could marry for duty and find a lover outside the marriage bed. He planned to provide for me as well because he did not want me to marry for anything less than love. *If I cannot marry for my happiness, chérie, at least you shall,* he said. My poor Michel! How I have dishonored his memory with my choices."

A tear spilled down her cheek, and she swirled the wine in the bottle.

"When they found his body at the front gate of his château, he was naked—drained of every drop of blood. His lover—some vampire merchant, the gossips said—had killed him and tossed his body in the street like some piece of trash."

Christ. No wonder she harbored a grudge.

"I swore vengeance, of course. Against his lover—a man I still do not know the identity of—and against anyone who would prey on another's weakness. Against vampires. *All* vampires," she said with conviction. "It's one of the reasons I joined the Order. And yet here you are. The most well-known vampire in all of Paris. Languishing in my wine cellar, drinking blood that I myself have served."

She said this last with only a slight hint of animosity, tilting her head at me curiously. She seemed struck by the absurdity of the situation. She chuckled to herself, but there was pain beneath it. Fresh pain, it seemed.

"Daphne." I reached for her, but she jerked her hand away. I cleared my throat again and ran my hand through my hair—unbound and tangled with the remnants of fevered sleep. "You could have staked me at any time or allowed me to die, just like the Order commanded. Why didn't you?"

She was quiet for a long moment.

"I suppose...even though you are a vampire, it seems that perhaps you are the one being preyed on."

"Tell me what happened. How did I end up in your wine cellar, of all places?"

"You don't remember anything?"

I shook my head. Flashes returned to me—a young woman, a strange taste, then blackness. Anxiety knotted my stomach. I'd been unaware of any biological weaknesses brought on by the plague, save for the sensitivity to sunlight; garlic; and, of course, wooden stakes. It seemed there was something else in this world that could wipe out my supernatural advantages—something unknown to me. The thought did not sit well. For someone who'd only just gotten used to the idea of immortality, I found myself remarkably concerned with it ending so soon.

"I sent you a message two weeks ago. You were to come here so that we could continue our investigation into Jeanne's death. Her missing ring. You arrived in the evening, but you were different—

very unlike yourself. Your eyes were red, and your behavior was..." She trailed off, sounding wounded.

I'd hurt her. My heart clenched at the thought.

"I was what?" I pressed.

"*Ungentlemanly*."

Hell. That could mean anything. I opened my mouth to find out more, but she hurried on.

"You were eventually overcome, and you fainted in my parlor. My staff helped me set up a bed here in the wine cellar—the only underground room in the château and the only place safe from the sunlight—and I sent for a doctor. I don't mind telling you that I had some time trying to find one who was familiar enough with vampire biology, but this doctor has proven to be very knowledgeable. She is staying upstairs in one of the guest rooms. I'm afraid I insisted that she remain on the grounds until you either expired or recovered."

I tried not to smile at her tyrannical tone. I was beginning to enjoy the high-handed way she managed her world.

At that moment, there was a knock on the heavy wooden door, and a curvy, dark-haired woman with spectacles entered. My brows rose in interest.

"Doctor Van Helsing," Daphne greeted. "Your patient appears to be recovering his faculties. I must congratulate you on your skill."

The doctor smiled and bustled over to me. She fussed about, examining my eyes and mouth, and pulled a red vial from her bag.

"Drink please, monsieur," she instructed through a thick Dutch accent. "This should help."

"What is it?" I couldn't keep the suspicion from my voice.

"Virgin's blood. It will help restore much of your strength. Mind you, don't spill a drop—it's hard enough to find a virgin in Paris these days," she complained.

I tossed the vial back and felt a surge of euphoric power rush through my body. *Mon dieu.* No wonder everyone was always banging on about drinking the blood of virgins. As restorative as it was, I still longed for more of the blood from the porcelain bowl.

"Now, then," the doctor said. "Do you remember the last person you drank from?"

Daphne was putting dishes on a tray, pretending not to listen. I felt strangely uncomfortable going into the details with her there, but I didn't think she'd respond well to my request that she leave. *Merde.*

"Vaguely," I hedged.

"Someone new?"

"Yes, why?"

"You were suffering from an acute attack of quicksilver poisoning. It enters the blood and affects the mind—usually resulting in brain fever and a kind of madness, which, when untreated, leads to a very unpleasant second death. Vampires seem to be more susceptible to its symptoms than humans, but not many people know that. The contaminated blood must be removed from the body of the infected, which is a very difficult procedure. You'll also feel weak, I imagine, for some time until you can feed enough to heal completely."

"How does one succumb to quicksilver poisoning?" Daphne asked.

The doctor handed me two more vials of blood.

"Take one vial just before sunrise for the next two days. You will recover entirely if you allow yourself the proper time to rest," she instructed. "As to the method of poisoning, I believe it was in the blood of the last person you drank from, which means they deliberately ingested it before you fed on them. At the risk of sounding dire, monsieur, I think you should make sure your affairs are in order. You seem to have a very formidable enemy who wants you dead."

7

DAPHNE

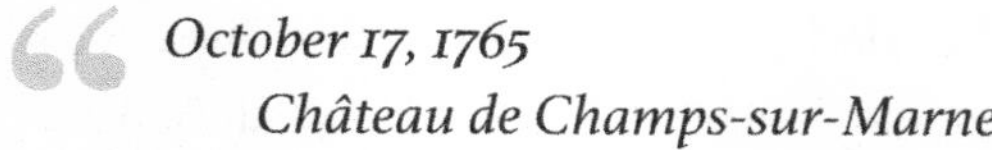

October 17, 1765
Château de Champs-sur-Marne

THE ORDER MUST HAVE SENT SOMEONE ELSE—ANOTHER ASSASSIN. I'D known it would happen eventually, but as usual, I'd miscalculated how much time I had, and Étienne had paid the price.

The two weeks that he'd been senseless had been some of the worst of my life. Not only had it delayed our investigation but seeing a powerful man laid low and raving through unconscious delirium was disturbing, to say the least.

"After this, he should be well enough to travel," Doctor Van Helsing said. She expertly bandaged the small cut on the inside of my arm and carefully handed the porcelain bowl of my blood to the cook. "Keep it warm," she instructed, ignoring the cook's queasy expression.

"Thank you, Doctor. I appreciate the care you've bestowed on the emissary," I said. I tugged my sleeve down over the bandage.

Van Helsing cocked her head and studied me, her bright-blue eyes made owlish by her thick spectacles.

"On the contrary, Your Grace. I merely treated the patient. He has you to thank for his care."

Uncomfortable with the insinuation that I cared for the vampire, I stood—somewhat unsteadily. Van Helsing caught my elbow and *tsked.*

"You've been feeding him for days now—you must take some time to recover your own strength. Red meat for your evening meal and early to bed, I say. And this should be the *last* that you feed him. Understand?" She fussed over me, looking more like an aging governess than the voluptuous, vibrant woman of thirty that she was.

"Far be it from me to disagree with a doctor's orders," I smiled, steadying myself. "I'm fine, Doctor, I promise. Nicole, if you'll hand me that tray with the blood, I'll see to our guest."

The cook nodded and handed me the tray, after half-heartedly offering to take it down herself. I brushed her off and descended the stairs to the wine cellar. Even though several of the household staff had offered their blood instead of mine, I'd refused. When Michel had been found drained, it had shocked and devastated our entire home—I had not grieved alone. I couldn't subject anyone else to something so unpleasant when I knew I had the strength to bear the burden. Besides, as long as Étienne was in my house, his care and feeding was my responsibility, though I preferred him being ignorant to that.

I knocked on the cellar door, and Étienne bade me enter. He looked vastly improved for a dead man. The hollows beneath his eyes had gone, and his gaunt features had evened out over the last several days, losing the sunken pallor of illness. He flashed me a grin and sat up straighter in bed, reaching for the tray in my hands.

"You must send my compliments to your chef—or whomever has kindly offered to sustain me. I must say, this is the best blood that I've ever had," he said, picking up the bowl eagerly.

I nodded and turned to leave, but he stopped me.

"Have you been in contact with your masters?"

I bristled. "My *what?*"

"The Order."

"They are *not* my masters. I simply work with them to address the more pressing threats to king and country," I said stiffly.

"Threats like vampires," he said, putting down the empty bowl. His fangs glinted in the candlelight as he dabbed at his mouth with a napkin.

"Yes. The blood plague is a threat to the country. People are dying, Étienne. Not every vampire leaves their victim alive after feeding."

"People are also dying of hunger, Duchess. Certainly, the plague adds to the numbers, but I have a hard time agreeing with the Order when their policy is to simply stake all the infected to prevent the plague from spreading. You're a smart woman. You can't tell me that you think it makes sense to kill people in order to protect them." He picked up the wine glass from the tray and sipped at it.

"If the deaths of a few will protect the many, then yes, that makes sense to me."

"And you think the Order has the right to determine that? What if the plague had only struck the aristocracy? Would you feel the same way? Would you be willing to lay down your life as a possible disease spreader in order to protect the lowly peasants?"

"I—well, yes, I would. If it was for the good for the many," I argued, folding my arms in front of me.

Étienne tutted. "Forgive me if I don't believe you. Trust me when I tell you that this condition—this burden—is not one to be taken lightly. The choice between infection and death is a near-impossible one, even for a disgraced wretch like me."

I narrowed my eyes. "At least you have an eternity to right your wrongs. To make amends."

"It's hard to make amends with the dead," he said quietly.

For the first time, I saw a flash of regret in his hazel eyes. I wondered who he thought of in that moment, and before I could catch myself, I felt a swell of sympathy for him. I knew what it was like to lose loved ones before you had the chance to tell them everything you wanted to. For a man who was surrounded by death, he must have felt that tenfold.

He cleared his throat and took a swig of wine. "Besides, who told you vampires were the minority?"

I stilled. "But, they are! There cannot be so many. The Order—"

He cut me off with an arched brow. "We are more than you think, Duchess."

His velvet tone implied he was referring to more than the number of vampires in France. I met his gaze and found myself thinking of his body pressed against mine, his kisses on my neck. I blushed. *I shouldn't have liked it—shouldn't have wanted it to continue.* I didn't trust him one whit, but that hadn't seemed to matter to my body.

Étienne stood from the bed, clad only in his loose linen shirt and breeches, and strode over to me. His eyes never left mine. When he was mere inches from me, he stopped.

"As am I," he murmured. He leaned forward, and I closed my eyes reflexively, fearfully prepared—*no, shamefully hoping*—for the kiss to come. My breath quickened. My lips parted.

But the kiss never arrived.

Instead, I felt him gently lift my hand to his lips. My eyes flew open. He pressed a chaste kiss to the back of my hand and smiled up at me through his lashes.

"Thank you for keeping me company while I dined this evening. I'm deeply indebted to you for your hospitality. I'll bid you good night, Duchess."

He opened the door for me, handed me the dinner tray, and bowed before retreating back inside the cellar. It took me some moments to recover my senses enough to make a rather incensed march back upstairs.

To distract myself from a whirlwind of confusing emotions—unspent lust, embarrassment, confusion, frustration, and no small amount of anger—I asked for dinner to be brought into the library and sat at my desk to tackle a mountain of correspondence that I'd been avoiding.

I put aside the apologetic missive from Philippe. I still didn't have any proof of Étienne's innocence, and I was loath to tell Philippe I was playing host, nursemaid, *and* dinner to the man I'd been sent to kill. Anxiety had rooted in my stomach at his suggestion that the Order would accuse me of having feelings for the vampire. Considering I'd been feeding him my own blood to keep him alive, that claim would be even more difficult to refute.

Days before, I'd finally gathered the courage to send a message to the Order and explain why I hadn't killed Étienne. I'd declined to tell them about digging up Jeanne's body and the recent events that brought Étienne to my doorstep—it made me uneasy to confront them about a second assassination attempt. Doing so would reveal that I was aware of it in the first place, and I didn't want to play my hand until I had all the cards.

I'd been surprised when they'd responded so quickly but no better off than I had been. While they'd agreed to allow me time to find proof of Étienne's innocence, they'd made it clear that I would be doing so on my own. I wouldn't have access to the resources or contacts that the Order possessed. I suspected they did so to limit the impact of what they believed would be my likely failure. The clock was ticking, and I was alone in my quest for truth.

So be it.

The last letter I had was from Charlotte, keeping me updated on the latest gossip at court. My cousin had an almost supernatural ability to gather information—far better than my own, even when I was collecting intelligence for the Order. Her cheerful nature and sparkling wit made her a natural ally and confidante, and I relied on her observations heavily when I wasn't at court myself. Reading between the lines, I started to pick up on a worrisome trend. Despite the king's more relaxed attitude toward having the nobility in residence at the palace, more and more courtiers were leaving their private châteaux to move into vacant apartments within Versailles. I thought back to Étienne's words. Were the infected no longer the minority? Were these moves motivated by the fear of what was happening around Paris? If so, who else knew that we humans were in a more precarious position than the king—and the Order, for that matter—would have us believe?

Étienne believed a reckoning was coming. For the second time since I'd met him, I was starting to believe he was right.

8

ÉTIENNE

> *October 18, 1765*
> *Château de Champs-sur-Marne*

I FLIPPED THE PAGES OF MY BOOK IDLY, UNABLE TO FOCUS. MY thoughts returned to Daphne and the expectant look on her face—the unmistakable desire I'd seen there. It had thrown me. She might not have believed what I was telling her about the plague and the people of France, she might not have believed I was innocent of involvement in Jeanne's murder, she might not have trusted me or my motives in the slightest—but I could sense that she was attracted to me.

It shouldn't have excited me as much as it did.

Feeling like a caged animal, I threw the book onto the bed and paced my makeshift room. I was sorely tempted to work my way through the dozens of wines lining the walls, but I figured that would be a temporary solution at best. At worst, I'd get drunk enough to become senseless again, and I didn't want a repeat of whatever transgressions I'd managed while poisoned.

I sighed. Perhaps a different book. Knowing it was after midnight, I listened carefully for the sounds of the household, not wanting to startle some unsuspecting housemaid. After I was certain the rest of the château was abed, I crept out from the wine cellar and padded silently through the halls. I hadn't bothered with a candle—my unfortunate supernatural condition afforded me the ability to see well enough in the dark.

When I located the library, I was surprised to see a thin ray of light beneath the door. I knocked softly, and Daphne's voice sounded from within.

"Yes?"

I went in. She sat at a large desk, bent over a pile of papers. Her hair fell over her shoulder in a thick, golden braid, and I glimpsed her white nightdress beneath her loose dressing gown. After a moment, she looked up, her eyebrows arching in bewilderment.

"Étienne! What are you doing out of bed? Are you well?" She stood to approach but paused, suddenly embarrassed by her appearance. She tied the belt of her dressing gown around herself and fidgeted with the knot. I'd never seen her look so unguarded—vulnerable, even. It was disturbingly appealing.

I grinned. "Forgive me for startling you. I thought everyone would be asleep by now. I merely came to find something new to read."

She nodded but did not sit back down. She gestured at the walls lined with books.

"You won't find a better selection of books anywhere—save, perhaps, Versailles. My father was a great collector and lover of the written word. Michel was too. Help yourself," she said, turning back to her letters.

I strode over to the wall opposite her, nearest to the fireplace, and perused distractedly. "What about you?" I asked.

The light scratching of her pen stopped. "What about me?"

"Do you share the same interests as your father and brother?"

The scratching resumed, then paused again. She sighed.

"I like books," she said evasively.

"The only books my father collected were about history,

weaponry, and military strategy," I said. "I never appreciated them, but I had little else to read. My mother snuck some romances into our collection—which I enjoyed more than the lessons on combat—but not by much."

"What do you like to read?" Daphne asked.

"Adventures. Travel, art, music, culture. Essentially everything that my father despised," I replied, with more than a touch of bitterness.

She was next to me now, leaning against one of the high-backed chairs that faced the fireplace.

"He was a soldier," she said quietly, more observation than question.

"A highly decorated general. A war hero, even," I replied, thinking back to the distant memories—and pain. "His last campaign was the battle at Dettingen in the war of Austrian succession. He was betrayed by two of his comrades, which led to his defeat. In the king's fury, my father was stripped of his title and most of our holdings. I'm sure you heard the rumors of our family's disgrace. *Vicomte* no longer. He died years later, broken and impoverished."

"I'm sorry," Daphne said, laying a hand on my arm. "I'd heard some of the gossip, but I didn't know the story. It was unjust for the king to punish your father so harshly—especially if it was the result of a betrayal."

"It matters little now. Louis knew exactly which strings to pull to coerce me into emissary service. My ancestral estate and holdings have been returned to me, at least. I don't care about the title. I shan't be having an issue to pass it on to anyway." Frustrated and resentful, I turned from the bookshelves and sat heavily in one of the armchairs before the fire. It needled me, if I let it—the inability to sire an heir. In my boyhood, when I was to inherit a title and the responsibilities attached to it, my father had worked tirelessly to drill a sense of duty and honor into my head. Even when I'd rebelled as a young man, I'd known that I'd return to the fold eventually. Find a wealthy, well-connected wife—hopefully pretty—and get her with child after child. We would enjoy family holidays in the country and seasons in Paris, try not to squander the fortune my father had carefully amassed and invested. I'd find some way to serve France, whether on the battlefield or in court. *Honor, duty, and responsibility, son. That's your lot in life. Do not waste it.*

And I almost had—but I was trying to make up for it now.

Daphne went to a sideboard, poured two generous glasses of cognac, and sat in the other armchair. She handed me a glass, which I took gratefully. I'd wanted company, but I hadn't expected to spill my life story. I swirled the cognac in the glass, unexpectedly self-conscious.

"Is that a...vampire problem?" she inquired awkwardly.

I nodded. "Hard to sire heirs when your body functions as a walking corpse. Did you and the duke never—"

"No," she cut in. "After a few months of marriage, I refused him. I would not consent to carry his bloodline." At this, she drank a sizable swallow of cognac. Her cheeks turned a fetching shade of pink.

"Was he—" I floundered for the right words, but she interrupted me again with an acerbic smile.

"He wasn't called *the Depraved Duke* for nothing," she said.

Things started to fall into place, then—rumors I'd heard about the brutal, predatory aristocrat. I hadn't realized *the Depraved Duke* was Daphne's husband. Horror filled me in a way I hadn't experienced in some years. The thought of her suffering the abuse of such a man made me see red. My fangs lengthened impulsively, and my muscles bunched, preparing to attack some unseen threat. Without warning, the cognac glass exploded in my hand.

"*Merde,*" I swore. Daphne jumped up, grabbing a cloth and a pitcher of water from a nearby table. She reached for my hand—tentatively. "I'm not going to bite," I chuckled. My fangs retracted. Daphne eyed me cautiously and started wiping the blood from my palm.

An uncomfortable silence settled between us.

"I heard from the Order," she blurted.

I arched a brow. "Good news or bad?"

"Both—or neither, depending on your perspective," she said. "They seem open to considering your innocence in Jeanne's murder, but they require proof. They've allowed me some time—but no resources—to settle the matter."

"How magnanimous of them," I drawled. She'd finished cleaning my hand and was using a clean scrap of cloth to bind it. Her movements were firm but tender.

"There's more," she said, gingerly picking up shards of glass from the floor. "I had a letter from Charlotte. It sounds like many of the nobles are relocating to the palace. I fear things are escalating. The aristocrats are worried."

This wasn't exactly surprising but certainly more concerning.

"What will the Order do?" I wondered.

Daphne went to her desk to throw the broken glass and bloody rags away.

"I don't know," she admitted. "I don't know about all of their plans, and I'm afraid if I don't find Jeanne's killer and bring them proof soon, they'll kick me out and I'll know even less."

I agreed. "We must hurry. I'm well enough to carry on. I'll send a message to some of my contacts in Paris and let them know we'll be in the city tomorrow night. We'll start with the ring."

Some relief shone in Daphne's face.

"That would be best," she said. "I'm eager to see this through and move on with my life."

"As am I," I said. I stood to leave, and she followed me to the door. "Tomorrow night, we'll need to play the parts of intimidating aristocrats. Prepare accordingly."

Daphne rolled her eyes. "I think I can manage that."

"I'll do what I can to keep you safe, but you should remain on your guard."

"I don't need you to keep me safe, Étienne," she snapped.

"Perhaps not," I conceded. "But I will try all the same. Should things go awry, I mean."

We were standing at the threshold of the library, the dark hallway yawning behind me. Daphne appeared at a loss for words and stood at the door, hesitating. The tightness around her mouth relaxed and she mumbled a soft "thank you."

"I'll say good night, then," I said.

"Good night, Étienne."

I didn't go. I waited a beat—taking in the flickering candlelight on her golden hair; the worn linen of her nightdress; the perfume of cognac, blood, and orange blossoms. Here, in this quiet moment past midnight, I felt an alien sense of comfort. It was unlike the plush rooms at Versailles, unlike my own château, even—with its haunting memories and ghosts of failure. It filled me with a painful longing—a hollow ache in my chest that I knew would linger long after Daphne's orange-blossom scent had faded.

Her eyes dropped to my lips, then, and her tongue darted out to lick her bottom lip. My restraint evaporated in an instant. Unable to stop myself, I pulled her to me and covered her lips with mine. Slanting my mouth over hers, I slid my tongue along the seam of her lips—a silent plea for her to open up to me. Almost straightaway, she melted into the kiss. When she opened her mouth and sighed, the sweetness of it overtook me, and I knew I was lost.

God help me—what have I done?

9

DAPHNE

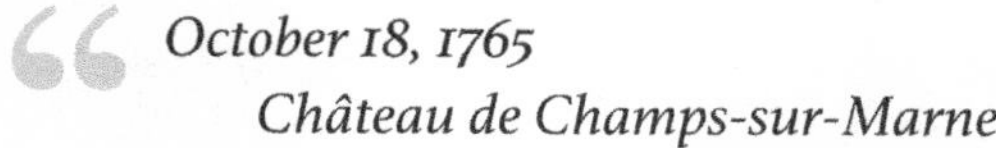

October 18, 1765
Château de Champs-sur-Marne

SOMEWHERE IN THE BACK OF MY MIND, A VOICE CALLED OUT TO ME, *Wrong. This is wrong. You cannot trust a vampire—especially this one.* I was dimly aware that I should be doing something—stopping this kiss. *This isn't kissing.* It was unlike the perfunctory and invasive attempts of Henri. It was *incredible.* Étienne brought his hand up to the back of my head and threaded his fingers through my hair, gently rubbing at the base of my neck. The pleasure of the touch rolled through me in waves. He tasted of cognac and something vaguely salty, but his lips felt so good against mine that I couldn't focus on much besides the feeling. *Dieu,* how he felt. My body craved more, but there was something stopping me from seeking it...

Do not trust the vampire. Remember all his women. Remember the blood. Remember Michel.

Finally, the thought beat back the surge of lust and I realized my mistake. I pulled away immediately, stepping back into the library. Confused by my desire for the man who represented everything I stood against, I couldn't help the force of my response.

"You kissed me!" I exclaimed. My fingers reached up to my tender lips as if to confirm the truth of the matter.

Étienne cocked a satisfied brow at me. "You kissed me back," he said.

"I—I didn't mean to! The cognac—and I haven't been sleeping, and I forgot myself, and *you* forgot *yourself!*" I stammered. *Damn it.* I didn't mean to sound so flustered. It made me even angrier. I fought for a steadying breath.

"It was a mistake," I gritted out. "It won't happen again."

Étienne's devilish grin slipped, and I could've sworn I saw a glimmer of hurt in his eyes. His face went blank. "A mistake. My apologies for being forward. As you say, it must have been the cognac."

I nodded, still not satisfied.

"We'll just forget it happened," I said, somewhat breathlessly. "And tomorrow, we'll resume our investigation. The sooner this is solved, the better."

Étienne bowed rigidly and turned down the hall. From the darkness, he called back to me.

"Sleep well, Duchess."

I wondered if we both knew that was unlikely.

The following day, I slept in much later than usual. I finally roused myself in the afternoon, ate a belated breakfast, and hid in one of the front parlors. My mind returned to the kiss over and over—how my body wanted him, but my mind couldn't trust him. Even if something happened to change that—which I reasoned was unlikely, given his scandalous reputation and supernatural state of being—I was not the kind of woman to take a lover, and as long as there were doubts about Henri's present whereabouts, I could not marry again. Besides, I was dedicated to the Order, and in my experience, men didn't tend to share well when it came to their lady's attentions. *It doesn't matter!* I chided myself. *The kiss was a mistake—a weak moment. Do you want to end up another name on some libertine's endless list of conquests? Certainly not.* My pride wouldn't allow it.

Still, I worried over the possibility that I'd started to care for him. It seemed truer now than when Philippe had first presented the possibility. One didn't aid in nursing a body back to health without forming some kind of attachment—an attachment that definitely needed severing.

I had to do it for the memory of Michel, for the sake of Philippe and Charlotte, for my duty to my king and to our dwindling human aristocracy. I had to admit that I felt less compelled to give him up for the Order now that they'd drawn a line in their support of my investigation.

I grunted. *Give him up.* As if you had him, Daphne. *As if I want him.*

Liar.

The rest of the day, I tried—and failed—to distract myself with letters, estate business, menu planning, and books before I finally gave up and went to change for dinner.

Eve helped me into my most somber-looking gray dress—a late mourning gown from when my parents had died, and then Michel not long after. It was severity in thread—soft wool with an infinity of tiny buttons. Wearing it made me feel serious and sad and hard-hearted all at once. It would be impossible for me to think of anything affectionate when it came to Étienne, and with the long sleeves and high neckline, I didn't think there would be anything that would remotely arouse his libidinous interests.

After I finished dressing, I twisted my hair in tight curls on top of my head, covered with a largely unflattering cap, and comforted myself by hiding an excess of stabbing implements in my pockets and sleeves.

If I came across anyone who meant me harm tonight, I'd take a great deal of pleasure in venting the maelstrom of destruction that seethed beneath my tightly reined exterior.

ÉTIENNE

I lay in my wine cellar bed for a while that evening, going over the events of the previous night in my mind. It was troubling to suddenly feel so unsure of myself—I'd thought the kiss was something we both wanted. While I knew Daphne had built an emotional fortress to protect herself, I'd sensed her desire and had felt it in her response. She'd wanted me as much as I'd wanted her.

...but what does that mean?

I hadn't been thinking about a future with her—or a future with any woman, for that matter. Women were delicious, wonderful playthings for me—food, pleasure, and tools to achieve what I needed to in court. With the disgrace to my name, the loss of my title, my inability to father children, and most importantly—the inevitable separation by time itself, if my paramour refused to infect herself with the plague—I had little to offer any woman beyond a few nights of passion. Frustratingly, I was beginning to feel that Daphne deserved more than that.

It didn't matter. I was recovering from a physical and mental shock, and I needed more than a few delicate porcelain bowls filled with donated blood. My lusty pursuit of this woman was likely the result of the euphoria I'd been experiencing from drinking virgin's blood. After our investigations ended, I'd go out and get something *properly* satisfying and leave the damned duchess Daphne to her melancholy.

As I was contemplating the strange turn of events my life had taken, someone knocked at the door. The butler Gaston entered with a set of shaving implements and a pitcher of warm water. He offered to help me shave, but I declined his assistance. After everything that had happened, I felt decidedly less comfortable allowing a stranger to hold a blade to my throat. He stood patiently by the door while I washed, lathered, and dragged the sharp blade over the light growth of whiskers I'd accumulated in my convalescence. When I was finished, he spoke.

"Her Grace instructed me to assist you with your dress tonight. If you'll follow me to the duke's bedchamber, we'll find something appropriate for you in his wardrobe," he said.

"Do you think the duke would object to my use of his clothes?"

Gaston glanced at me, eyes wide in surprise.

"His Grace is...gone," he said, fumbling for the right word.

"Yes, so I heard. What *exactly* does that mean, I wonder?"

Gaston didn't answer. We reached a sumptuous bedchamber decked in dark wood and burgundy velvet. It reminded me of the color of Daphne's gown the first night we'd met. The room seemed a tad stale, as if it hadn't been opened in some months. There were strange, lingering scents in the air that I struggled to name: faint wisps of opium smoke, the cloying reek of vomited brandy, the musk of ancient lovemaking, and—disturbingly—the metallic tinge of old blood. I'd smelled rooms like this before—in the dank basements of brothels that specialized in pain over pleasure. I couldn't imagine Daphne willingly submitting to such debasements, and I started to understand her fears. The hairs on the back of my neck stood on end and my fangs lengthened.

"What happened in here?" I growled. On some level, I already knew. A rush of protective indignity coursed through me when I imagined what Daphne had endured. *So, the gossip about the Depraved Duke had been true.*

A deep sorrow filled Gaston's gaze.

"We do not discuss it, monsieur." Shame and regret radiated from him.

"Just tell me this, then," I bit out. "Is the duke dead?"

If he isn't, I will amend that promptly.

A long-suffering sigh escaped him while he pulled ornate jackets, breeches, and matching waistcoats from a large ebony armoire. "We do not know, monsieur. But we do not think he will be coming back."

"Why not? He has one of the most influential duchies in all of France, a fortune almost as vast as the king's, this exceptional château, and a rather formidable wife. Even with the requisite carousing of the aristocracy, they're usually quite dedicated to at least some of the responsibilities of the peerage. Siring an heir is the most pressing one that comes to mind," I grumbled, then remembered Daphne's words from the night before. Her refusal to carry on the duke's bloodline. *Brave girl,* I thought. *Considering procreation is the only important preoccupation of titled women.*

I selected a charcoal-colored velvet coat adorned with silver embroidery. Despite the duke's obvious predilection for depravity, his taste in clothing was impeccable. He'd obviously enjoyed the slighter stature of the nobility and the coat was tight across my chest and shoulders, but I thought it would do for our outing tonight.

"You look very fine, monsieur," Gaston said, offering me a selection of shoe buckles to choose from. "Most satisfactory for *l'émissaire vampire.*"

I arched a brow at him. "You know who I am?"

"*Bien sûr.*" His reply was tight with stifled affront. "You've been a guest with us for some time now, monsieur."

"Ah, so madame has told you about me?"

"No, of course not. Her Grace does not share everything with us. But we know—all the same. We've been with her since she came to this house, and we are loyal to her," he said tersely. He finished tying back my hair in a silver ribbon.

He offered me a matching hat and shiny ebony walking stick, which I took with a nod.

"It is possible that you know my reputation," I said a touch more defensively than I would have liked. "But I assure you I'm not here to take advantage of your mistress."

"As you say, monsieur."

I made to leave but stopped at the door.

"And I did not kill Madame de Pompadour."

"*Oui.* As you say, monsieur," he said, his expression unreadable.

I didn't know why, but it bothered me immensely that Daphne's household thought ill of me. They likely believed I was as much of a villain as the duke. *As much as Daphne does.*

My mood was dark as I went downstairs. *Damn the Order. The sooner I can find Jeanne's murderer, the sooner I can put this mess behind me.* It might've been time for me to take an extended trip abroad and leave Paris entirely. Perhaps ride out the winter months in the south of France or even Italy. Even if I couldn't enjoy the sunshine, I could enjoy the warmth of an evening or the smell of the sea. They were better substitutes for light than the stifling candlelit ballrooms of Versailles.

Daphne cleared her throat behind me. "Are you ready?"

Even with her drawn expression and her severe gray attire, she was still the most luminous thing I'd seen since I'd been banished from the sunlight. Her self-assurance and confidence emanated from every curve of her body in a way that seemed positively magnetic. The determination in her violet eyes hid every other emotion I knew she kept contained, daring me to try to rile her—to remind her of our kiss. *I will not.* We had work to do—and she was not for me. I could not afford to let her presence distract me and keep turning me into some mindless, rutting beast. I was above that.

"Indeed. After you, Duchess."

We got into her waiting carriage and crunched down the gravel drive. She stared out the window, avoiding conversation, until the feel of the street changed, and we rumbled into the louder, grittier neighborhoods around Paris. Sounds and smells changed to an earthiness that I doubted Daphne had experienced before.

"We're going to the jeweler first," I said. "Perhaps you should wait in the carriage for me."

"Why?" she asked.

"Because I don't want to worry about protecting you while I'm trying to focus on getting information from this man."

"Protecting me?" she scoffed. She stuck her hand in her pocket, and I heard the unmistakable click of a pistol cocking.

I rolled my eyes. "Are you any good with that thing?"

She cut her gaze to me disdainfully, then flicked her wrist. A small silver dagger shot forth and embedded itself in the seat half an inch to the left of my head.

"Almost as good as I am with that thing," she said with a cheeky smile.

"Very well, then. I suppose I should have known better. No offense meant."

She lifted a shoulder in a shrug. "No offense taken. I am used to being underestimated."

The carriage stopped outside a small shop on the main street. We got down and knocked on the door, seeing only darkness inside. Some minutes passed with no one coming to let us in.

"Perhaps they're closed for the evening?" Daphne suggested. "It's very late."

"No, it isn't. Most of the shops and vendors have changed their hours to keep pace with their increasingly vampiric clientele. You'd be hard pressed to find an establishment that closes before midnight around here." I gestured to a sign by the door—a hastily scrawled *We welcome our immortal brethren.*

Daphne's brows rose in surprise, but she said nothing. Finally, the bobbing light of a candle broke through the gloom and a corpulent man in a leather apron unlocked the door.

"Ah, *Monsieur l'Émissaire*! How fortunate to see you here this evening. And I see you brought a new—ah—friend!"

"*Bonsoir*, Georges. *Duchesse de Duras*, allow me to introduce the finest jeweler in all of Paris—Versailles included," I wheedled. I hoped that Daphne would take my wink as instruction to follow my lead.

She did, indeed. Tilting her chin up haughtily, she sniffed.

"We shall see about that." She offered Georges her hand to kiss, and I noticed him instantly eyeing the necklace of expensive black pearls at her throat. His piggy eyes sparked with hunger.

Georges led us into his shop and went around lighting all of the candles. Jewelry and unset gemstones glittered up at us from velvet-lined cases atop a counter.

"How may I be of assistance, Your Grace?"

When he turned to open another box of necklaces, she caught my eye and I nodded to her encouragingly. If she could get information out of him without me having to use force, so much the better. Besides, I was curious to see how well this lady agent handled herself.

"I'm looking for something special—very special. I have a new gown being made for an upcoming ball at Versailles, and it's in the loveliest shade of pink. A soft pink, like the inside of a shell, you know. Normally I would pair a pink gown with my pink diamonds, but I feel as though I need something new and dazzling. Something to win the right amount of attention from His Majesty, you understand. I couldn't go to the court jeweler, of course—he is already designing pieces for several other ladies, and I simply cannot wait. I thought I was forsaken! Then, as luck would have it, *Monsieur l'Émissaire* told me that he knew of just the man to accept such a commission." She blushed prettily and gently touched his arm. He reddened to an unflattering, mottled purple and stared up at her with pure adoration. *He was hooked.*

"Of course, madame, of course! I am at your disposal. What sort of piece do you have in mind? A necklace? Some new earrings? A new brooch for your bodice, perhaps?" He licked his lips and stared at her breasts. Anger and a fierce possessiveness crept through my veins.

"Oh, la! No, I have all of those things. A ring, I think. A ring with a pink pearl at the center. I will be just like Madame de Pompadour, God rest her soul. Pearls—they come in pink, do they not? I have seen them in every other color at court. Have you ever done something like that before? With pink pearls, I mean?" She ran her fingertips along the black pearls of her necklace, drawing his attention—and mine.

"Pink pearls? Yes, yes. They come in pink. They are rare though, madame. It would take me some time to acquire the necessary—"

"Oh, but I don't have the time, monsieur. I simply must have it as soon as possible. I will, of course, be happy to pay for any trouble you have in trying to find the very best materials. In fact, I will double your usual fee. My husband, the *duc de Duras*, is rather generous with both his pocketbook and his oversight." She arched a brow suggestively and leaned forward. I was certain both Georges and I cursed the high neckline of her dress.

"Perhaps, Georges, you might find the gems at a more ready source," I offered. "I know that Madame de Duras is—shall we say—less than particular about the provenance of her jewels."

Daphne nodded emphatically. "You must understand how important it is for me to present myself at court in the height of fashion. And I will do anything to get what I want." Her long lashes fluttered, and a coy smile spread across her lips. *God, she is magnificent.* My cock twitched in the duke's too-tight breeches.

Georges' attention was fixed on Daphne's mouth. I had a sudden urge to remove his eyes from his skull.

"I have employed such methods before, madame," he oozed. "Don't you worry your pretty head over that. I understand you perfectly. I have—perhaps—heard of something that may help *expedite* the process. But it is not yet in my possession. Give me seventy-two hours to attempt to acquire it," he rasped, clutching at her hand. He was beginning to sweat, and his breath was coming in heated pants.

"You have thirty-six," Daphne snapped icily, breaking the spell of sensuality. "Or I shall take my custom to another jeweler. Oh—

and this should go without saying, but this arrangement is entirely confidential. I shall remain anonymous. If I find out you've told anyone about this, I will deny everything and have your tongue cut out for slander. Do you understand?"

Georges nodded vigorously and bowed. "Of course, Your Grace. Of course. You may trust Georges!"

Daphne smiled coldly at him and left. I tipped my hat to the quivering man and followed her out.

When we were alone in the carriage, I let out a bark of laughter. "You did not need to be so rough with him at the end, Duchess."

She bristled. "He does not have it, and yet he will try and sell it to me! The ring of my brutally murdered friend. Without a thought to her memory, he will try to find someone to dig her up and take it, and then sell me something that was once so precious to her. I do not regret dashing his ill-mannered hopes. Besides, he was entirely inappropriate to a lady in mourning attire."

I knocked on the carriage roof to signal our driver. "He's just trying to earn a living, not an easy thing to do in these times. I'm sure if he had the meager luxury of not worrying about feeding himself or his family, he would leave a dead woman's jewelry alone."

"Perhaps," she said stiffly. "It's still wrong."

"So, in your estimation, it is wrong to take from a dead woman in order to feed oneself and it is wrong for the peasants to become vampires so they do not need to eat. What do you suggest they do, Duchess? Wait for the scraps from your table?"

"It cannot be so dire," she insisted. "I refuse to believe that there are no alternatives to surviving than to rob graves and drink the blood of the living. I myself have had to think laterally in order to avoid destitution."

I could not help but laugh. "As the emissary between a largely impoverished vampire class and the declining human nobility, let me assure you, Duchess, that the destitution of the aristocracy is very different from the destitution of everyone else."

"An empty belly is an empty belly regardless of the body's social status."

"The difference is that you had the opportunity to marry a wealthy, titled duke. Most other women do not."

She continued to stare out the window, but I saw a flash of anguish in her eyes. She was quiet for long moments, and when she spoke, it was so low I almost missed it beneath the noise of the street.

"Had I known what kind of man was saving me from hunger, I would have starved to death a thousand times."

10

DAPHNE

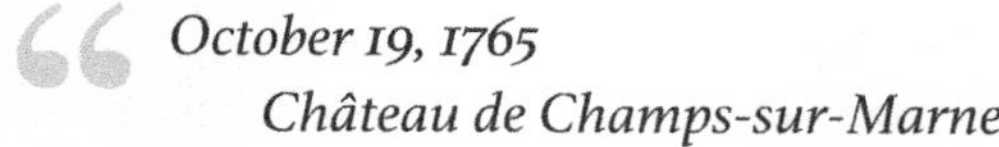

October 19, 1765
Château de Champs-sur-Marne

I DIDN'T HAVE MUCH HOPE FOR A LEAD FROM THE JEWELER, GEORGES. If Jeanne's ring had made its way to some black-market jewelry merchant, I suspected we would have had some inclination about it by now. We were no closer to Jeanne's killer.

After our outing into Paris, we'd returned to my château to regroup. We decided our next move would be to hunt down the woman who'd poisoned Étienne. The more I thought about it, the more I wondered if she *had* been on assignment from the Order. As far as I knew, I was still the only female member, though I supposed she could have been hired or coerced by one of the other male agents. Either way, we needed to find her and question her.

In an effort to regain some of my lost influence with the Order, I'd also sent them a message about what I'd learned in Paris—the late hours of the merchants and their willingness to do business with the vampires—and told them I suspected a change in the attitudes of the people. *Are the other agents aware of this? If so, what is the plan to deal with it?* I left out several details, not wanting to damn the unfortunate Georges, but made it clear that my investigation was progressing regardless of their assistance. I hadn't received a reply, but I didn't really expect one either.

Étienne had refused to tell me where our investigation would take us tonight and had become somewhat agitated in response to my questions, so we'd been careful to avoid each other for the rest of last night and the first part of this evening. While I didn't know what to expect, I was sure we would find ourselves in yet another dark and dangerous part of the city, so it seemed silly for me to be bathing now, but I didn't care. Relaxing in the hot water helped me shore up my courage—and I'd spent so much time worrying over Jeanne's murder, the Order's grand plan, and Étienne's recovery, this was my first opportunity to enjoy time to myself and let my swirling thoughts still.

At least, I *had been* enjoying it until my infuriating houseguest knocked on my door.

"*Go away!*" I shouted.

"I've come to apologize," he called. "I'll tell you where we're going tonight, but I'm not going to yell at you through this door."

"Well, it will have to wait," I replied.

"We're already losing evening hours—I don't believe it can," he said and forced the door open.

I shrieked and ducked beneath the bubbles, covering as much of my nudity as possible. His face lit with a pleased grin.

"There had better be an exceptional reason why you're here," I growled. "Otherwise, I'm going to call Dr. Van Helsing again and have her put the quicksilver *back* in your blood."

Étienne chuckled and sat on a chaise opposite the tub. He stretched out his long legs before him and leaned back, making himself comfortable. His manner was no longer dark and brooding—rather, he seemed extraordinarily gleeful.

"We're off to the Maison des Nymphes on the Rue Saint-Denis," he said, his eyes never leaving me. "I'm sorry I didn't tell you sooner. I was...*uncertain* about allowing you to accompany me. You are, after all, a duchess."

"Rue Saint-Denis? We're going to a house of ill-repute?"

"The finest in all of Paris." He winked.

"And you're worried that will offend my delicate aristocratic sensibilities?" I scoffed.

"Certainly not. I'm worried you'll offend the ladies within. I must insist you be on your best behavior," he drawled, eyeing me up and down.

If the water was warm before, I was set to bring it up to boiling in my ire.

"We're going to a bordello that you patronized, and you think *I'm* the offensive one?" I gritted out.

"Well, you do have a firm set of opinions and a rather sharp tongue, Daphne. Not that I'm complaining. In fact, I rather like your tongue."

Lust heated his gaze, and he smiled wickedly.

The audacity of the man!

"I'm sure I don't know what you mean, monsieur. If you're referring to that *mistake* in the library, I've quite forgotten it. And just because you had the misfortune of succumbing to your poisoning in my house does not give you leave to address me like one of your mistresses or your meals. Now, gather up your arrogance and get out."

"*My* arrogance?" He laughed. "Duchess, you are quite possibly the most arrogant woman I've ever known."

"And yet—remarkably—still less arrogant than nearly every man on Earth."

"I can't argue that," he conceded, standing up. Just when I thought I'd won, he proved me wrong and started to disrobe.

"Did the poison damage your hearing, Étienne? I told you to leave."

His eyes sparked as he casually unbuttoned his cuffs. "Have you really forgotten it?"

"Of course. I remember the cognac and nothing more," I grumbled. *Liar.*

He took off his shoes and pulled his linen shirt up over his head. I opened my mouth to yell at him again but froze, strangely mesmerized by his bare torso. Taught, sculpted muscles flexed beneath smooth, pale skin. A thin trail of dark hair descended from his bellybutton into his breeches, hinting at some dark, secretive virility. Infuriated with myself, I found it impossible to look away. Henri hadn't looked like this. There wasn't an ounce of softness to Étienne, merely hard planes and smooth angles. My fingers fidgeted with the desire to touch him.

Beneath the blood rushing through my ears, his voice carried like a devilish hymn.

"Do you like to watch, Duchess?"

His movements slowed as he caressed his abdomen and stepped toward me. His hands were on the buttons of his breeches, undoing them one by one. I needed to leave—to put a stop to this, go get dressed, and find Jeanne's killer. Restore my place in the Order. Figure out what the blood plague was actually doing to my city.

Why aren't I leaving?

Étienne's breeches slid down his hips and to the floor. My breath shuddered on an exhale as he stood before me, naked, sinfully handsome, visibly aroused. He grinned down at me, fangs extended, hazel eyes glowing. He stepped into the large copper tub, facing me, and began a slow, predatory drift in my direction.

Get out, my brain screamed. *Get out of the tub, Daphne. This is wrong. He is a libertine and a rake. He will throw you over when he is done, and you will be just another one of his conquests.*

I stood abruptly, water sloshing down my naked body. Modesty forgotten in the face of my anger, I stepped from the tub and pulled a towel from the chaise. Instantly, Étienne was behind me again, pressing his hard body against my back. His arms snaked around my waist.

"Have you not come to care for me, Duchess?" Étienne whispered against my neck. "At least a little?"

I squeezed my eyes shut.

"No," I breathed.

He chuckled at the lie. *Merde.*

Soft, wet lips pressed against the back of my neck. Desire and wild curiosity paralyzed me. I couldn't believe he'd had the temerity to enter my bedchamber in the first place, let alone the brazenness to strip before me and insinuate himself in my watery sanctuary. I fought to ignore the heady thrill I felt at the press of his hard cock against my backside. It was almost dizzying feeling how much he wanted me.

What would it be like? To be with a man who wasn't Henri, to feel intimacy without pain and humiliation, to have a man touch me with more than his own pleasure in mind, to be worshipped and caressed and not used or brutalized.

His cool body sent little shockwaves of pleasure through me when he brushed against my skin. He ground his hips harder against me, and he let out a guttural moan that made heat pool at my core. When my lips parted, the bridled tension between us snapped, and he whirled me around to crush his mouth to mine.

His kiss was rough with urgency, his soft lips covering mine entirely. He was a man dying of thirst in a desert and I was his only oasis. I'd never felt such passion before, having long believed that after Henri that part of me was a cold hearth full of ashes. My desire rekindled, some distant joy erupted within. *Perhaps there is hope for me yet.*

My thoughts of protest seemed to dilute in the ocean of lust swirling between us. He shoved one hand into my hair, scattering pins across the floor. He pulled at my curls gently, massaging my scalp with his fingertips. I whimpered at the exquisite pleasure of it. His lips left mine and he kissed my jaw, working his way down. His other hand stroked my breast beneath the towel, lightly at first, then with more insistence. He rolled my puckered nipple between his fingers, and I became a bottomless pit of sexual need.

Then came that eerily familiar, warm wet stroke along my neck as he licked me.

Just like his night of madness—his poisoned mind. The shame of that night returned to me—the thought of wanting him even when he was sick and disturbed. *Dieu.* What did that say about me? *It says you will probably suffer the same fate as your brother—too easily seduced by a man who will turn you out when he's done with you.*

I flinched and froze. As quickly as it had come, my lust evaporated. He stopped immediately, pulling away with a question in his eyes.

"Daphne, what—?"

I pulled away and shoved him back—hard. His eyes widened with shock and offense.

"I cannot do this," I ground out through gritted teeth. Shame and guilt powered my anger and I stood before him, wrapping the towel tightly around me like some kind of armor against my own desires. "I will not do this. I will not be another woman who lines up before you to be fucked and feasted upon. I will not fall prey to your charms just so you can use me and take from me and then discard me like some forlorn, dried-up husk of a woman. I am more than food. I am more than a warm place to put your cock. I am more than some gossip-trading courtier looking for a tryst. My purpose on this Earth is greater than your base needs, monsieur, and you shall remember that from now on, or so help me God, I will stake you and not bother to brush your dust from my skirts."

"Daphne, wait! What happened?" he called, but I had already stormed from the room.

It occurred to me in some vague part of my mind that I was—perhaps—overreacting. Perhaps I was punishing Étienne for the sins of Henri and the tragedy of Michel's death, and that I was frightened—not because Étienne was a vampire but because he'd awoken things in me that I'd long assumed dead or destroyed. Yes, all of these things whispered through me, but the most resounding thoughts were sheer instinct. *Protect, endure, survive.*

Eve helped me dress in a plain gown of lavender silk. Like last night, I pinned up my curls and comforted myself with a variety of weapons tucked against my body. When I met Étienne in the drawing room downstairs, he said nothing—simply nodded and escorted me to the waiting carriage. His expression was unreadable, but his manner was dark, as if he were being followed by a little black rain cloud. It didn't do much for my own feelings of anxiety, and a whisper of regret went through me.

We drove down a street in a shabby neighborhood of Paris, lined with prostitutes calling out to men. Unbeknownst to Étienne, I was already familiar with the area, having had to come collect Henri from countless dens of iniquity when he'd rendered himself senseless from opium or alcohol. My stomach soured when I remembered it. I felt overwhelmed by regret and shame. When I'd refused to allow Henri to torture me and torment the ladies of my household, he'd inevitably wound up here, visiting his evil upon women too disadvantaged to say no. It broke my heart and made me feel sick at the same time. I only *just* managed to convince myself that my queasiness had nothing to do with the jealousy over Étienne coming here to be with other women.

"Why have we come here?" I demanded. "Is your would-be assassin a prostitute? Is that how you feed?"

He laughed at me then. A warm, full-throated chortle that crinkled his eyes and showed his dazzling white teeth. I would have felt abashed if some part of me wasn't charmed by how sweet and boyish he looked in a light mood.

"What an inappropriate question! Are you jealous, Duchess?"

"Don't be absurd. I simply want to know why you've brought me here."

"If you're uncomfortable, you are free to wait in the carriage. In fact, perhaps that would be best. I don't need you upsetting the ladies with you in all your *state*," he said with a grin. The carriage pulled up to a large building at the end of the street—a once-grand home that had been turned into a modest hotel.

Étienne got out of the carriage. When I made to descend, he stopped me on the step.

"I meant what I said, Duchess. I won't have you insulting or upsetting the women here." The good humor had left his face, and his hazel eyes bored into mine.

Since I didn't trust myself to speak without some sharp retort, I merely nodded and followed him. Instead of approaching the front door, he went around to the side and entered through the kitchen.

"Étienne! You've come to visit me! And have you brought me sweets?" A blur of chestnut curls and matching brown wool hurled itself at him and jumped into his arms. The girl—likely no more than six—was covered in flour, which resulted in a soft puff of white enshrouding the two.

"Marie, *mon dieu*! You are covered in enough flour to bake an entire loaf of bread." Étienne laughed, reaching in his pocket for a gold coin. He palmed it and made it appear behind her ear. She squealed a giggle.

"I don't have sweets on me today, but this will do—our little secret, okay? Where is your *maman*?" Étienne kissed the girl's cheek and stood.

"She is upstairs in the sewing room. Come, I'll take you—and your pretty friend!" Marie danced from foot to foot as if she had more energy than a swarming beehive.

"Manners, Marie! This is the Duchess—"

I cut him off. I bent to the girl and stuck out my hand.

"Daphne, *chérie*. My friends call me Daphne." The girl beamed at me and shook my hand. Étienne eyed me warily, but he said nothing.

Still gripping my hand, Marie tugged me through the house, which was humbly furnished but clean, warm, and comfortable. Up the small staircase lay several rooms on either side of the hallway. The lilt of feminine laughter sang from every closed door. If this was a brothel, it was unlike every brothel I'd ever entered. *What is this place?*

Marie paused before a large oak door, brushed some of the flour from her cheeks and dress, and knocked politely.

"*Entrez-vous!*"

"*Maman*, Étienne is here! And he has brought a Daphne!"

A round woman with soft red curls pinned on top of her head turned from her sewing. It looked like she was stitching a small repair in the skirt of a buttercup-yellow dress. She smiled at Marie and Étienne, then stood to greet me with a polite curtsy. Marie scampered back through the hallway, closing the door behind her.

"I imagine, madame, you should be addressed as more than just Daphne," she said. Warmth shone from her smile, and she had startlingly familiar hazel eyes. *It can't be...*

"Perhaps elsewhere. But here, tonight, I am just Daphne."

"I am Josephine," she said. "Welcome to the Maison des Nymphes. But I'm sure Étienne has already told you that—if he has brought you here."

I glanced at Étienne, who was watching our interaction with guarded interest. When I didn't reply, she tutted and whacked Étienne's shoulder.

"This imbecile is my brother."

I gaped. Étienne rolled his eyes.

"Half brother," he corrected.

Josephine tutted again and waved her hand. "Half, quarter, cousin, whatever. Half brother by blood, but full brother, indeed."

Seeing my confusion, she threw a withering glare at Étienne.

"You did not tell her, *mon frère*? Oh, you are *impossible*! Fine—I shall do so." She settled down on a chair in the corner and motioned for me to do the same.

"Josephine, please don't. We are in a bit of a hurry," he grumbled.

"So, you bring a woman of your own here for the first time, and you tell her nothing? *Quel crétin!* What are you on about? Are you ashamed all of a sudden?"

"You know I'm not. We just don't have the time tonight, and Daphne is not interested in our family dramatics—"

"Yes, I am," I interrupted and grinned at Josephine. "Tell me, please, madame."

"Josephine!" Étienne cautioned.

She ignored him. "Our father, you see, was the *vicomte de Noailles*. At least, he was born and raised as the *vicomte*. Étienne is the only legitimate heir, but we have at least six half siblings, three of whom live abroad. *Papa* had so many mistresses around the world, we are forever finding new relations. It wasn't as bad as it sounds, of course. He was not a bad father, really—not as bad as some men. We were always provided for, even if we were just his bastards. But then he suffered that humiliating loss at the Battle of Dettingen, and the king was so angry…"

"Yes, Étienne told me. I'm so sorry," I said.

Josephine patted my hand. "Well, as you would imagine, funds became a little short. Étienne was off in Italy or England at the time —I don't remember which—so it was just me, Noelle, Anne, and Nicole left here in the city. We'd never had much to begin with, but then we had even less. We had but one way to make ends meet—to start selling our company."

My jaw dropped. She spoke of prostitution openly, without shame or regret. Étienne, however, was less than pleased. His jaw clenched, and he strode to look out the window.

"Well, we were doing okay—not great, but okay—and Étienne came home to find his identity seized, his entailment demolished, our father on his deathbed—the shock, you know, the poor thing—and his impoverished half sisters running a brothel. You can imagine his temper!"

"Enough. She doesn't need your life story, Josephine," Étienne growled.

"You mean, you don't want her to know *your* life story, eh?" Josephine teased. "He must really fancy you, then, *chérie*."

He turned from the window to fix her with a glare. "*Josephine,*" he warned.

She sighed. "Another time, then. *Alors, mon frère.* Why are you here tonight? It cannot be good."

"The woman from earlier this month—the new arrival. Is she still here?"

"The blonde one? Brigitte? No, I'm afraid not. She packed up and left in the middle of the night a little over a week ago. No note or anything. Just picked at her dinner—didn't eat much, the little mouse—went to bed, and then *poof*. Gone the next morning."

"You didn't go look for her? What if she's in trouble?" I asked.

"It is a common thing, madame. The young girls come here looking for a place to stay. Sometimes they want to work as a light-skirt or a bleeder—we give them a safe place to ply their trade—but many of them find other work. Laundry, sewing, even a few governesses. They come here to find a degree of comfort and security while they get on their feet. But many come and go, just as easily. It is their choice. We do not indenture them here. Brigitte was not the first—nor dare I say the last—to come and go so quickly."

"What's a bleeder?" I asked. Josephine turned disbelieving eyes on me. Étienne scoffed.

"You do not know, madame? But they are all over the city—there are so many now. Perhaps even more than the light-skirts." She was baffled by my ignorance.

Embarrassment pinked my cheeks. "I'm afraid I don't get out much in the city."

Étienne threw the explanation over his shoulder at me as he began pacing. "A bleeder is a common term for a woman who sells her blood. A blood-whore, if you will." He glared at me in irritation, then turned back to Josephine. "You have no idea where she went?

Did she have family? Where did she come from?" Seemingly unable to stand still, he resumed his pacing.

Josephine arched a brow at him. "You know as well as I that the women here are free from the shackles of their past, Étienne. I knew almost nothing of the girl, except that she was anxious to make your acquaintance."

"She was?" I asked. "Was she particularly interested in him?"

"Of course! All the ladies are, especially the new ones. They hear the stories from the older girls, and all have the same hopes that the dashing vampire emissary will one day come and fall madly in love with his meal," she chuckled. "The saps. Incurable romantics, the lot of them."

Étienne crossed his arms and harrumphed.

"Well, whose fault is it that these poor girls have such notions? I try to divest them of their false ideas that you are anything but a tried-and-true rogue, but they don't listen. Anyway, why are you asking after her? Has something happened?"

While Étienne stewed in frustration and embarrassment, my mind worked.

"That's what we're trying to ascertain. May we see her room, please?" I asked.

"Suit yourself. Lucky for you I have not had time to clean it and turn it out properly. We haven't had need of it yet, but inevitably, some new wretch will show up on our doorstep soon." Josephine put her sewing down and led us out to the hallway. At the far end was a smaller staircase that wound up to an attic with low ceilings and a small bed. A cacophony of noise erupted below, and Josephine excused herself to go determine the cause, leaving Étienne and me alone.

"Well?" he challenged tersely.

"Well, what?" I started opening drawers in a small bureau to see if Brigitte had left anything behind.

"Aren't you going to ask me a thousand insulting questions about my family? My past? My failings as a brother and as the heir of an unseated *vicomte*?" He sounded petulant. I recognized it as the irritation commensurate with a close sibling relationship. It lent him an air of vulnerability and—more than that —*humanity*.

"No."

The drawers were all empty. I went to the small writing desk to see if she'd left any papers or letters.

"No?" Étienne asked in an incredulous tone, and did I detect a hint of disappointment?

"Well, yes, actually. When you were here with Brigitte—"

He cut me off with a laugh. "Oh no, Daphne. I didn't come *here* for her. I sent for her. She came to me. I wouldn't feed or...do anything else here. Certainly not in Josephine's home."

"What else do you know of her? Did you converse at all? Were there other clues to her identity or anything?" I felt the underside and the back panels of the writing desk. *Nothing.*

"We didn't speak much," he said. "We had other things to do."

My exasperation grew. Étienne smirked at me. Peevishly, I went to the small bed and felt around the sheets and pillow. *Still nothing.*

I swore. This was proving to be another dead end.

"Can you give me nothing that would help? This woman tried to kill you, Étienne. I'd think you'd be a little more interested in finding out more about her," I muttered.

He sat on the bed, thwarting my search of the sheets and blankets.

"Very well. She was blonde, her name was Brigitte, and she tasted strange," he said unhelpfully.

"That'll be the quicksilver, I wager. And she didn't say anything else? Nothing seemingly innocuous about a previous customer?"

"Daphne, there's nothing here. My interactions with her were minimal and professional. She obviously didn't live here long enough to leave anything behind."

"Get up," I said with a spark of inspiration. "Get off the bed. I want to check something."

He sighed and stood. I hefted the lumpy straw mattress off the bed frame.

"You're really not going to ask me anything about Josephine? About this place?"

My annoyance finally won out.

"Étienne, if you wish to tell me about your past—your father, your sisters, your turning, this home for wayward women—please do so. However, I will not pry. I believe in what Josephine said. One should be free from the shackles of one's past, if given the chance. My only interest right now is in the truth—in this woman Brigitte and her vendetta against you, in Jeanne's killer, and in the blood plague devastating our city. So, if asking you questions you do not wish to answer will only derail me with falsehoods, then I will not waste time for either of us."

Ignoring his piercing gaze, I studied the bottom of the mattress. There, in the lower corner was a small seam that did not belong. A three-inch long tear that had been hastily stitched back together. Hands shaking in near triumph, I took out my dagger and slit it open.

A small, black leather pouch fell out and landed on the floor.

Étienne picked it up and sniffed it.

"It's him," he said, stunned. "It smells of Jeanne's killer."

11

ÉTIENNE

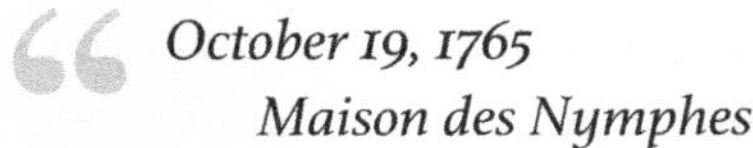

October 19, 1765
Maison des Nymphes

Daphne took the pouch from me and opened it with the excitement of a child opening a present. She removed a small glass vial and two squares of parchment. She passed me the vial and, as expected, there were minuscule droplets of quicksilver sliding around inside.

"*Drink two hours prior to bleeding,* says the first one. Instructions from someone. The handwriting doesn't seem familiar to me. Do you know it?" she asked.

I shook my head. Thick, black script ran jaggedly across the paper. It was either an ill-educated hand or an educated hand trying to disguise itself.

"What does the second one say?"

"It's an address. I don't recognize it, do you?"

"I know the street. It's at the other end of the city in the plague district." Foreboding snaked through me.

"I thought that area was abandoned." Daphne frowned.

"It was, back when the plague first arrived and people still feared it. Now that the poor have embraced it, they've repopulated the deserted buildings and shops. They call it le Quartier Sanglant. It's the only neighborhood in the city that's inhabited entirely by vampires."

Daphne's mouth dropped open in astonishment.

"I had no idea," she breathed. "The people...the state of things. I wonder how many in Versailles know."

I laughed bitterly. "Many of them, I'd wager. The king certainly does, as well as his closest advisors. They just don't want to admit as much to the rest of the court because they fear a panic—or worse, an uprising."

"An uprising that you already believe is coming," she murmured.

I nodded. "It is inevitable."

She scrubbed her face with her hand and checked her pocket watch. "We have three and a half hours before sunrise. Do you think that's enough time to make it across town?"

I looked at her warily. "I think I should go alone. If you walk in there, it would be like ringing the dinner bell, and I cannot protect you from an entire district hungry for blood, literally *and* figuratively."

"Then we shall have to be quick and careful," she said. "Face it, Étienne, I'm not going to wait in the carriage while you walk into a dangerous situation. It would be easier on both of us if you just accepted that. I recognize the peril though, so I promise to do exactly as you say."

A hint of desire flickered at the idea of Daphne submitting to me in more ways than one. I dashed it away before it could distract me. I folded my arms across my chest.

"Impossible woman," I sputtered. She was unmoved.

We made our way downstairs and found Josephine in the kitchen with Marie. I kissed them both and stuck a purse full of coins into Josephine's pocket.

"I'm afraid we made a bit of a mess in Brigitte's room," I said.

"This should make up for it. Be careful, *ma sœur*. If anyone comes asking after me—or Daphne, for that matter—you have not seen us. Understand?"

Josephine nodded, worry etched on her face. I tried to smile.

"Unless it is a very beautiful woman," I said with a wink. "Then, please do send her my way."

Daphne snorted a laugh. "Isn't that how you got yourself into this mess?"

Josephine giggled and hugged her. Daphne left to give us some privacy and stepped out into the night.

"I like her," Josephine whispered. "Don't fuck it up, *d'accord*?"

I glared at her and followed Daphne to the carriage.

"Quartier Sanglant," I told the driver. "Quickly, please. We're in a bit of a hurry."

Daphne watched me in the darkness of the carriage, her expression unreadable.

"How long have you been a vampire?" she asked.

Her question took me by surprise. I didn't often speak to others about my turning. Despite appreciating my abilities and accepting my lonely fate, turning had been one of my life's low points. I looked on it as a moment of weakness and shame, brought on by the stupidity and impetuousness of unruly youth. It was one evening's mistake that I would be paying back for a thousand lifetimes.

"Twenty years."

"That is before the plague swept Paris," she observed.

"Yes. I was not turned here. And before you ask, *no*, I did not bring the plague to the city. By the time I returned from my travels abroad, it had already taken hold."

"I did not think—" she defended.

I cut her off. "Yes, you did. I don't blame you. You're not the first to wonder such a thing, particularly because I'm the oldest vampire in the city, as far as I know. I contracted the disease while traveling through Hungary. It took hold in that region long before and has been slowly spreading east for some time now. The wars that Louis has been fighting all over eastern Europe have advanced the spread faster than *la grande vérole*, thanks to all the eager soldiers."

"*La grande vérole*? The great pox?" Daphne sat forward. "Syphilis!"

I arched a brow. "...yes? What about it?"

"Quicksilver!" she said with excitement. "Don't you see? Quicksilver is a treatment for syphilis."

I could see where she was going with this, but it still wasn't enough. "Yes, but anyone can get their hands on quicksilver these days, not just physicians. Any corner chemist will have it."

She sat back, defeated. "Yes, you're right. I was hoping we could match the handwriting on the instructions to a receipt—maybe a signature or a prescription. Perhaps a chemist would recognize it. But that would take too much time—questioning every chemist and physician in the city. The quicksilver and the ring seem to be dead ends for us at the moment. So far, we know that someone murdered Jeanne and stole her ring. It's possible that same person is familiar with vampiric poisons, knows Josephine's *maison* is connected to you, and sent Brigitte after you. Oh, and that if it is the same person, they want you dead."

"You don't think it was the Order?"

She shook her head. "I considered it at first, but it doesn't fit. They might want you out of the way, but they wouldn't chance sending another agent into my assignment. It would be too messy. Much of their power lies in their ability to operate in shadow, so they only authorize operations that can be easily and thoroughly covered up. Besides, if they suspect that you're under my protection at the moment, they won't run the risk of antagonizing me."

I was taken aback by the matter-of-fact way she spoke about her abilities. Given her marriage, I was sure her confidence had been hard won, and I felt a peculiar sense of pride in thinking that she didn't fear the men in the Order—rather, that they should be intimidated by her. That was the truth. I smiled.

"Am I under your protection?"

Her eyes narrowed. "When it comes to the Order, you are. *At the moment.* And I shouldn't need to remind you, but that doesn't mean you're safe from *me* indefinitely."

I chuckled. "Promises, promises."

We sat in companionable silence for a while. Finally, the carriage came to a stop across from a dark alley.

"Put on your cloak," I instructed. "Pull the hood up, and do *not* remove it for any reason. Do not speak. Do not touch anything. Do not go anywhere without me. In fact, do *not* leave my side. If things should go wrong for any reason—well, let's just hope they don't."

Fear clawed at me. Certainly not for my own safety, but for Daphne's. This was a terrible idea.

"Are you ready?" I asked. *Last chance to wise up and back out, Duchess.*

She nodded once, steel in her eyes. *I should have known.*

I sighed, resigned.

She pulled her hood up, obscuring her face. I was less concerned about her being seen and more concerned with her being smelled. Beneath the mouth-watering orange-blossom-and-vanilla fragrance wafted the sweetness of her blood. At this time of night, I hoped most would have already found their food and entertainment. Dawn would soon approach.

We stepped from the carriage and hurried down the alley. Daphne clung to my arm, and a thrill went through me, though I suspected it was less to do with any fear or desire she felt and more to do with the fact that she could not see as well as I in the near blackness of night. I could hear carousing down a few side streets and smelled blood, both fresh and stale. We passed by a knot of people outside a tavern, and I picked up our pace. Just as we cleared the group, a man called out to me.

"Monsieur! Fancy sharing your bite?" He cackled drunkenly. A few others turned.

"Not tonight, my good man," I tried jovially. Daphne stiffed beside me.

"Aw, come on," he jeered. "Be a sport. She looks tasty, and I haven't had anything this evening. I won't take too much, love."

"I'm afraid I'm too hungry to share, and I've already paid for the privilege," I said. I moved Daphne along as quickly as I could without drawing more notice. Unfortunately, the man followed with two of his friends.

"That's not very brotherly," he sang. The others laughed.

Nearly jogging, Daphne and I made a sharp right down a narrow street. Only one window at the end of the street flickered with candlelight, casting a dim pool of dingy amber on a stone wall. *A dead end. Merde.*

I pushed Daphne behind me and faced the men. Two would be no problem. Three would be troublesome. I could smell their newly turned blood, which meant I had the advantage of increased speed and strength. They would probably fight recklessly, as most new vampires did, which made them dangerously unpredictable. I leaned casually on my walking stick, affecting an air of nonchalance.

"*Mes amis,*" I began, silk in my tone. "Surely you don't want to fight me for this old slip of a thing? She's an aging widow, too wizened to survive more than one bite in an evening. Come, take my advice—there are far better meals wandering around tonight."

"But she's already right here," one of them said. "That's dead convenient."

The three guffawed uproariously at the wordplay.

I sighed. "So, you aim to take her from me?"

"If you're too selfish to share, then we'll have to teach you some manners," the drunkest said. "Some brotherly love, if you will."

One of them lunged at me. I sidestepped his charge and tripped him with my walking stick. Before I could turn to him, the other two were upon me. One punched my stomach, and the air left me. I doubled over with a wheeze. The other grabbed my hair and hauled me up, landing a punch on my jaw. I whirled around and grabbed one man's arm, breaking it easily. He screamed and fell to the ground. The second aimed another blow at my face, but I saw it coming and ducked. His fist smashed into the stone wall behind me and he shrieked. He got back up but froze, stunned by something behind us.

I turned to see Daphne pirouetting gracefully away from the first vampire, then bringing her fist up to smash him squarely in the nose. He grunted with the impact but reached out again, trying to grab the blonde curls that had come undone from beneath her hood. She leaned back, using his momentum against him, and dodged out of the way while he fell forward. Then, with a speed that rivaled any vampire I'd encountered, she jumped onto his back, yanked one arm behind him and bent it upward in an immobilizing hold. She flicked her empty wrist, and a thin wooden stake slid from her sleeve into her palm. She held it threateningly above the prone vampire's back—exactly above his heart. The whole fight was over in a matter of seconds.

"*Enough!*" she yelled. "Étienne, are you all right?"

"*Mais oui.*"

Fierce energy rolled off her crouched form. I'd never desired another woman more.

"You!" She jutted her chin at the man standing next to me. He cradled his broken hand and looked at her fearfully.

"Pick up your friend with the broken arm over there and go *now*, or this one is dust."

She started to slowly sink the wooden stiletto into the vampire's flesh, and he yelled a stream of profanities that shocked even me.

They scrambled down the street at a dead run, not daring to look back.

"Now," she said to the man. "My friend and I have some questions, and I think you're in an excellent position to answer."

"Get drained," he growled.

Daphne *tsked* and twisted the stake in farther. The man howled in pain.

"First question: What do you know of Madame de Pompadour?"

"Who?"

"The king's mistress. The rumors say that she was killed by your kind."

"I don't know anything about that!" The man screamed again. Tendrils of smoke began to curl from his wound.

"No? Because we followed the trail of a bleeder to an address around here. Rue des Oubliés. What do you know of it?" Daphne leaned on the man's arm.

"It's nearby, but no one goes there!" he shouted. "Please, release me. It burns—*putain de merde*—it burns!"

"Why does no one go there?" she demanded.

"Ease up, and I'll tell you. I swear, I'll tell you," he gritted out. By the look on his face, he seemed close to passing out.

She lessened the pressure on his arm and slid the stake partway out. The man panted.

"No one goes there because it's haunted," he gasped.

Daphne leaned forward again and hissed at him. "Do you think I'm stupid? *Haunted?* There's no such thing."

"Just like there's no such things as vampires?" he wheezed with a laugh. "Look, lady, I don't know if it's real ghosts or not. People don't go there because they say it's haunted. Strange noises. Awful smells. Unnatural darkness. It's a bad place."

"How do we get there?"

"Three blocks down, then turn right. You'll know it when you come to it."

Daphne released the man's arm and pulled the stake from his back. Brandishing it in front of her, she stood and took her pistol out and held it aloft for good measure. The man got to his feet slowly, threw a curse at the both of us and hobbled away. As he turned the corner to the street, I heard him mutter.

"*May the ghosts take you.*"

12

DAPHNE

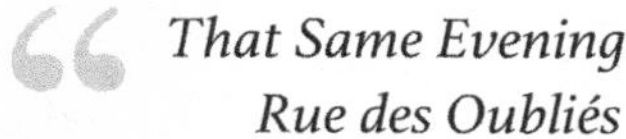

That Same Evening
Rue des Oubliés

"THAT WAS...*IMPRESSIVE*. YOU COULD HAVE KILLED HIM!" ÉTIENNE remarked as we followed the drunk's directions.

"Well, I should hope so, otherwise I'd be a poor excuse for an agent. You said the Order has tried to kill you before. Hasn't everyone you've met with fought with the same skill?" I clutched his arm to avoid stumbling over the uneven cobblestones.

"No," he said. "The way you fought was... Well, Daphne, you were magnificent."

A blush warmed my cheeks, and I was grateful he could not see my face beneath my hood. His appraisal gave me immense pleasure, but I feared dwelling on it.

"Thank you."

"How many—ah—*assignments* have you had?"

I sighed. "In the beginning, the Order used me for intel. I sent them reports on the happenings at Versailles. Nothing treasonous, mind you. They just wanted to know what people were saying—the state of the war; who was sleeping with whose wife or husband;

who was spending what on clothes, jewels, properties; that sort of thing. The whole time I had tutors coming to my home to teach me various fighting arts. My first few assassinations were newly infected vampires who preyed on young women—draining them and leaving their bodies in the streets or making them disappear altogether. Housemaids and other servants, prostitutes, tavern maids, and the like. Women too lowly to attract much notice."

I had to pause to calm my rising ire. Étienne's arm rose as if he were going to reach out and touch me. Right now I wouldn't be able to withstand his touch, so I went on.

"Those women deserved justice. The parasites I killed would've continued to murder and feed indiscriminately. Tell me, Étienne, how do you justify your fight for vampire rights when those you protect are, by their very nature, predators? How many young girls should die so that your vampires may live free?"

"I won't deny that some of the infected are corrupt," he said. "But to lay the blame at the blood plague itself is irresponsible. Murderers existed before vampires and will continue to exist after we've all been extinguished. I seek to bring education to the infected. If so many have been turned and are continuing to turn, they should know how to manage their supernatural state. Right now, the desperate feel they have no alternative and are forced into a choice that they're not prepared to make."

"Education. That's what you're after?" I said with surprise. "Not the total eradication of the nobility at the expense of your vampire majority?"

He laughed again, warm and genuine. "If that's what the Order has told you, I'm afraid I have far less respect for your sources of intel. I don't want to eradicate anyone. I have already seen more death than I care to. My efforts have been to *prevent* a revolution, not incite one."

I was quiet in the wake of this revelation, realizing again that I'd once again misjudged him.

"Why did you join in the first place?" he asked suddenly.

The cold seeped in through my clothes, and I huddled against him. I thought we were getting close—the air had changed. I considered his question. He'd been so exposed by our trip to Josephine's, I felt like I owed him some of my own truth.

"Michel's death devastated me, and I did want revenge," I admitted. "But I suppose that's not the whole reason. I wanted to be...*useful*. I wanted to have purpose. I wanted to be able to defend myself from men like Henri. I only learned about the Order a couple of years ago—whispered rumors at court about an old religious sect that had been revived to combat the blood plague and save the city—and perhaps the world. They did not want me to join at first. They said they had no need of women. Ha! With Philippe's help, I convinced them to let me prove my usefulness."

"Did the duke know?"

"No, he was gone by then," I said. "Not that he would have known when he was here. We did not enjoy the same leisure pursuits and thus spent very little time together." Cold sliced through me at the thought of Henri. The wind picked up, and I bent against the frigid breeze, then pulled up short with a cry of pain. *The damn drunk vampire had probably cracked one of my ribs.* Before I could react, Étienne's strong arms encircled my waist and hauled me upright. I grunted in pain when he squeezed the tender spot on my abdomen.

He dropped his hands like he'd been scalded.

"Did I hurt you?" The concern in his voice startled me.

"No," I huffed. "That damned drunk landed a kick in my side. It's fine. I'll have to forgo stays for the next couple of days, but it'll heal well enough."

"Are you certain nothing is broken?" He ran his hands along my ribs, feeling for swelling. My heart hammered in my chest.

"Oh, *mon dieu*! Don't fuss, Étienne. I've had worse before, I assure you." I batted his hands away and straightened my cloak.

"So you've said," he retorted, his voice dark and vaguely threatening.

"I'm fine," I insisted. "We can continue."

Suddenly, he turned me until my back was pressed against the wall of the alley. I gasped in surprise. I could feel the hardness of his muscles beneath the velvet of his clothes, and my desire ignited instinctively. Gently, he tipped up my chin, and I could just see the outline of his face in the moonlight.

"You are not indestructible, Duchess," he whispered, his mouth inches from mine.

"Neither are you," I breathed. Conscious thought fled. The chill of the night air; the low temperature of his body; his clean, fresh smell—if I closed my eyes, it was like I was standing in a snow-blanketed forest. I didn't feel cold though. My body blazed with heat.

Before I could talk myself out of it, I was setting my lips to his. Beneath my kiss, I felt him smile. Unlike the assertive ardor from earlier, his touch was tender and languid. His tongue played slowly against my lips until I parted for him. I stroked against him, tasting the metallic tang of blood.

I pulled back, my breath coming in ragged pants. "You're bleeding."

He traced delicate kisses across my cheek and my jaw, lingering at my ear. He tugged at my earlobe, sucking at it gingerly. My nipples tightened, and desire spiraled through me to my core. I whimpered at the delicious torment.

"Shall I stop?" His words were punctuated with little licks along the outer edge of my ear.

"Bleeding? Yes, if you have the power to command that sort of thing."

A throaty chuckle escaped him, and he leaned his forehead against mine. Perhaps it was the waning aggression from the fight, but I realized with a jolt that I wanted him rather badly. I found myself cursing my earlier reluctance in my chamber. *He was naked before you, and you cruelly rejected him. Why? What are you so afraid of, Daphne?*

Losing him, came the reply. I pushed it aside.

"Should we continue?"

"Yes," I moaned, tilting up to meet him again.

His breath caught, and his tone became pleading. "No, Daphne, I meant we should continue to the Rue des Oubliés."

I froze.

"...ah. Yes, of course."

I tried to pull away, stung by his words and embarrassed by my own behavior. *Idiot!*

"Damn it, Daphne, wait. Stop. This is *not* a rejection. You must know that. You must know how desperately I want you. I cannot even *think* without wanting you." He pressed his hips into me, and I felt the hard length of his arousal. I stifled a groan at the thought of him sliding into me.

"You see? I would give anything to have you. But not here—not like this. We are running out of time." He reached up to stroke my cheek, and I looked up.

Merde. He was right. The pitch blackness of the sky had already begun to lighten to a deep sapphire. Dawn was coming. We needed to hurry.

I offered him a chagrinned smile. "*Allons-y!*"

We took off at a rapid clip, closing the distance to the street we sought. Nearing it, a chill ran up my spine. The drunk had been right. There was something *off* about this part of the neighborhood. Our steps slowed as we approached.

"This is it," I said. "How far down is the address?"

"Not far," he replied, gripping his walking stick more tightly.

A thick silence blanketed us as we walked down the street. We saw no light from beyond and heard nothing but the sounds of our footsteps and our anxious breaths. Even the air seemed stagnant—like it, too, waited for something malevolent.

Étienne stopped before a storefront with a boarded-up door and broken windows. I squinted up at the sign above the door but couldn't make it out in the gloom.

"It's a bookshop," he offered. He lifted his nose in the air and inhaled.

"What is it?" I whispered.

"It smells of the murderer. Stay close, and keep your pistol cocked."

He wrenched the boards from the door frame, and they came away easily. He beckoned me to him, and we entered the shop together.

"What do you see?" I whispered. We stepped over broken glass and a few discarded books. Most of the shop's contents had been looted, it seemed. I picked up one of the remaining books from the floor and held it up to the moonlight to read the title.

"Étienne," I said, fear building in my gut. "This is a book of dark magic. I don't think this is a normal bookshop."

He sniffed the air again and tugged me to the back of the store. An open door—probably a storage room—gaped like a tall, dark mouth.

"There's something in there. I can't see it, but the smell is getting stronger from that direction."

"Should we light a candle? I won't be any help to you if I can't see what I'm fighting," I hissed. In that moment, I wished for supernatural abilities of my own.

"I don't want to give us away," he whispered back. "Just hold on to me."

I didn't need to be told twice. I held on to his coat and willed myself calm. I had been trained for this, after all.

We crept forward to the doorway, and Étienne paused, listening. I couldn't hear anything, but I was beginning to detect the smell Étienne had tried to describe to me. A stinking, burning, rotting smell, like a tannery on fire. It made my insides twist with nausea.

"Well?" I pressed. "What is inside?"

"A stairwell going down. I can't see all the way though. The drunk was right. There is something unnatural about this darkness," Étienne said.

Navigating the stairs proved to be incredibly difficult. We were forced to move slowly. After an interminable amount of time, we finally reached the floor below. It felt like hard-packed earth beneath my feet. *Is it some kind of cellar?*

"Étienne, what do you see?"

He was quiet while he surveyed our surroundings.

"I can't be sure," he began. I sensed an undercurrent of unease from him and started to grow nervous. He pulled away from my grip momentarily and bent down, then straightened again. He struck a match, lit a small stub of a candle, and handed it to me.

I held it aloft and looked around. I'd been right on one count—we appeared to be in some kind of root cellar beneath the bookstore. It was strangely empty, except for a few wooden crates stashed to one side. In front of us, drawn on the floor in something suspiciously blood-like, was a circle filled with a pentagram and numerous symbols. At each point of the pentagram sat a glass jar containing a different object.

I picked up the jar closest to me and gasped. "Étienne! It's Jeanne's ring!"

He stooped to look in the jar opposite and growled an oath. The jar contained a pink ribbon garter stained with fresh blood.

"It's Brigitte's," he said. "She was wearing it when we... Her initials are stitched onto the side."

"Check the other jars," I ordered, trying to stem the tide of panic. "I'll see what else I can find."

I ran to the crates along the wall. At the bottom of one was a large, leather-bound book with the words *Pseudomonarchia Daemonum* written in black. Dread gathered inside me. I picked up the book and flipped it open to the middle, where a gold ribbon marked a page titled *The Demon Asmoday*. What did it all mean?

"Two of the jars are empty," Étienne said. "One of them contains a gaming piece from a casino in Venice. It, too, is bloody. I recognize it, but—"

Without warning, the door upstairs slammed shut. A dry, hot

gust of wind rushed in, blowing the book closed and extinguishing the candle. The rotten, sulfuric smell grew worse until I could barely breathe. Étienne leaped for me across the room, but as soon as he stepped over the markings on the floor, an invisible force hurled him back against the wall. He slammed into it with a violence that would have killed any human.

"Étienne!" I screamed. He moaned shakily.

"Daphne," he coughed. "Run!"

From all around us—yet nowhere at all—a dry laugh echoed through the room.

"Run? Before introductions? How...impolite," the voice rasped, whispering like sand across stones.

"Who are you?" I yelled. Anger warred with my fear.

That bone-chilling laugh came again. I scanned the room frantically but couldn't find the source of the voice.

"What do you want?" I shrieked, louder this time. The demonic wind was picking up in the cellar, lashing my hair against my face and whipping my skirts around. I edged along the wall toward Étienne, who was still slumped on the floor. When I reached him, I covered his body with mine protectively.

"Daphne, go! I'll be fine!" he mumbled.

"In the name of God, what are you?" I whispered, more to myself than to our invisible attacker. Abruptly, the wind ceased, and the foul odor disappeared. A heavy stillness pressed in upon us. I helped Étienne to his feet, and just as we turned to the stairs, a familiar cloying perfume floated through the room. It was a scent I knew intimately, and it frightened me a thousand times more than any supernatural entity.

No longer rasping, the disembodied voice drawled in a frigid baritone.

"Oh, *ma petite Daphne*! Don't you recognize the voice of your own husband?"

13

ÉTIENNE

"*October 20, 1765*
Rue des Oubliés

The terror in Daphne's eyes was unlike anything I'd ever seen. The blood drained from her face, and she froze, too stunned to move. That cold, evil voice laughed again, and I didn't fancy waiting around to see what else it had in store for us. I tugged hard at Daphne's arm, yanking her forward up the stairs. I smashed the door at the top of the stairs with my foot, showering us in tiny wooden splinters. As I hauled Daphne through the streets toward my waiting carriage, I could still hear the dark laughter taunting us from a distance.

The sky was paling to a fair lavender by the time I reached the carriage and threw Daphne inside. Dawn was upon me, and if I didn't get underground soon, things would become dire indeed.

"Daphne." I knelt before her in the carriage. Her face was still pale—her gaze unfocused and her teeth chattering. *She is in shock.*

"Daphne, we need shelter. You're going into shock, and I need to get underground. My home is nearer to us than yours, so I'm having my driver take us there. When you're recovered, I'll send someone to escort you home. Do you understand?"

She didn't respond, merely stared ahead at a fixed point behind me. I stripped off my coat and wrapped her in it, laying her back against the carriage seats. The ride seemed to take ages, but we finally arrived at my château. I scooped her up and carried her inside.

My father's château was one of the few things left of my family's once grand legacy. When I'd returned to France after my travels abroad, much of the grandeur of my family home had fallen into disrepair—the result of my father's decimated fortune and his broken spirit. After his passing and my royal appointment, I'd labored tirelessly to restore the upper floors to their former magnificence and taken the opportunity to renovate the cellars into a comfortable suite of apartments for my vampire needs. For my own safety and for my self-indulgent sense of privacy, few outside of my architect and household staff knew of my secret chambers. I usually entertained others—notably women—in the upper part of the house. *Not today*.

I carried Daphne to the door hidden behind a floor-length tapestry and opened it. Another set of stairs descended below ground, though this one was not so dark. Candlelight flooded the corridor from dozens of glass fixtures that I insisted remain lit while I was at home. Sometimes, if I closed my eyes, it almost felt like my memories of sunlight.

I brought Daphne into my bedchamber and set her on the bed. Her eyes had closed at some point, hopefully in a dreamless sleep. I tucked her in beneath the thick silk coverlet and went to my wardrobe to change. I washed quickly in the basin—tomorrow I would indulge in a long, hot bath. For now, I needed the healing power of sleep to mend my wounds and refresh my mind. I'd pulled off the borrowed jacket and waistcoat as well as the shoes, when I heard Daphne stir. She sat bolt upright and let out a ragged, shattering scream.

She babbled incoherently, unable to form intelligible words in her panic. Tears streamed down her cheeks when she at last mouthed the name like an oath.

"Henri!"

I rushed over to her and seized her shoulders. "Daphne, he's gone! You're safe now, understand? It's just us. We are here in my home, far away from le Quartier Sanglant. Be easy, Duchess. You are safe."

Wild-eyed, she continued to sob. "He isn't gone, Étienne. *He isn't gone.*"

Her body shook, and she fisted her hands in her hair, then brought them down to hold herself. She rocked back and forth, whispering prayers I'd long since forgotten.

Cautiously, I put my hands on her tear-streaked cheeks.

"Daphne, look at me," I soothed.

With effort, her wide violet eyes met mine.

"You are safe," I repeated. "It's just us here. Safe."

"Safe," she whispered. The word slowly took root, and she ceased rocking. I climbed into the bed next to her and put my arms around her, holding her as tightly as I dared. She drew a shaky breath and nuzzled against me, her eyes drifting closed again.

"Safe," I repeated. "I'm not going to let anything happen to you. You are safe here with me. With Étienne."

I rested my cheek atop her silky blonde curls and stroked her arms and her back. Eventually, her taut muscles loosened, and her breathing slowed to a deep, steady rhythm. I blew out all but one candle on my bedside table and leaned back against the downy pillows. Sleep claimed me almost immediately.

When I awoke some hours later, Daphne was curled against me. The candle had burned out at some point, but I could see well enough in the dark. Her eyelids fluttered in sleep, and she murmured something unintelligible. I pushed her hair from her face and kissed her forehead. Startled, she opened her eyes and tensed but relaxed when recognition dawned.

"Étienne."

She didn't pull away but continued to stare at me.

"So, it was not a nightmare," she said.

"No."

She rolled away from me, wincing at her bruises, and stretched her arms above her head. Her panic appeared to have diminished slightly, and she blew out a breath.

"You know, I never really believed he was dead. I just hoped he was. After he fled to Italy, I hoped he'd debauch himself into oblivion. Yet it seems the rotten bastard was too ill-tempered to simply lie down and die, and now his ghost will haunt me...just like his memory."

"Why did he leave?" *How could he leave you?*

"I'm surprised you don't know. The king offered him the emissary position—your position. This was a couple years ago, before the court was fully aware of your turning. No one wanted the emissary post, least of all my wastrel husband. Henri left the country before the king could order him to take the post. I haven't heard from him since. Well, until tonight."

I turned onto my side to face her. She continued to stare at the ceiling. Tears leaked from the corners of her eyes, and I wiped them away with my thumb.

"What is he, Étienne? A ghost? A vampire? A demon?" she wondered, her voice barely a whisper.

"I do not know," I admitted.

"Whatever he is, I'm still married to him. He was a monster before, and now..."

The realization gutted me. *She is taken. She is not mine. She cannot be mine.*

She turned to look at me, the despair on her face devastating. "You weren't injured in the cellar, were you?"

I pursed my lips to avoid lashing out. I was angry at her foolishness—she could have been killed, and here she was worrying about me—but now was not the time to chastise her. I swallowed my ire and brushed a lock of hair from her face. "No. Nothing lasting, at least."

"What is it like? Being able to heal so quickly. Is it painful?"

"No. It is... Well, it's hard to describe. Would you like me to show you?" I'd never spoken of my abilities with anyone, but a thread of mutual vulnerability now stretched between us in the dark.

"I don't know. I do not want to be a vampire," she said.

"That is not what I'm offering, Duchess."

"What do you offer, Étienne?"

"A taste." My fangs lengthened. "I cannot heal all wounds, but bruises are an easy feat. Show me your side where you were kicked."

I expected protests, denials, disdainful refusals—everything but compliance. Perhaps it was the blackness of the room that made her feel comfortable. Perhaps it was the traumatic experience we'd just shared or—as my anxious mind suggested—the eagerness for physical strength and power over her husband, our new enemy. Whatever it was, she nodded to me and sat up on her knees to begin disrobing. The slow, sure movements of her fingers on her buttons were a sweet torment that I found unbearably arousing. I would watch them play out over and over in my head when I thought of her, marveling at the sainted restraint I exercised in keeping myself from ripping her clothes off. She untied her skirts and petticoats, letting them fall to the floor beside the bed. At last, she knelt before me in her stays and chemise, and paused.

"Do you need help with your stays, my lady?" My voice sounded husky and strangled.

In response, she turned her back to me to allow me access to her laces, which I undid with trembling fingers. When the last lace had been loosened, she let out a small breath of relief as the garment fell away. I swallowed, my mouth suddenly dry.

I'd seen her nude form in her chambers, but here, now, in her sheer chemise, she was baring herself to me of her own free will. It was the single most erotic moment of my wretched life. I wanted to make her crest with pleasure—to bury myself in her in a thousand different ways. I bit the inside of my lip hard enough to draw blood, forcing myself to focus.

"Lie back down, Duchess," I instructed. "Relax."

She did as I asked, but she was far from relaxed. She was on edge, ready to jump out of her skin at the first touch. To comfort her, I clasped her hand.

"This is something not many vampires learn until they've had the time and inclination to practice. It may feel a bit...*strange*, but I promise it will not hurt you. I would never hurt you, Daphne."

She took a deep breath and smiled tightly. I pulled her chemise up over her hips, fighting every instinct to dive between her legs and wring climax after climax from her. *Focus, Étienne.* The bruise was the size of a melon, covering much of her side down to the curve of her hip. It was already darkening to an angry purple. *The bastard.* I should have ripped his head from his body for daring to lay a hand on her.

I delicately ran my fingertips across the discolored skin, and she shivered.

"Relax," I murmured again. I leaned forward and licked the bruise. Her sharp inhale hinted at her pleasure, and I smiled against her skin. I dropped wet kisses over her side and slid one hand up her thigh, then bent and lightly scored the tender area with my fangs. Daphne elicited a soft whimper, stoking my desire. I sucked at the small scrapes, tasting her blood. *Orange blossoms, vanilla, and—God help me—desire. And something familiar...*

"It was you," I said against her skin. "It was your blood in the porcelain bowl. You fed me from your own veins."

Her eyes searched for mine in the dark.

"Yes," she whispered.

Somewhere in the back of my mind, it seemed fitting that this woman—this vampire-hating, strong, beautiful, untouchable woman—would be the best I'd ever have. The thought drove me nearly mad with desire and terror. She'd sustained me in my weakness, tried to protect me from the evil we'd encountered, was the most delicious, and yet she was not mine. *Could* not be mine. I'd be damned if I let her go back to that bastard husband of hers, but I'd at least have to let her go back to the Order and the life she wanted—while I wandered throughout eternity, hunting for some other woman just as good. Not just to feed from, but...*but what?* I didn't know. All I knew was that as delicious as she was, my need for her felt *different*. She was not food to me. She was the angel sent to drive me to utter madness with wanting.

When I'd finished sucking the damaged blood from her injury, I licked the top of the scrapes again, and they healed over immediately. The bruise was gone completely, and her porcelain skin was once more unmarred. Daphne was panting when I lifted my head.

"Well, Duchess? What does it feel like to heal in such a way?"

She stretched out on the bed and moaned her reply. "It feels warm, hot. I feel...peculiar."

I chuckled. "Yes, *peculiar* is one way to describe supernatural abilities." She twisted on top of the sheets, testing my strength and sanity.

"I feel rather good actually," she said, trailing a hand up her torso. "Powerful. Exhilarated." Her hands moved across her body, lifting to her breasts. Her eyes met mine, hazy with desire.

Every frayed thread of my restraint snapped, and I could not bear it any longer.

"Allow me," I begged in a gruff whisper. When she moaned her assent, I ripped the chemise down the middle and stroked her body from thigh to neck. She slid her fingers into my hair and pulled my face down to hers for a desperate, searing kiss. She sucked at my tongue and tugged at my shirt, frantically trying to pull it over my head. I eased myself away from her to remove my shirt and breeches, then crawled back across the bed to her. I kissed my way up her legs, pausing just below the blonde curls covering her sex.

"Daphne," I said, my voice raw with need. "Are you sure you want this?"

Please say yes. Say you'll be mine—if only for tonight.

"You tried to save me," she murmured. "Back in the cellar."

"You tried to save me *first*," I argued, slowly caressing the inside of her thigh. Her breath hitched. "And you didn't need me to save you anyway."

"No," she agreed. "But it was...nice. The thought, I mean."

I ran two fingers along her sex, dipping one into her slick folds. She whimpered.

"Will you allow me to demonstrate some more *nice thoughts* I have?" I begged.

In answer, she pulled my face to hers again and caught my lip in her teeth, then hooked one of her legs behind mine and arched her hips up, seeking friction from my hardness. At the feel of her wetness sliding across my cock, I abandoned my attempt at chivalry and uttered a string of oaths. Dieu, *I would give this woman anything.* Everything she asked for. *But she is not yours.* I shoved the thought away and turned my gaze back to her.

She is tonight.

Setting my lips to her breasts, I reached one hand down, trailing along her abdomen, back to the slick seam between her legs. She cried out when I circled one fingertip against the bud of her pleasure and dipped another finger inside her, stroking as she bucked against my hand.

"More," she moaned. "Étienne, give me all of you."

My self-control already past its breaking point, I positioned my cock at her entrance and stopped again, my thumb working her core with firmer and firmer caresses.

"Tell me you're certain. Tell me you want this."

Her eyes snapped open and a sultry smile crossed her lips.

"Yes," she cried. "I need you, Étienne." She wrapped her legs around my waist and arched her back again.

Thanking God, Lucifer, and the universe itself, I sank into her ready heat on a moan from us both. She felt tight and hot and wet around me, and I ached with the pleasure of it. I moved inside her slowly at first, trying to regain control of my sanity, all the while stroking that tight bud where her climax would peak. Her hands slid down my back, grasping my bottom and pulling me into her deeper, harder. Soon, her cries reached fever pitch and I felt her orgasm crescendo and break, and she came apart around me. Unable to hold back, I followed her over the edge, letting wave after wave of bliss roll through me.

I collapsed on top of her, our bodies a tangle of sweat-slicked limbs. My fangs were slow to retract—I couldn't remember the last time I'd made love without feeding. Daphne tilted her head to me and smiled shyly.

"I can see why the ladies in court gossip so much about you," she said. "That was— Well, I've never had—you know, with a man —and—" She covered her furious blush with her hands.

Daphne, I would pleasure you for every day of my eternity. The thought turned me cold with panic. *She is not yours,* that dark voice of reason echoed.

I gathered her up and pulled her in to my embrace, kissing her temple.

"I'd prefer they didn't, you know," I murmured. "Gossip, I mean."

She chuckled, and the vibrations from her mirth reverberated through me like a plucked harp string. A phantom ache started to build in my chest.

"It's scandalous, to be sure, but mostly good. You're forbidden fruit to them, even once they've had a taste," she said with a yawn.

"Forbidden fruit?" I laughed. "More like a shiny apple that's rotten at its core."

Daphne's eyes drifted closed. She snuggled closer into the crook of my arm and drowsily grunted at me.

"That's just what you want everyone to think," she mumbled. "I'm beginning to know better."

With that, her breathing slowed in the satisfied sleep that always followed intimacies and her muscles relaxed against me. As she slept in my arms, my thoughts took off like a bolting horse. Instinctive protectiveness pulsed through me—something I'd not experienced with a woman in a long time. A sense of sick dread began to take root, and I cursed my carelessness. How had I allowed myself to become so attached to this woman? She'd said it herself—ours was a temporary truce. I remembered the loathing on her face the night she'd tried to kill me. Would that hatred return when our investigation concluded and she returned to the arms of the Order? Would she regret this intimate act later on and feel as though I'd pressed my advantage during a moment of weakness?

On top of all that, she was a pillar of the *tonne* and a married duchess. Even with my position at court and the changing populace of Paris, I was still leagues beneath her. She'd be risking everything to be seen with me outside the bedroom. Sadness and doubt bloomed in my chest and refused to be uprooted.

You cannot have her. You don't deserve her. She is not for you.

I knew the truth of those thoughts. It did me no good to chase after one woman—a man in my position needed more. I needed to feed. I needed more aristocratic allies for my cause. Those were hard to get without the freedoms of bachelorhood.

Obviously, it had just been too long since I'd been with another woman. I needed distance from Daphne. *What I feel is not real.* At worst, it was some kind of temporary infatuation.

Even as we lay there together, naked and entwined, I felt the thread of vulnerability between us break. I eyed her sleeping form, so beautiful and still, and felt my resentment and frustration reach a crisis point. Things needed to go back to the way they'd been, but I couldn't move forward while I felt so bound to her. I needed her out of my arms and out of my bed. I needed her away from *me.*

I shifted myself from beneath her, gently but firmly, and she stirred from her sleep. She yawned and stretched, blinking up at me with wide, expectant eyes.

"It is getting late in the day, Duchess. I need my rest," I said.

A flash of some imperceptible emotion crossed her face, but she nodded. "Of course. There is much I need to do today as well." She paused, perhaps covering the sting of my dismissal.

Guilt surfaced, but I swallowed it. "I believe you'll be safe for the day, at least. I can't imagine Henri would endanger you so quickly after the events last night. If he hasn't come for you before now, it seems there is some other endgame that he plots."

"I will be fine, Étienne. I can take care of myself," she returned stiffly, but I could tell from her manner that she was covering her fear.

"Still, you should not be alone. Perhaps you can call upon a friend or family member. Maybe stay with the *comte* and *comtesse de Brionne* for a few days," I suggested.

"I said I'd be fine," she bit out, then sighed and rubbed at her temples. "Do you think the Order will believe me when I tell them about him? About Henri, I mean. I don't know what exactly to tell them, whether he's some monster or otherworldly spirit, but that he's back in some form and seems to be connected to all of this," she said, her brows knitting together.

I scoffed, irritated that she'd seemed to pluck one of my worries from my head. *Already she is thinking about the Order again.*

"Hardly. They'll probably accuse you of being hysterical. In fact, I don't think I'd tell them at all."

She sat up and the sheet fell away from her breasts. My body responded immediately, but I turned away and rose from the bed.

She stiffened. "I must, Étienne. Do you not wish to have someone attest to your innocence? To try and convince them there is something darker afoot than a rogue vampire?"

"I don't need your protection," I snapped. My temper had crept up on me, goaded on by the fear and mistrust of my own feelings. "I'm not a fool. The Order has wanted me out of the way since I took the emissary appointment—perhaps even since I first returned to Paris. We were enemies long before you showed up with your stake in hand."

She watched me guardedly. Her breath hitched slightly when she whispered, "Enemies?"

"Apologies, Duchess. I don't know if there's a better word for people who want you dead."

Her eyes narrowed. "I am not your enemy, Étienne."

"Don't you understand? If you're with them, you will be."

"No. I'll tell them the truth. We'll figure things out, and you will be exonerated. I swear it."

"And risk your life's purpose? *Please,*" I sneered. "What happened to revenge against all vampirekind? You say I'm not your enemy, Daphne, but I represent them—all of them. I'm fighting for their rights, not the least of which is the right to exist. Your work with the Order sets you against me. Besides, it won't be long before they manage to convince you that we're to blame for every evil in Paris."

"You believe my mind can be changed so easily?"

I laughed cruelly and gestured at the rumpled sheets. "I believe you told me you'd rather fuck Lucifer himself than me."

Anger flashed in her eyes, chased by regret. Whether it was for her earlier words or our intimacies, I didn't know. Minutes of tense silence passed between us until she finally stood and retrieved her clothes. The disappointment in her eyes made me feel a thousand kinds of wretched, but it was better this way. I half hoped she would argue—hurl some acerbic insult that I rightly deserved, but she didn't. I watched mutely as she dressed, pinned up her hair, and left the room without a word.

14

DAPHNE

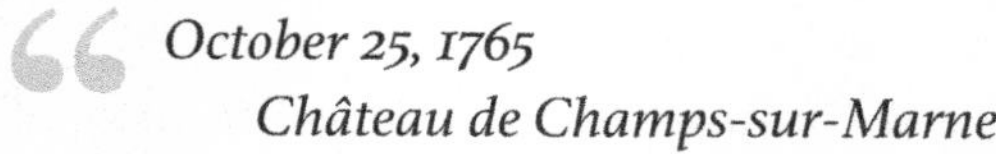

October 25, 1765
Château de Champs-sur-Marne

JUST A LITTLE FARTHER…ALMOST THERE…GOT IT! I SEIZED THE BOOK from the top shelf in triumph, then promptly stumbled off the library ladder when a shrill voice startled me.

"*Mon dieu*, Daphne, what the hell are you doing?" Charlotte yelled from the doorway.

I righted myself and dropped the book to the floor, then stepped down from my perch.

"Nothing! Well, reading," I replied, feeling like a child caught misbehaving.

Charlotte strode into the library in a gown of vibrant chartreuse that glowed in the dim light of the rainy afternoon. She narrowed her eyes in suspicion at the pile of books I'd collected.

"Daphne, *none* of these appear to be salacious novels. In fact, these are all religious texts and— What's this? *Malleus Maleficarum!* Have you taken up an interest in the occult?" she said with a raised brow.

"No! Of course not." I rubbed at my temples, trying to ward off the ache building in my head. Charlotte folded her arms in front of her and waited expectantly.

"Well, perhaps a bit," I hedged.

She gasped, her eyes sparking with excitement, and clapped her hands together. "Fantastic! I've always wanted to learn how to cast a spell. What have you learned so far?"

I sighed as she fluffed her skirts out around her and sat upon the floor. She picked up one of the books and flipped through it. I collapsed to the floor beside her and closed my eyes. I couldn't remember the last time I'd had a decent night's sleep, and I felt stretched and threadbare.

"Can we find a spell that will help my husband become a better lover? You know, help him keep it up longer." She tossed the first book aside and picked up the second one. "Or perhaps there's a spell that will help him be able to find my—"

"*Charlotte, please,*" I begged. "I am not in the mood to hear of Philippe's failings in bed."

She set the book aside and studied me. "Darling, what's wrong? You look positively dreadful. Shall I call for some tea?"

I sat up on my elbows and grinned at her. "Fancy a proper fucking drink?"

She leaned over, her expression grave, and felt my forehead. "Well, you don't *feel* feverish. I can only deduce that you've well and truly cracked, and to that I say, *it's about fucking time.* What shall we drink, *ma chère amie*? Brandy? Cognac? Whisky?"

"Oh, hell. Let's go drink some of my bastard husband's good wine." I grabbed the stack of books, and we made our way downstairs through the kitchens to the wine cellar. I hadn't had the bed removed yet, and Charlotte's eyes grew wide at the sight.

"Daphne, you know I'm one for a fair tipple most of the time, but if you're sleeping in your wine cellar, it occurs to me that you may have a drinking problem." She sat on the bed and leaned against the pillows. "Although this *is* damned comfortable."

I handed her a dusty bottle of champagne, and she popped the cork with practiced efficiency. She took a swig from the bottle and passed it back to me as I sat down next to her.

"It's a long story," I said. I drank deeply. "Tell me, Charlotte, do you believe in ghosts? Demons? Otherwordly apparitions?"

"Of course I do," she said earnestly. "I believe in everything." She chugged a good deal of champagne and burped, then laughed at her own rudeness.

"Do you think it is possible to kill them?" I asked.

"Probably. Everything dies eventually. I assume demons and spirits do too. Why?"

"I think Henri is alive. Or un-alive. Or he's a ghost. He exists, somehow." I took the bottle back from her and drank again.

"What, like a vampire?"

"I don't think so. More like a phantom."

She snorted. "Figures. He was so much of a fiend that even Satan didn't want him in hell."

"I'm serious," I insisted.

She peered at me curiously. "Well, I don't think you kill a ghost, *chérie*. I believe they need to cross over. Demons certainly must be exorcised. Vampires need to be staked, and I'm fairly certain I've heard werewolves need to be killed with silver—somehow. Have you spoken to a priest?"

"No. I'm worried they'll think me mad or a witch. I don't know who else to talk to."

She drained the last of the bottle and stood to choose another one from a rack on the wall.

"You know, if you're really interested in things supernatural, there is *one* person you could ask," she offered.

Her singsong tone told me she was thinking of Étienne. I cringed inwardly. Since our night of passion, I hadn't been able to stop thinking of him. I couldn't settle my mind on what exactly had gone wrong. One minute, I'd been enjoying the most passionate time of my life, and the next, Étienne had completely shut down—gone cold. I was distraught that he thought I would so easily go back to being his enemy after everything we'd shared. Clearly, the connection I felt had not been mutual.

Even when I wrote to him inquiring about our investigation, his correspondence was taciturn and monosyllabic—as if I was inconveniencing him with every missive. *Had he heard from the jeweler?* No. *Was Josephine well?* Yes. *Had anyone seen Brigitte?* No. *What should we do next about the sudden and unnatural appearance of my evil husband, and how was he connected to Jeanne? Did the jars of objects in the basement mean Brigitte was dead? And what of the gaming piece from the casino?*

No reply. Every night I waited, either for Étienne to appear at my doorstep or for some foul wind bearing Henri's cruel voice to blow through my home. I needed to find out what was going on. What *was* Henri? How was he back? Was he dead or not? Was he alone responsible for Jeanne's death? If so, why? What did he have to gain? If he was working with someone else—someone who had a more intimate understanding of things supernatural—who was it? Why murder the king's mistress? And if Henri was back and taking part in some kind of nefarious plot or revenge scheme, why hadn't he come after me?

I found myself frustratingly desperate to speak to Étienne. I wanted to figure things out with him, but his silence and sudden indifference made my head spin even worse than my ceaseless questions about our investigation. Plus, as much as I didn't want to admit, I wanted some kind of reassurance that I hadn't acted like a complete fool with him. It appeared that was not an affirmation I was likely to get.

In hindsight, I reasoned that I must have ended up as one of his short-lived conquests after all—the very thing I'd been trying to avoid. I felt completely humiliated. To have behaved so wantonly, allowing myself to be touched by his dark powers and practically begging him to make love to me... I couldn't believe I'd let it happen. When my final message went unanswered, I cried a river of bitter shame and chalked up my behavior to the vulnerability I'd felt after such a horrifying evening. I'd learned the hard way that the rumors had indeed been true—he was a reckless libertine who used women for one thing or another. I was lucky to get out from under him when I could. If he didn't want to work with me to figure out our predicament, I would carry on alone. I didn't need the Order's help, and I certainly didn't need Étienne de Noailles.

"I don't think so. Just because he is a vampire doesn't mean he knows about everything supernatural."

Charlotte pulled the cork from the bottle and sniffed it. She nodded to herself and sipped the dark burgundy liquid. "He's the supernatural emissary to the king, Daphne. If *he* doesn't know about whatever metaphysical mystery you're dealing with, he probably knows *someone* who does."

"Perhaps he does. I'd much rather do it on my own. After all, if someone is going to get to the bottom of Henri's schemes, it will be me. He made my life miserable before he left, and I'll be damned if I'm going to let him make my life a misery again. No...ghost, demon, monster, or plain old murderer, I'm going to see that his reign of terror finds an end," I muttered.

"So, you will not ask Étienne for help?" Charlotte inquired, offering me the bottle.

"Certainly not," I huffed.

She leaned in close to my face and stared into my eyes.

I backed away, alarmed. "What?"

"I knew it! You slept with him! Of course you did! I'm so proud of you. What was it like? Was he as masterful as everyone says? Come now, you must tell me everything."

I almost denied it, but the champagne and Charlotte's comforting presence unlocked something within me. A tear slipped down my cheek, and I sniffed.

"Oh no! Was it horrible? He didn't take advantage of you, did he? I will kill him myself if he did!" Charlotte gripped the wine bottle threateningly in her hand, and burgundy droplets splashed out onto her skirts.

I took the bottle and drank, shaking my head. "No, it was... Oh, Charlotte, it was wonderful. I felt things I've never felt with any man. But I fear I did something wrong because afterward...he just shut down on me. Now I'm afraid that I just became another name on his list of mistresses. Women of the court to use and toss aside."

The tears flowed more freely, and Charlotte tutted affectionately. "You poor thing! Why do you feel like you did wrong?"

"I don't know!" I wailed. "All I know is that we made love and then he just went cold! What if he's lost interest in me because he finally succeeded in getting me into bed and the chase is over? Either that or...well, I've only ever been with Henri, and his tastes were *unusual*, to say the least—what if it's because I am horrible in bed? He was likely disappointed with me, otherwise he wouldn't be avoiding me, right? I'm so furious with myself, Charlotte, I could just explode! I was doing so well resisting him and his charms, and in the midst of *one* weak moment..." I growled and gulped the wine.

Charlotte patted my back. "My darling, I'm certain you performed admirably. Men just behave this way sometimes—they don't have much experience dealing with anything beyond their own set of immediate needs. Goodness, if I want a bit of a cuddle after sex with Philippe, you'd think I was asking for the moon. He was probably overtired or hungry! Men can be such strange creatures, to say nothing of *supernatural* men. Don't fret over it."

She took the bottle and drank. I blubbered a bit more, and she leaned her head onto my shoulder.

"Do you want me to punish him? I could have him ousted from the *tonne* or spread vile rumors about him. I could tell the women at court that he has *la grande vérole* and his manhood has become black and shriveled."

I wiped my face and giggled. "No, but thank you. I suppose I'm just embarrassed about it all. And it feels strange...being with a man who isn't Henri. And, rather regretfully, there was nothing shriveled about him."

Charlotte cackled and nearly spilled the bottle of wine. We

dissolved into drunken fits of laughter, and my tears were soon forgotten.

On a sigh, Charlotte tossed the second empty bottle across the room. "*Alors*, tell me about your ghost. Is it his room? Your château isn't haunted, is it?"

"No. Charlotte, you must never repeat what I'm about to tell you. Our very lives may depend on it."

"Cross my heart."

I took a deep breath. "I am investigating Jeanne's death."

"For the Order?"

My jaw dropped. "Charlotte! How did you— What do you know of the Order?"

She laughed. "If you think Philippe is smart enough to keep that big of a secret from me, you seriously underestimate me, *chérie.* I have known since we were married, and I know that you are also with them. Do not worry! I have kept it to myself for this long. Your secrets are safe with me. Now, go on. Tell me of the ghost."

My shock waning—*of course Charlotte would figure it out...Philippe has no talent for espionage and Charlotte has a mind like a whip*—I cleared my throat and continued.

"Right. After Jeanne was murdered, they believed Étienne was responsible—"

"What utter rot!" she interjected. "That man seduces women, he doesn't murder them. If he murdered women, there would be fewer pussies for him to—"

"Yes, well, there was a report of Jeanne's death and it said *vampire bite*. I was supposed to administer justice on their behalf, but—"

"You mean stake him?"

"Yes, Charlotte, *please* stop interrupting. I'm getting to that."

She selected another bottle of wine and sat primly at the foot of the bed. I told her everything about the investigation and about Étienne, from our first meeting in the hedge maze to the graveyard to his poisoning to our encounters with the jeweler, Josephine, and the drunks, and finally the black magic bookshop basement. I told her about making love to him, though I left out the part about his healing abilities. For some reason, divulging that felt like a betrayal of something strangely sacred. When I finished, the third bottle of wine sat abandoned on the bedside table and her face was a pale, inscrutable mask.

"Well?" My nerves crackled as I worried about how she would respond.

"I cannot believe you've been through all that in the last few weeks," she said. "Firstly, I retract my earlier defense of Étienne's behavior. He is certainly an ass. Secondly, this book you found in the basement—what was the title again?"

"*Pseudomonarchia Daemonum*."

"You must be dealing with a demon of some kind," she said, her brows furrowing.

"*Dieu*, I know nothing about demons! The Order won't help me, and it's been far too long since I've set foot in a church..." I groaned.

"I think I know where we may find a copy of that book," she said, her eyes sparkling with intrigue.

"No! Where?"

"The library at Versailles."

"That cannot be. King Louis would never have such a heretical text in his library," I said with a frown.

"You are right. It wouldn't be in *his* library, but it would be in Jeanne's."

"What? Charlotte, you aren't making any sense. Jeanne was a devoted Catholic, just like Louis."

"Yes, but she was also a grand patron of the arts. She attended salons with some of the most liberal thinkers in France. She was friends with Voltaire, for God's sake. The library in her apartments is said to have a much more *enlightened* and *progressive* catalogue of texts. Did you never hear the rumors of her interest in life beyond the grave? There were even whispers of her holding a séance at court."

My mind worked. I'd always thought Jeanne was an innocent victim in all of this. Was it possible she'd been caught up in something dangerous and otherworldly?

"But her apartments have been closed up," I said. "Even if she had a copy of the book, it would be nearly impossible for us to get inside that wing of the palace without attracting too much attention."

"Well, then, it's fortunate indeed that we have the perfect excuse to skulk around Versailles in the middle of the night next week!" Charlotte nearly fell off the bed in her excitement. Seeing my confused expression, she groaned in exasperation. "Oh, Daphne. Tell me you haven't forgotten about the midnight masquerade on All Hallows Eve. You told me ages ago that you were thinking of the perfect costume."

Merde.

15
ÉTIENNE

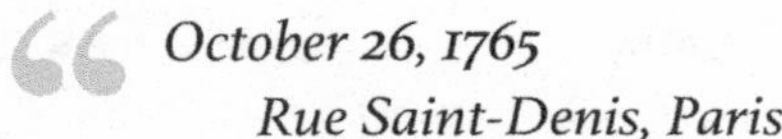

October 26, 1765
Rue Saint-Denis, Paris

"I THINK YOU'VE HAD ENOUGH THIS EVENING, MONSIEUR. WHY DON'T you go home and sleep it off, eh?" The barkeep tugged the empty tankard from my clammy grip. My fangs extended and my eyes darkened.

"Another," I snarled at him. He sighed and waved to one of the curvy barmaids at the back of the tavern. Nervously, she brought me a fresh ale and hurried away before I could unleash my ire upon another undeserving person. A month ago, she would have been winking at me and refilling my drinks with overt displays of her impressive cleavage. I would have taken her to bed for pleasure and blood.

Not anymore, I thought sourly.

After Daphne had taken off into the afternoon, I'd fallen into a restless sleep and promptly woken at sunset, tormented by growing fears that I'd been wrong and somehow Henri or the thing bearing his voice had made its way to her. I'd rushed over to her château but, once there, refused to allow myself the pleasure of meeting her in person. Instead, I'd miserably patrolled her grounds, hunting and sniffing for any putrid whiff of the murderer's scent. When I'd been satisfied that he hadn't been here—and I'd caught a vexing glimpse of Daphne seated at her library desk—I'd turned from the estate and sulked all the way back to my own home.

I'd returned the next night and two nights hence to perform the same ridiculous ritual of ensuring her safety.

The evening of the fifth day, I'd decided to forgo my warped desire to prowl around her home and dressed instead to seek different company. I'd gone to all of my favorite haunts—upper class gaming clubs, bourgeoisie taverns, even a few questionable brothels, but nothing had appealed. Woman after woman had solicited my attention, but each one had left me feeling cold and uninspired. I'd sated myself with drink and gone home hungry. The next night, I'd suffered the same disappointments.

Necessity had forced me to find someone to feed upon. Shamefully, I'd found a bleeder with golden hair and light eyes, but even when I'd had her naked in front of me, I could not bear to pursue any carnal pleasure. Angry with myself, I'd told her to dress and drank what I'd needed from her wrist. Since then, I'd given up seeking pleasure with other women, at least until the damned duchess Daphne was out of my system. I'd been enamored before. I knew it was only a matter of time and distance before she was forgotten.

Unfortunately, Daphne was not making it easy on me. She'd sent me several letters asking reasonable questions about our investigation. *Where should we go from here?* Damned if I knew. I suspected there was something much more demonic and less ghostly to the Departed Duke's appearance, but I couldn't concentrate long enough to figure out my next steps. Every thought circled back to Daphne—to her strength and wit, her soft skin and shimmering hair, her beautiful violet eyes glittering with desire. It was infuriating. Trying to screw her out of my mind was supposed to work, to help, but then message after message arrived, smelling of orange blossoms and vanilla, and I'd inevitably lose an evening caressing myself with memories of her velvet heat.

It was pathetic.

So, I'd decided the only acceptable plan of action was to keep myself in the throes of a drunken stupor until enough time passed that I could think about anything other than Daphne. *Daphne.* Things were—it must be said—not going well, but I was immortal. I had all the time in the world.

"Monsieur, you look so hungry! Do you care for a bite?" The woman next to me stroked her neck seductively, showing off half a dozen bite marks in various states of healing. Her arms, too, were covered in scrapes and punctures. She grinned lasciviously with a mouth full of brown, rotten teeth. My gut churned, and bile rose to my throat.

"Not tonight, my lady. Find another gentleman," I slurred. I stared into my ale.

"What's wrong, *mon cher*? My blood is as sweet as any aristo's! Just a taste, then, on the house." She pouted and shoved her wrist under my nose. I pulled away from her and slipped off my chair, falling to the floor. The bleeder laughed heartily and extended a hand to help me up, but I batted her away. I supposed that was enough humiliation for one evening. I stumbled out of the tavern, tossing a handful of coins at the barkeep and one to the bleeder. I bowed unsteadily amid guffaws of drunken laughter from the other patrons.

"My apologies for my unseemly behavior, good people." Their laughter followed me out the door and carried a good way down the street.

I wandered the streets for a while, not wanting to go home. I didn't know if it was worse to have my sheets smell like her and dream in torment or if it was worse to feel the tightness in my chest when each day, her scent lightened a bit more. I swore and ran my fingers through my hair, yanking it out of my customary queue. This was madness. My immortal life was in danger from some obscured threat, and here I was—one of the greatest lovers of Paris—reduced to a simpering pup over some prissy courtier who was completely wrong for me. *No, you fool, you're the one who's wrong. Wrong for her!*

"Get ahold of yourself, Étienne!" I yelled. A few street urchins eyed me and backed away from my ravings. *Pity,* I thought. *I could do with a good fight.*

Unaware of the path my feet took, I found myself drifting aimlessly in the direction of Daphne's château yet again. I stopped to reorient myself, realizing I was near the Faubourg Saint-Germain and some of the wealthiest town homes in the city. I quickened my pace, worried that I'd be seen in my disgraceful state by some gossiping lord or lady out for a moonlit stroll. Because good fortune seemed to have abandoned me entirely, it wasn't long before I heard a familiar trill at my back.

"Monsieur de Noailles! Oh, monsieur! Yoo-hoo!"

I stiffened and attempted to straighten my cravat, frowning at the spilled ale and blood on my waistcoat. My dark hair hung in loose waves around my face, and I hadn't bothered to bathe or shave. I probably looked like some sort of wild man who'd only just found his way to civilization. *Well, nothing I can do about it now,* I thought with a grimace.

I turned and bowed to the *comtesse de Brionne* and her petulant husband. He looked an impressive mix of haughty and irritated as his wife tugged him forward in my direction. She, however, seemed beyond delighted to see me, given my disheveled appearance. Her eyes flashed with humor and feminine conspiracies.

"Charlotte, it seems Monsieur de Noailles is having himself an unsavory evening. I suggest we continue on our way home and leave him to his debauchery."

"Nonsense, Philippe! One must always say hello to one's friends when out and about. Is that not so, Monsieur de Noailles?" She extended her hand to me to bow over, but her husband yanked her arm out of my grasp.

"Do not touch her," he hissed at me. "Carry on your way, monsieur. Come along, Charlotte—*now.*"

The threat in his tone would have stayed many a woman, but Charlotte just whacked his shoulder with her folded fan. "Philippe, *please.* I apologize for my husband's rudeness, monsieur. He has just lost a tidy sum at the card game following the duke's dinner party and will be in an unbearable temper for the rest of the night." Philippe glowered murderously, and I smothered my laugh.

"From whence do you come, *Monsieur l'Émissaire*? Working late in the evening? Maybe leaving a new paramour? Or perhaps, as my husband says—a night of well-earned debauchery?" Charlotte's tone was light, but the scrutiny in her gaze sent a fresh wave of hot shame through me.

"The latter, I'm afraid, though it was hardly well earned. How fare you on this fine October evening?" I tried for the smooth coolness of my courtly tone, but it came out gritty and flat.

"Oh, fine, fine! You seem somewhat out of sorts, monsieur. Are you certain nothing is the matter? You look a little sick—*or is it lovesick?*" Her piercing eyes took in my rumpled appearance with a hint of sympathy.

I bristled. "No, madame. I assure you that is *not* the case."

She eyed me for a moment, unmoved by my protest. I hid a grimace when her lips split into a wide, self-satisfied grin.

"Well, I wish you the best with your mystery lover. As I said, we've just come from the duke's little get-together. It was lovely, of course, but they served *stewed fruit* for dessert—can you believe that? Really, what are we, *English*? I felt it was incredibly unpatriotic, don't you? I'm sure the other guests were scandalized as well, don't you think, Philippe?" She laid a soothing hand on her husband's arm, but his icy glare did not stray from me. He gripped her arm tightly.

"Well, we've paid an acceptable call upon Monsieur de Noailles, darling, and it's time we let him return to his evening. Come along, Charlotte," he growled between gritted teeth.

"Philippe, *mon cher*, not so tight, please. You shall wrinkle my gown. *Alors*, Monsieur de Noailles, my husband is right! We must away, but do tell me, are you planning on attending the All Hallows Eve masquerade next week? I understand it's meant to be a rather *spirited* evening," she said, giggling at her own joke. "I will be glad to have Philippe by my side, in case I become frightened. It is good, I think, to have one you love close by on such a night, don't you agree?" Her intense expression hinted at some secret meaning that the alcohol prevented me from understanding just then.

"I hadn't thought to," I answered. "I'm really quite busy at the moment. I don't know if I have time for—"

"Well, that's very nice, monsieur. Thank you for your time. *Bonsoir,*" Philippe muttered. Charlotte glared daggers at him and yanked her arm from his grip.

"*Philippe. Arrêtez!*"

"Damn it, Charlotte, go get in the carriage! We will discuss your behavior when we get home. *Let's go!*" Without a glance at his wife, he whipped around and stomped over to their waiting carriage.

Charlotte turned wide eyes on me and flicked open her fan. Her hands trembled—no doubt at her husband's outburst—and she dropped the ivory accessory on the ground. Reflexively, I bent to pick it up and nearly fell backward when she bent down to meet me.

"Gather up your courage, monsieur," she whispered. "If you do not attend the masquerade, I daresay you will disappoint some very important people."

"*Mon dieu*, Charlotte! Get in here, now!" Philippe yelled from the darkness of the carriage.

"Oh, la! *Monsieur l'Émissaire* was just retrieving my fan for me, darling!" Charlotte called back to him. "You know how clumsy I can be after champagne *and* sherry at dinner," she laughed. She gave me a dazzling smile and a saucy wink, then plucked her fan from my fingers and bustled away.

"*Bonsoir, monsieur, et bonne chance!*"

I swayed slightly and blinked at the retreating carriage. Already, my head was beginning to ache from the drink and Charlotte's unsettling insinuations. I turned around and walked back the way I'd come, seeking my waiting carriage back at the tavern. I tried to sort through the *comtesse*'s words, but ale would not wear off until I fed. Forcing my despair down, I re-entered the tavern and beckoned to the bleeder from earlier. Without a word, she took me into a dingy room above the bar and sat on the bed. I stopped her from undressing and knelt before her, taking her wrist gently. When I'd drunk what I needed, I licked the wound closed and paid her handsomely. She smiled weakly, and I made my way back out to my carriage, lost in thought.

The warm fingers of sunrise trailed across the sky, and I felt painfully weary. One thought seemed to return over and over as I neared my home. Charlotte's teasing words were seared into my mind. *Lovesick.* What was she suggesting? That I was in love with Daphne? *Impossible.* She was a passing infatuation, that was all. Did it matter that I thought of her constantly; that I worried for her safety; that for the first time in my life, I found myself *unworthy* of a female? Of course not. Certainly, I wished for her safety and her happiness, but any gentleman with an ounce of chivalry in him would. Disappointment flared. I did want to protect her, but that job was not mine. She'd told me so many times that she could protect herself, no doubt because she'd been doing so from the moment she'd had to marry the Depraved Duke. She'd had to guard herself against his cruelty and brutality before, and now she would have to do it all alone yet again because my heart couldn't bear to be near to her.

The memory of the scents in his awful bedchamber resurfaced in my mind. Henri—whatever he was, whatever he'd become—was dangerous. Just because he hadn't come for Daphne yet didn't mean that he wouldn't come for her still. The thought gripped me in a panic that I could not assuage. *Damn it all.*

If she'd been able to endure his sadism for so long, surely I could endure the pain of being near her in order to help protect her, at least until we'd brought this whole horrible investigation to a close. She deserved that much.

I couldn't do that acting like an inebriated imbecile. It was time to straighten up and honor my responsibilities—to the country, to my reputation, and to Daphne. Then, when this investigation was finished and she was safe, I could well and truly move on.

Satisfied with myself for the first time in ages, I hurried inside my château and called for my butler and valet. "François, Robert, have a bath prepared downstairs immediately. Then while I rest, send for my tailor. I'll need something appropriate to wear to the All Hallows Eve masquerade at the palace. Spare no expense—just tell him to have something ready for me by sunset on the thirty-first."

"*Oui*, monsieur."

"*Bon. Merci, mes amis.*" I stripped off my soiled clothes on my way down to my apartments. I entered my bedchamber and tossed the clothes to the side. My men followed and, to their credit, did not bat an eye at my carelessness. I'd managed to retain most of the staff after I'd been turned. A few of them had chosen to leave, understandably, but many of them felt a sense of familial obligation. My father had been well-loved, even in his dour twilight years of failing health.

"Do you wish for us to change the bed linens now, monsieur?"

"No!" I barked, startling them and myself. Daphne's scent still lingered, but it would be gone in a few more days. She'd be safe by then, and I could let her go—orange blossoms and vanilla and all. "No, thank you. When I am ready for new linens, I shall strip the bed myself."

"As you wish, monsieur."

I nodded gratefully. Two footmen appeared carrying the large copper tub and started the laborious process of filling it. Sinking into the hot, lavender-scented water, I allowed myself to revisit the memory of Daphne's bath. I hardened, fantasizing about the episode ending differently. I should've checked my need and moved more slowly—kissed her and stoked her and made love to her until her cries shattered the steamy silence.

What a fool I've been about her. I groaned, gripping my cock and thinking of her passionate words. *Étienne, give me all of you. I need you.* Desire arrowed through me, closely followed by the remembered pleasure. This was the last time, I told myself. It had to be the last time. I did not love her. I could not love her.

I should not love her.

16

DAPHNE

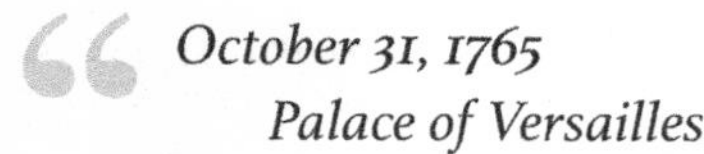

October 31, 1765
Palace of Versailles

"DAPHNE, YOU LOOK ABSOLUTELY GORGEOUS! SURPRISINGLY VIRGINAL for Aphrodite." Charlotte laughed.

"*Mon dieu*, do I look like I'm supposed to be Aphrodite?" I cursed. "I was going for Artemis."

"Oh, really? But you're covered in all those pearls."

"Well, yes, but they're supposed to symbolize the moon. Did the bow and arrows not give me away?"

I peered at my reflection in a back corner of the Hall of Mirrors. I'd decided on a shimmering silk gown in the palest blue, so light that it almost looked silver. I wore a spiked silver tiara to represent a crown of moonlight and had adorned a matching satin domino mask with several large pearls. I'd strapped a bow and golden arrows to my back as well.

"It doesn't matter. You are breathtaking, *chérie*! I'm sure your dance card will be full in no time."

"*Merde!* I don't want to be the center of attention, Charlotte. We're supposed to be sneaking into Jeanne's library."

Charlotte rolled her eyes. She was dressed in a gown of fine plum silk that was almost dark enough to be black. She'd attached matching silk wings to the back of her gown and wore a black mask with high, pointed ears.

"Charlotte, I thought you were coming as a peacock," I said.

"Well, I was, but then I had this moment of divine inspiration! I changed my costume at the last minute and decided to come as a bat. Oh, Philippe was *furious* about the expense!" She chuckled and to illustrate her point, she held her arms out and the wings unfolded beautifully. She did, indeed, look like a lovely, mysterious bat.

"How clever you are! You look beautiful," I said with a smile.

Philippe joined us and held out two glasses of champagne. He'd come dressed as Apollo, resplendent in gold brocade with a glittering mask and crown. A papier-mâché lyre hung from a belt at his waist.

"Daphne, you are certainly the most beautiful Aphrodite—lovelier even than the goddess herself," he gushed.

I scowled at him.

"She's Artemis, *mon cher*," Charlotte said, nudging him with her elbow. "See her bow and arrows?"

"Yes, of course," Philippe said, though his mouth was twisted in confusion.

I sighed and sipped the champagne. I tried to avoid looking around the room nervously, but it was difficult considering the last several days had me in a tangle of raw nerves. Sleep had all but eluded me over the past week, and I'd taken to prowling the moonlit halls of my château, gripping my pistol and a vial of holy water, waiting for Henri's return. Add to that the simmering resentment I felt at Étienne's abandonment, and it seemed that it would be a long time yet until I could drift off in some sense of peace.

I had no idea if Étienne would be coming tonight, but I hoped not. I didn't think I could restrain myself from issuing a very thorough dressing-down. I held on to the anger as best I could, mostly because it covered the hurt I couldn't seem to overcome. Besides, if he was here, I'd end up thinking of his dreamy, golden eyes and his hard, muscled body, and I wouldn't be able to properly focus on the task before Charlotte and me tonight.

If only I could focus now.

I'd thought of him ceaselessly since our night together and found myself squirming in bed, dreaming of his lips and hands on me. I reasoned that it was only natural, since the only physical love I'd ever known beyond my own explorations was with a man who couldn't climax without the sight of blood. Of course I would feel some sentimental attachment to Étienne. I wasn't made of stone. *Regrettably,* I thought.

"Might the humble Poseidon fill a slot on Aphrodite's dance card?" A courtier in sea-green silk bowed before me. He stroked his trident pruriently and winked behind his mask. I looked around for Charlotte, but she had wandered off.

"Oh, well, I—" Panic had me stuttering and backing away from the unpleasant overture, until I came up against a solid wall of man. I shut my eyes. My body knew him immediately.

"I'm afraid the lady Artemis has a full dance card tonight, Your Grace."

That voice—velvet across my skin. The smell of soap, cedar, and peppermint. Snow-covered pine trees. Cool, smooth skin and lean, hard muscle making me burn with desire.

Putain.

Poseidon prowled away, grumbling. I opened my eyes and spun around. For all the angry words I wished to lash against him, I was ill-prepared for the impact seeing him would have upon me. He was clad in a suit of deep-burgundy velvet and wore a leather mask topped with a small pair of black antlers. His sensuous lips curved up in the hint of a smile, and his warm hazel gaze scorched me in its intensity.

"Étienne." His name came out more breath than sound. Of its own volition, my body arched toward him, magnetically drawn to what it wanted most.

"Duchess." He took my hand and bowed over it, then turned it over and pressed a lingering kiss to my wrist. Lust blazed through me, wild and urgent. I stared—gaping like a ninny at his seductive beauty. Try as I might, I could not form the sharp retorts I'd been clinging to for the past days.

Étienne smirked. "Perhaps we should make our way to the dance floor? I'd hate to have Poseidon accuse me of lying. I believe that's actually the *marquis de Balay* beneath that hideous mask. I can't believe he adorned his wig with *real* seaweed. In an hour, this room is going to reek of low tide."

Despite myself, I chuckled. Étienne's hand found the small of my back, gently guiding me to the other dancing couples. I drew in a breath, fighting for calm—fighting to remember my anger and disappointment.

"I'm surprised you bothered," I managed.

"Pardon?"

"What do you care if the *marquis de Balay* asks me to dance? You made it abundantly clear you want nothing to do with me—after *everything*," I sneered, hating the petulant tone of my voice and the undisguised hurt that bled through.

A look of pain flitted through his eyes but was gone quickly. He opened his mouth to reply, but the strains of an allemande began, and he grasped my hand to start the dance.

"Though I suppose you're not here for me," I goaded. "Probably just back to your regular hunting grounds now, eh? Isn't that how it is for you, Étienne? Use one up, then move onto the next—a little sex, a little blood, a little influence. The Order isn't sending another agent after you because of my interference, so I suppose that's all you needed from me, then."

The dance swirled us away from each other for a moment, and

when we came together, he was white lipped with anger. When we clasped hands again for a turn, his grip was rough.

"What do you want from me?" he hissed. "By your own admission, our alliance was only ever meant to be temporary."

"That doesn't mean I appreciate being cast aside like another one of your conquests! For a moment, I thought you were...I thought I was...I thought *we* were—" I cut myself off, too afraid to say the words out loud. *I thought you were different. I thought I was special. I thought we were...something.*

Étienne paused, missing a step in the dance. He stared at me, his eyes unfathomable behind his demonic stag mask. Couples spun around us, and I started to suffocate in the stifling room. I needed to get out and get some air. *Breathe, Daphne.*

Without another word to Étienne, I fled the room before the dance ended. I barreled through the other revelers, fighting my way to the doors that led out to the gardens. I was grateful for the sharp bite of late October chill. The bracing cold allowed me to regain the composure I seemed to misplace whenever Étienne was around. I stared out at the dark garden beyond, dotted with guttering torches. Had it only been five weeks since my encounter with him in the hedge maze? It felt like a lifetime ago.

"You never answered my question."

The words at my ear made me jump. Once again, I marveled at his stealth. He came up to stand next to me, looking out into the inky blackness.

I blew out a breath and watched it condense in a cloud of frost before me.

"I want what I've always wanted," I answered. "The truth."

He turned to face me, raising his fingertips to my cheek.

"Is that all?" he murmured.

"Yes," I whispered, leaning into the feel of him. *No. I don't want to live in fear of Henri's return. I want to be able to sleep at night without dreaming of your hands on me. I want to feel like I was something to you.*

He chuckled. "Liar."

I shut my eyes against the truth of his words.

"We will get to the truth," he said, taking a step closer to me. His legs brushed against my skirts. "Daphne...whatever happens, you will be safe from Henri. I swear it."

"And then?" I asked.

He swallowed. "And then you will go back to the Order and continue your life as an agent. I will go back to my duties as emissary, trying to convince the king to see reason, trying to convince the court to accept the blood plague as our new reality. We'll go back to work, Daphne, and Jeanne's spirit will be at peace."

His words formed an ache in my chest that spread through my entire body. *But why? Isn't that exactly what I wanted?* I knew it wasn't—not anymore.

"What if that's not enough?" I whispered.

Étienne sighed. "Daphne, it has to be. You're a smart woman. You understand what it would take for us to be together. I'm immortal—eternal. I will not watch you wither away with age and die, and I hardly think you're leaping at the chance to sacrifice a lifetime of sunrises on me. You must understand. It's better this way."

A sharp pain chased the ache away, followed by an overwhelming numbness. I swallowed back tears I didn't want him to see. He was right. Even entertaining the idea of there being something more between us made me feel foolish. What had I been expecting? I didn't just want a passing fancy, but the reality was we couldn't be anything more.

I swallowed and nodded. The look of anguish in Étienne's face nearly unraveled me. I turned to head back inside, but he caught my arm and pulled me to him.

"Daphne, I wish it could be another way," he said, wrapping his arms around me. "I won't dishonor you by asking you for more, but you must know you were never just another conquest to me."

He tilted my chin up and set his lips to mine. There was no lightness to the kiss, just the untamed unleashing of need and a thousand shades of passion. His arms around my waist tightened, and I clung to him, holding on as if I were adrift in a storm. I pressed him back against the stone balcony railing, painting my body against his.

He groaned against my lips. “Daphne, I can’t—*mon dieu*—I can’t do this. I can’t keep doing this. I have to let you go.”

But his hold on me tightened and his lips found mine again, and the only time he paused was to feather kisses against my cheeks, jaw, and neck. His arousal pressed against my belly, sending fire straight to my core.

“Why do you have to?” I panted against him, nearly faint with desire.

He pulled away to look at me, staring hard into my eyes. “Because, Duchess, you are not mine.”

He tilted his head down to resume the kiss, his lips inches from mine, when a rough voice called my name. The look in Étienne’s eyes went cold. At the interruption, I froze, panic snapping my mouth shut. I straightened and backed away from him.

“Daphne!” Philippe called again. “Daphne, Charlotte needs you, darling. Over there. Now, please.” He pulled me firmly away from Étienne. “She was most insistent.”

The look in Philippe’s eyes was murderous. I burned with embarrassment at being caught, but Étienne stood straight and narrowed his gaze at Philippe. A heavy silence descended upon the three of us.

“Daphne,” Philippe prodded. “She said it was important.”

I nodded and stepped back toward the ballroom. Étienne bowed stiffly at Philippe and followed me.

“I believe the ladies would like to be alone,” Philippe said, staying Étienne with a hand on his arm. Étienne glared but let me go.

Rather than get in the middle of whatever unpleasant altercation seemed about to take place between them, I hurried inside the palace, searching for Charlotte.

The candlelit corridors blurred as I careened forward, quietly calling for her. Finally, a door cracked open, revealing a thin stream of amber light. A familiar head poked out and beckoned to me.

"Daphne! Come here! I've found the library!" Charlotte ducked back inside the room and quickly closed the door behind me.

I ripped off my mask, throwing it onto a desk beside Charlotte's bat mask, and crumpled into a nearby chair. Seeing my pink cheeks and breathless manner, Charlotte threw her head back and laughed.

"Oh, *chérie*! Tell me what happened with Étienne."

"*Mon dieu*, Charlotte, I have no idea!" I shook my head in confusion as tears started to well in my eyes. "One moment, I was arguing with him on the dance floor, the next I was outside trying to get some air, and then I found myself before him again, wondering *what if we could be together?* But we can't because he will live forever and I can't become a vampire, and so we have no future—and then it was as if we were saying goodbye to each other, but then we were kissing, and then Philippe found us and he's just *furious*, Charlotte —I don't think I've ever seen him so angry!" The words rushed out of me as the tears started to fall, dropping onto my shiny, pale skirts.

"Hush now, *ma chère amie*! You are fine now, are you not? Philippe and his temper are out there, and we are safe in here. And as for you and Étienne—well, what do you really want?"

"I don't know!" I wailed.

She tutted and hugged me, but her tenderness only made me cry harder. I buried my face in her shoulder and sobbed almost as hard as I had when Michel had died. *What is wrong with me?*

"You must figure that out first, *chérie*. Otherwise, how will you know what to ask him for?" she soothed, pulling a flask of brandy from her garter. "Here. Have a drink of something medicinal."

I sipped at first, enjoying the sweet warmth of the liquid. Then, at Charlotte's insistence, downed the rest of the flask.

"I don't know what I want. I don't understand my feelings for him, Charlotte. I want to hate him. He makes me so crazy! And he's a *vampire*! Just like the ones that killed Michel."

"But he did not kill Michel," Charlotte pointed out. "And you know, darling, I don't think he's really like *all* vampires, any more than one man is like *all* men. Why are you so confused by these feelings? You simply thought he was one thing, and then you got to know him and learned that you were wrong. And now you must figure out if you want him at all, if you love him and will make it work or if you think it's best to part ways and move on with your life."

"It's not that simple," I argued.

"*L'amour* rarely is. But for now, we have work to do, so no more tears, *d'accord*?"

"Yes, yes, I know. *Merde*. It's fine. I'm fine, really."

"Good," she said, taking the empty flask. "Now that you are fortified, we shall look for the book. I would love to hear of your troubles and your heartache, *chérie*, but we don't have much time before the silly men come looking."

She was right. I stood and forced Étienne from my thoughts, intent on finding a copy of the book. I blew out a breath and took a candle from the desk.

"Thank you, *chérie*. As always, you are right." I offered her a wan smile. "You start over by those shelves, and I'll start on this side."

We perused the bookshelves lining the walls, standing on chairs to reach the uppermost volumes. Unfortunately, they didn't seem to be in any kind of order, which meant we'd have to individually check every book. I groaned. This room wasn't as large as the formal library at Versailles, but it was big enough to take us all night.

"I should have brought more brandy," Charlotte muttered. "Do you think I should go and get us some?"

"No! It'll take us long enough to search together—it'll take twice as long if we're drunk."

A soft knock startled us both. Before I could climb down from the chair, the door opened. We froze.

A pair of antlers poked in, followed by the rest of the man I wanted to see the least.

"Étienne!" I gasped. "What are you doing here? Get out before someone sees you and finds us in here!"

I jumped down from the chair and hurried over to him.

"My, my," he drawled. "What have we here? Two sneaky little vixens hiding away in Madame de Pompadour's private library? What *will* the king say?"

I started to push him out the door, but it was like trying to move a block of solid stone. He chuckled at my feeble attempts and removed his mask. Charlotte narrowed her eyes at him but suddenly gasped and pulled him farther into the room.

"Charlotte, *what* are you doing?" I whispered.

"Daphne, he can help us look!"

I scowled.

"Look for what?" Étienne glanced from me to Charlotte, then back to me again.

"Nothing!" I whispered. "It's nothing. If you want to help, go keep watch and leave Charlotte and me to work. You haven't exactly been the best partner in this investigation lately anyway."

He peered down at me, his expression unreadable.

"No," he said.

"No—what?"

"No, I don't want to leave. The *comtesse de Brionne* has asked for my assistance. I will stay to help." He faced Charlotte and smiled charmingly at her. "What are we looking for, madame?"

I seethed with anger. Charlotte raised her brows at me.

"*Pseudomonarchia Daemonum*," she said.

"Traitor." I folded my arms against my chest.

Étienne's smile dropped.

"Daphne," he said in a warning tone. "This is extremely dangerous. You have no idea what you're getting into."

I raised my chin haughtily. "Oh, and you do? Well, by all means, share it with me. You forget, Étienne, I was in that cellar too. I want to know what we're up against, be it ghost, supernatural beast, or demon. Whatever it is, I will defeat it. We have no other leads to follow, and I don't think I need to remind you that time—and the Order's patience—is running out."

"The Order's patience? Because it's not enough to simply find Jeanne's murderer—we have to do it so that your masters will welcome you back into their good graces," he scoffed.

"How dare you!" I growled. "If it wasn't for my intervention with the Order, you'd probably be returned to dust from some other assassin's stake."

Charlotte rolled her eyes. "Stop! Both of you. We're wasting time. Help us look for the book, Étienne, and then you two can spar all you want."

Chastened, I returned to my spot at the bookshelves. I resolved to ignore Étienne as best as I could, but it was difficult with him smiling smugly a few shelves over. I cut my eyes to him. He was scanning the titles with inhuman speed, and I swallowed an oath. Charlotte had been right to ask him for help. I'd almost forgotten about his supernatural speed. I could only hope I found the book first, just so that he wouldn't have the satisfaction of—

"Found it," he called.

Merde.

He pulled a thick, leather-bound book down and placed it on a table near the middle of the room. It looked almost identical to the one from the cellar. Without hesitation, I flipped through the pages, looking for the one that had been seared into my mind.

The Demon Asmoday.

Charlotte and Étienne stood on either side of me, reading over my shoulders. The page detailed horrifying rituals for summoning and controlling a demon. In exchange for sacrifices of blood, the demon Asmoday was said to bestow wealth, charm, power, and all-compelling allure upon his summoner, in addition to granting any number of requests. The demon could appear in his own form but had the power to both remain unseen and inhabit bodies. With the illicit gifts listed, I could suspect any number of people of summoning him—especially at court. Who didn't wish for wealth, power, and the lust of others? The only thing that didn't make sense to me was Henri's involvement. Why would he have summoned a demon to give him everything he already had?

"What does this mean?" Charlotte's humor had faded, replaced with a look of horror.

"We're dealing with a serious force of evil here," Étienne said, turning the page. "Someone has summoned the demon Asmoday, and somehow, he is connected to Henri's body—or his spirit. I can't be sure which. We will need to petition the Vatican for an exorcism. That's the only way to defeat the demon."

"Are you certain? There has to be another way. Holy water, prayers, silver—something like that," I offered, desperate and starting to panic.

"Well, I don't know for certain about the holy water and prayers, but I believe silver only works on werewolves," he said thoughtfully.

"We don't have time to petition the Vatican," I said. My voice sounded on the verge of hysteria, even to my own ears. *Henri is connected to a powerful demon! As if he wasn't terrifying enough as a mere mortal man. What has he sought and gained in this new supernatural state? Strength? Immortality? Other unnamed dark powers?* Each prospect became more terrifying than the last, but I willed myself calm with a steadying breath. "You read the text. There will be more deaths—more sacrifices until the summoner has what he wants. If we don't stop him, who knows what will follow? To stop Asmoday, we must stop the summoner."

"How do we do that?" Charlotte asked. Worry lines creased her forehead.

"We don't," Étienne said emphatically. "We must have help—someone who has performed an exorcism before. I've certainly never done one, and I doubt either of you have. I do know that if it isn't done properly—*safely*—it can go very, very wrong."

I ignored his words. "Perhaps there's another book in here...a book about exorcising demons. Charlotte, help me look!"

"What the hell is going on in here?" Philippe threw the library door open, knocking several books from their shelves. He tore off his mask and threw it aside, face purpling in anger. His eyes lit upon Étienne, and he practically vibrated with violence.

"Philippe!" Charlotte laughed to cover her nerves, but her voice shook. "Nothing, *mon cher*, nothing! I was just having a quiet moment with Daphne when Monsieur de Noailles came in and—"

"Not another word, Charlotte. Not another lie shall cross your lips tonight. Get your things. We are leaving."

"Philippe, please, it was my fault. I—" I stepped toward him.

He held up his hand to stay me. "No, Daphne. I've had enough of this. It is your life—your decision—if you choose to remain under Noailles's influence, but I will not have you dragging my wife down with you. I feel like I can't trust you anymore, and if I cannot, then neither can the Order. I'll be writing to them this evening and telling them that you've been compromised. Do not send them any further messages."

Shock slammed into me. I felt rooted to the ground. My heart pounded with the speed of a runaway horse. I swallowed and opened my mouth, but no sound came out. *Out of the Order?* I couldn't believe it. Charlotte's worried gaze met mine, and she shook her head, eyes warning me to be silent. She sighed deeply, picked up her mask from the table, then came to kiss my cheek.

"It will be all right, *chérie*. I will call on you in a few days when all of this has blown over. *D'accord?*"

Then, straightening with as much grace as the queen herself, she exited the room. As she passed Philippe, she looked at him and said in a voice more chilling than I'd ever heard from her, "Apollo always was a silly, jealous god."

A muscle in Philippe's jaw ticked, and he slammed the door, leaving Étienne and me in devastated silence.

17

ÉTIENNE

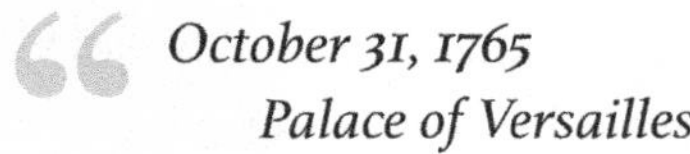

October 31, 1765
Palace of Versailles

It was some moments after the *comte* and *comtesse de Brionne* had left before Daphne finally exhaled. She sat heavily in one of the chairs and raised a hand to her forehead, rubbing a spot of tension between her brows. The defeat in her posture left a hollow ache in my chest, and the mask of detached composure I'd been struggling to maintain began to fracture.

"Daphne..."

She closed her eyes and held up her hand to silence me.

"Please," she murmured. "I have lost much tonight. I do not wish to lose my temper as well. Go away, Étienne. I cannot bear your presence just now."

Frustration tumbled through me. I was desperate to pull her into my arms, kiss away her sadness, and move heaven and hell to right her world, but those promises would tie me to her and to a future I knew we could not have. A future she did not want. *No.* The best way to help her would be to deal with the demon and his summoner and leave her to the luxurious life she rightly deserved.

Emboldened by that sense of rightness and quelling the selfish wrongness I felt at letting her go, I knelt before her and cleared my throat.

When she opened her eyes, they were shimmering with unshed tears. For all her exquisite beauty in her angelic silk, there was something tragic lurking in the depths of those large violet pools. After a beat, I was able to find my voice again.

"Have you encountered demons before in your work with the Order?"

She shook her head.

"We must find someone who knows how to perform an exorcism. The demon is the greatest threat to us now. If we remove him from the equation, the summoner is temporarily impotent. If we go after the summoner first, who knows what will happen. The demon may become untethered to hell and be unleashed upon our world with nothing left to control him. Right now, he is bound by his ties to the summoner."

"We don't have time to wait on the Vatican. I don't suppose you know of someone who can help?" Her voice had lost its ragged edge and was frosty with irritation.

"Unfortunately, I do not often engage with men of the cloth," I said wryly.

She ignored my attempt at levity.

"I'm afraid I rather lost my faith after Michel died," she said. "I don't have many friends in the church. I would have sought assistance from the Order—they have several members familiar with some of the more indelicate religious practices—but I can't count on their help right now."

"Is there no one you could ask from the Order? Even if you do not petition the group as a whole..."

She looked at me murderously and gestured to the door. "Yes, there was! And there he goes! If you hadn't been here, Étienne... If you just would have gone when I'd first asked, I could have convinced Philippe that Charlotte and I had snuck away to be in each other's confidence. Why did you follow me?"

"My apologies," I said, more curtly than I intended. "I wanted to make sure you were all right after our little balcony tête-à-tête."

She stood and paced around the library, her skirts swirling in a soft rustle that sharply contrasted the resonance of her anger. I leaned against the desk, attempting to calm my own emotions.

"Yes, fine, thank you. Being caught kissing at a party is actually the least of my worries right now," she huffed.

"That's not what I was referring to," I said. I thought back to her words, *What if it's not enough?* Of course it wasn't enough—certainly not enough for me. But the possibility that the end of our investigation and return to our old lives was not enough for *her* filled me with a perverse kind of hope. It was the hope for a future neither one of us could have and that I didn't deserve in the first place.

"Oh, that. Yes. You're right, of course. It doesn't make sense—the two of us. It was foolish of me to think..." She trailed off, her voice barely a whisper.

"Foolish to think what?" I pressed. *Foolish to think there was something more for us? That, perhaps, you wanted me as more than a throwaway lover like the rest of the women at court do? Foolish to think that you'd be willing to sacrifice so much to be with me?* My heart thudded in my chest, anticipating the rejection I knew would come.

"Nothing," she lied. "You were right is all I'm saying. But we can't just give up on this investigation now. Especially not with... with Henri emerging. I've given almost everything to come this far, and I won't stop until it's finished. If I do, I will have betrayed my friends, the Order, Michel's memory, and myself in vain."

She turned her back to me, and her shoulders slumped in fatigue.

"I don't know why you came tonight, Étienne. After everything I gave you, I left you to your solitude. I came here to finish things on my own. But you are back, wanting me to let you in again and to just pick up where we left off. I don't know if it's out of guilt or self-preservation or morbid curiosity or perhaps so you can feel like you have some kind of strange sexual power over me. Whatever it is, *I do not know*," she stressed. "But..."

She faced me, tears gone, her face a study in fierce determination and exquisite beauty. Whether it was her pearlescent gown or the force of her will alone, she seemed to glow with an unnatural light. *She is magnificent.*

"What I do know, Étienne, is that I do not need your blessing or your approval to finish what we started. I will do it on my own—for Jeanne; for Michel; for the people of Paris; and, most importantly, for me. Your involvement, or the lack of it, will not stand in my way. And if it becomes necessary, I will go through you."

She stepped toward me, eyes narrowed and chin raised in defiance. She squared her shoulders and crowded me back against the desk. "Now, tell me, Étienne. Why are you here? Why did you come tonight? What do *you* want from *me*?"

Everything, Daphne. I want everything. I want your body, your mind, your heart. I want to make love to you every dawn before I sleep so that I will dream of you every day. I want to spend my nights finding ways to challenge your incomparable wit and trying to draw forth that small smile that makes my icy heart melt. I want to give you pleasure and happiness and all that my wretched body and damned soul has to offer. I came here tonight for you—to see you safe and to protect you so that I can let you go, but God help me, I don't think I'm strong enough.

I briefly considered prevaricating, but the bold frankness on her face prevented me from lying to her outright. I met her gaze unflinchingly, a cool smile on my lips. It was becoming harder for me to affect an air of detachment when every part of me felt like it was reaching for her. She waited for my answer, but because I couldn't lie and I wouldn't tell her the truth, I had no other alternative.

I pulled her to me and kissed her.

I could taste her conflict—torn between her body's desire for me and her mind's recoil at that need. I didn't give her time to think

—to object. I licked her lips, and she opened to me on a resigned sigh, meeting my tongue stroke for stroke. She tasted like brandy and fire, igniting every nerve in my body. I tugged at the neckline of her bodice, gently lifting her breast from the satin. I lightly caressed her pretty, pink nipple until it hardened beneath my touch. Breaking from the kiss, I bent and put my lips to it, sucking at it delicately until Daphne threw her head back and moaned in a rough tremor. I scraped my teeth across it and lifted her other breast from her gown, kneading it softly in my hand. She gasped, and the sound went straight to my cock, already stiff and straining in my breeches. Mindless with want, I almost didn't hear her tortured, soft-spoken words.

"So, this is what you want from me. I hate you for it, Étienne, because—*damn us both*—I want it too."

I ignored the guilt snaking through me, resolving to devote myself solely to her pleasure in this moment. I lowered my hands to her waist and pushed her back against the wall of bookshelves in the darkest corner of the library, then dropped to my knees. For once, it felt right for me to be here, kneeling before this powerful, luminous goddess.

"Étienne, what are you—?"

I bunched her gown and lifted it, gazing upon pale-blue stockings and the leather garter that strapped her flintlock pistol to her upper thigh. A growl of desperate lust issued from my chest at the sight of the contrast. Delicate, proper undergarments topped with lethal practicality. If that didn't sum up Daphne as a woman, I didn't know what did.

Her hands had threaded their way through my hair, and I took them in my own. I handed her the bundle of skirts.

"Keep it there, Duchess," I purred, sliding my hands up her legs. "I'm going to need both of my hands for this."

Her eyes danced with excitement, but her mouth was a tight line.

"You say I have some kind of sexual power over you?" I blew a stream of cool air against the thatch of blonde curls at the apex of her thighs. Her knees trembled.

"Perhaps you do," she gasped. "Perhaps it is this way for all of your women."

Pleasure thrummed through me at her ill-disguised jealously, and I slid my hands farther up her thighs, caressing her curls with my thumbs.

"Perhaps you are afraid to admit that you desire me, Duchess," I said, lightly rubbing my index fingers along the outer folds of her sex.

"I am not afraid." I watched a blush creep across her chest and cheeks.

"Then say it." The command was as much of a challenge to her pride as it was a need for me. I looked up at her, meeting her eyes above her gathered skirts. One long, languid stroke of my finger through the wet seam of her entrance and her eyes snapped shut, her mouth falling open on a whimper.

"I desire you," she breathed.

"Brave girl," I chuckled, rewarding her by finally setting my tongue to her, licking every sweet, perfect inch of her. I circled the peak of her pleasure, and her soft cries became louder, more insistent. She fell back against the books, and I held her hips to my face, worshipping her feminine perfection with lips and teeth and tongue. One of her hands dropped the bundle of satin, and I felt her fingers wind through my hair again. She bucked against my mouth, driving for the friction against the places where her pleasure grew. Her instinctive pursuit of her own bliss made me wild.

"Am I the first man to touch you like this?" I panted, sliding a finger into her soft, wet heat.

"Oh, yes. Yes." She fisted her hand in my hair, pulling my lips back to her sex.

A primal sense of possessive triumph coursed through me as I pulled one of her legs over my shoulder. I dropped an airy kiss to her tight bud, then sucked it between my lips and worked it with firm strokes of my tongue.

"*Oh, mon dieu. Putain de merde,*" Daphne swore, guttural and lewd. I nearly spent in my breeches.

Fighting the animal urgency to take her hard and fast, I focused instead on her—on the beautiful way she embraced her sensuality. The way she looked above me, eyes half-closed in hunger yet watching me bring her to the brink. I slid a second finger inside her, and her other hand let loose her gown, draping me beneath the weight of her skirts. I did not mind. I wanted to watch her come apart from every angle, and soon I heard the escalation of her cries telling me that I was succeeding. Her pleasure crested, and she screamed, clutching my head as her legs gave way. In a moment of selfishness, I let my fangs extend and nipped at the vein in her thigh—not to feed, but just to taste. *One last taste of perfection.* She cried out again as a second orgasm rolled through her—my favorite benefit of drinking from this part of the body.

Dieu, *how could I live without this?*

You must, logic argued. *For her.*

I licked the wound closed and caught her as she fell, holding her tightly and laying her down on the thick Persian carpet.

For one satisfying moment, she lay sated and panting in my arms. I still ached with need, but it was a small price to pay for such a thorough distraction from her damaging line of questions. She sighed, slung one arm over my chest, and nuzzled into my shoulder. My heart stuttered at the tenderness in the gesture. She looked up at me, eyes finding mine in the flickering candlelight.

"As enjoyable as that was, you never answered my question, Étienne. Why are you here tonight?"

Putain.

18

DAPHNE

> *October 31, 1765*
> *Palace of Versailles*

THE PANIC THAT FLASHED ACROSS ÉTIENNE'S FACE ALMOST MADE ME laugh. *Poor thing.* He'd really believed he could just kiss me into forgetting my questions. What kind of a simpering fool did he take me for?

He was quiet, staring fixedly at my bare breasts, eyes hazy with lust and his breathing still shallow. I knew he wasn't going to answer me—or if he was, it would be some kind of falsehood. It didn't matter. If he thought he could control me by using my lust as a weapon, he'd just learned that I was not so easily victimized.

I sighed and sat up, tugging my bodice back into place and smoothing the wrinkles from my gown. Étienne stood, helping me to my feet. I blushed at seeing his rather conspicuous excitement, and he smiled predatorily at me.

"How fitting that you would come dressed as vestal Artemis and I as the poor, hapless stag," he chuckled, his voice a low rumble that vibrated through me. "Actaeon stumbling upon his lovely goddess, only to be struck down and ripped to pieces by her hounds."

I smirked and tied my mask back on. "Oh? And here I thought you showed up as a stag to engage in some mindless rutting with some poor, unsuspecting doe."

"It is never mindless, Duchess," he purred.

"Well, it's lucky for you I left my hounds at home, then."

He came up behind me and kissed the back of my neck. "What is your plan?"

"Why?"

"Because I'm going to help you. You cannot face Asmoday and the as-yet unknown summoner by yourself, Daphne, which is what I know you intend to do. It would be *ungentlemanly* for me to go back on our original agreement. Consider the last several days a temporary setback in our progress." He bowed with exaggerated gallantry.

Irritated, I adjusted my crown and re-pinned a few of the curls that had come loose during our tryst.

"*Our* progress? Forgive me if I'm misremembering, Étienne, but it's been by my wits alone that we've made *any* progress at all. Bringing Van Helsing to you was my idea, as was searching Brigitte's bedroom, as was seeking out the book that led us to Asmoday. Well, I had Charlotte's help for that, but my point is, monsieur, that you overestimate your usefulness to me."

"Oh, you think so? I hate to disappoint you, Duchess, but if I hadn't brought you to Jeanne's grave, you'd still be laboring under the false information supplied to you by the Order. And how would you have found Brigitte and the bookshop if not for me?" Étienne's temper flared as he straightened his hair in its queue.

"We were led to Brigitte because you fucked her and she tried to kill you, Étienne. Perhaps that's how we should proceed, then. You can hump your way to the truth and seduce Asmoday and his summoner all the way back to hell. While you're at it, why not visit the Order as well? You might find your way off their hit list, and then the whole useless lot of you can stand around and stroke each other's massive egos while Paris bleeds around you."

Hurt flashed in Étienne's eyes, but was gone almost as quickly as it had appeared. "You sound rather bitter for someone who seems to enjoy my seduction so well."

I bristled. "Yes, well, given my past, I'm sure I would have enjoyed myself with any man who didn't leave me bruised or bleeding after the act."

"Your low expectations of lovers don't insult me, Duchess—what is it you so often say? 'I assure you, I've heard worse.' Especially here, at court. They call me 'a delightful beast,' you know. Not a paramour. Not a vampire. Not a man." His cocksure manner slipped, and for the first time, I saw him radiate sadness, insecurity, and loneliness.

"Then, why do you do it?" I asked.

"You said it yourself, Duchess. Food. Influence."

I knew exactly what that was like. I'd heard scant rumors of Henri's cruelty before I agreed to the match, but it was only after we were wed that I fully understood the depth of his depravity. My marriage had saved me from one kind of hell, only to usher me into another. Étienne seemed to be in a similar hell, though not necessarily one of his own making. I felt a swell of empathy for him and immediately regretted some of my words. Yes, I was angry and hurt and incredibly tired of being underestimated by the men in my life, but that was no excuse to lash out at Étienne. Truthfully, I treasured our intimacies, but I was afraid of being strung along by a notorious rake who was only interested in saving his own skin.

Étienne leaned against the desk again, his handsome face inscrutable. I didn't like the hiccup in my pulse when I looked at him, all those taut muscles sheathed in sumptuous burgundy velvet, the antlers on his mask making him eerily demonic in the candlelight. He was a devil—born of fire, to be sure, but much of the fault lay within me for being so ready and willing to burn.

"So, Duchess. Where do we go from here?"

I sighed and shook my head. An ache was building at the base of my neck, and I needed quiet and clarity to think.

"I don't know," I said. "But I won't figure it out sitting in here."

I smoothed my skirts and left, casting the barest glance back at him. He remained motionless, obviously lost in thought—still so handsome, still so tempting, still so dangerous. I walked down the hall back toward the ball, though I knew I wouldn't stay long without Charlotte and Philippe to keep me company. Halfway there, I felt a cold draft of air blow through the hallway, and I stopped. To my left was another narrow hall that led to the courtyard and gardens beyond. At the very end, I could see one long curtain swelling and fluttering with the breeze. *Curious.*

Why would someone leave a window open in the chill of October? I crossed slowly into the hall, the hairs on the back of my neck standing up.

This is wrong.

My shoes crunched over broken glass, and I saw that the window hadn't been opened—it had been broken. Flecks of blood dotted pieces of glass that trailed outside into the frigid Paris night. Something bad had happened here.

Dread gathered in me when I realized that Philippe and Charlotte had been the only other people in this wing of the palace. Had there been some kind of accident?

"Étienne!" I called.

He was there in an instant, taking in the scene with a bright, intense gaze.

"Was it like this when you came through to the library?" I asked.

He shook his head. "No. It must have happened after I came through."

"Do you think—" I swallowed the lump in my throat and tried again. "Do you think it is Charlotte's or Philippe's blood?"

Étienne picked up one of the glass fragments and inhaled, then licked the droplet of blood staining it. His pupils dilated to black pools, and his fangs extended.

"I do not know who the blood belongs to, but I can tell you that it is a man's." He sniffed the air again and cast his eyes about, looking for something unseen. He walked to the billowing curtain and bent to pick up something on the floor.

I gasped in horror when he held it up.

"Charlotte's mask!"

Étienne approached me, our argument forgotten, his face etched with concern. He took my hands in his and looked into my eyes.

"Daphne, there is something else," he hedged.

Frightened, mind racing, I braced myself for what I knew would be devastating information.

"I smell the murderer here. I don't know if it's the demon or Henri or the summoner, but I smell it on the glass."

The world spun on its axis, and I shut my eyes tightly. *No, Daphne. You cannot faint. Keep it together! You must—for Charlotte.*

"What else do you detect?" I whispered.

"A few things I cannot place," he said. "Some things I recognize from the bookshop. But, Daphne, if he—it—took Charlotte and Philippe, they're probably still alive. Remember what the book said."

"We have to go after them now! Before it's too late!"

"We don't know what we're walking into, and we don't have any way to fight a demon. If we go in there ill prepared, it'll be four corpses, not two. We have to come up with a plan."

I wracked my brain, wildly grasping for a solution. *How can you fight a demon?* The obvious answer seemed to be a priest, but Étienne didn't know any and the only ones I knew were in the Order. *When was the last time I was even inside a church?*

Suddenly, I remembered. I turned a half-crazed smile on Étienne.

"I know where to find a priest," I said.

He eyed me skeptically.

"Come on," I said, tugging at his arm. "This time, I'm leading the way."

He didn't argue or challenge me, and although his face was stern, I swore I saw the glint of amusement in his eyes.

⚜

The carriage ride was silent with repressed tension. Étienne watched me from beneath long sweeps of lashes but did not speak.

Uncomfortable with the insults I'd hurled at him back at the palace, I cleared my throat.

"Étienne, I—" My voice rasped. "What I said back in the library, it was—"

Mon dieu, *why was this so hard? Out with it, Daphne!*

Étienne's lip twitched. "*Unladylike?*"

"It was wrong. You were right. If it hadn't been for you, I would probably still believe the worst of you—that you murdered Jeanne. The progress we've made has been *ours*, not mine alone. On top of that, you saved my life back at the bookshop, and I'm grateful to you for that. I said those things out of anger, and I shouldn't have. I am sorry."

He remained quiet but nodded once. I held my hand out to him, hoping to put the awkward mess behind us.

He regarded my outstretched hand. Grinning wickedly, he took it and pulled me onto his lap.

"Étienne!"

"What? I was just going to tell you that I forgive you. Shall we seal it with a kiss?"

I wriggled against him, trying to extricate myself from his grip. I felt his arousal through my skirts. He tipped his head back and moaned.

"If you keep that up, Duchess, I shall seal it with more than a kiss."

The carriage slowed, and I looked out the window. We were near the abbey.

"We are here," I said.

Étienne swore. He brought my face down to his for a quick kiss, then released me. He looked out the window and swore again.

I hesitated. "Can you enter a house of God?"

He laughed. "Of course I can. I just try not to. With all of my sins, it's a wonder I'm not struck down the very moment I set foot on holy ground. I feel as though I'm tempting fate."

"We'll have our fair share of tempting fate tonight," I muttered. "No point in avoiding it now."

"As you say, Duchess. *Alors*, shall we go in? I am yours to command tonight, *chérie*."

We approached the heavy oak doors, and I stopped for a moment. Shoring up my courage, I knocked loudly. It wasn't long before the door swung open and we faced a young and somewhat rumpled-looking priest. His close-cropped brown hair stood out at odd angles, and he had a shadow of whiskers on his face that badly needed a shave. He blinked blearily at us but, seeing our extravagant dress, straightened his robes and bowed.

"Madame. Monsieur. How may I assist you?"

Without waiting for an invitation, I swept past him into the nave. Candles flickered in the darkness, but it was still possible to be awestruck by the beauty and grandeur of the building.

"Do you know who I am?" I demanded of the priest, who was shutting the door behind us.

"No, madame, I don't believe I've had the pleasure."

"I am the *duchesse de Duras*. My husband and I were married here four years ago in a wedding presided over by *Cardinal de Bernis*."

The priest's eyes widened, and he looked at Étienne in confusion. Étienne grinned at him, showing a good deal of fang. The priest let out a noise somewhere between a squeak and a gulp. He bowed again.

"I've come here tonight to seek his help. It is a matter of grave importance, and I'm afraid it is rather urgent. Would you be so kind as to direct me to him?"

The priest shook his head. "But, madame, His Eminence is not here."

"No, I didn't expect he would be *here.* But I do expect that you'll be able to help me find him," I said, glaring at the quivering man.

"You do not understand. His Eminence has been retired for some time. He no longer resides in Paris—he is at his home in Soissons." The priest swallowed and darted his eyes over to Étienne.

"Retired," I huffed.

"Well, yes. For some time now...as I said."

Nervously, the priest shifted and wiped a droplet of sweat from his forehead. Not looking away from Étienne, he forced a laugh.

Blocking out the rest of the priest's stammering, I sat on a pew and sighed. *So much for my stroke of genius. How will I defeat the demon Asmoday now?*

Étienne sat down next to me and put his hand on my knee.

"I'm afraid we won't be able to make it all the way to Soissons tonight. Even if we could, the chances of Charlotte and Philippe being alive by the time we returned would be slim. I fear I've let them down," I said.

Étienne sighed. "It was a good idea."

The priest stepped forward, apparently taking pity on me.

"Madame, is there anything— I mean, I am certainly not as capable as His Eminence, but I am a man of God and...is there any way that I might assist you?" He produced a rosary from his pocket and toyed with the beads.

"What is your name, monsieur?" I asked.

"Father Clarence."

"No, Father Clarence. I don't suppose you can be of assistance—unless, of course, you are somehow adept at performing exorcisms and banishing demonic entities from this earthly plain," I quipped humorlessly.

His eyes flicked to Étienne again, who growled at him.

"Not me," he said.

"No, of course not, monsieur," he stuttered. "Well, what I mean to say is that I can, of course, perform an exorcism—it is one of the rites that we must all know, you see—but I would not dare to do such without the express permission and assistance of the Vatican. To do so would be dangerous and practically blasphemou—*erp!*"

Father Clarence's skittish ramblings abruptly ended, and I looked up to see Étienne holding him one-handed by the front of his robes. He lifted him easily until the priest's feet dangled above the ground. Eyes darkening, fangs extended, Étienne hissed an oath that made Father Clarence blanch.

"Monsieur! This is a house of God!"

"Do you think he will come home before I can separate your head from your body and drain the blood from your corpse?" Étienne thundered.

Father Clarence whimpered.

"Étienne, I don't think that is necessary," I said. He ignored me.

"What happens if you perform an exorcism without the knowledge of the Vatican?" Étienne demanded. His voice was low and threatening.

"It is not done!" Father Clarence choked out. He kicked his legs futilely. "I could lose everything—be excommunicated! It could go all wrong!"

Étienne's eyes had blackened to solid pools of onyx. As I watched in horrified fascination, his handsome face started to morph into something monstrous—his gaping mouth expanded, showing off rows of needle-sharp teeth. His tongue snaked out, forked and flittering like a snake's. His cheekbones and jawline sharpened, and two horns started to protrude from his forehead. When his transformation stopped, he looked just as satanic as the pictures of Asmoday. Had I not known the man he was and—admittedly—enjoyed such sensual pleasure in his arms, I would have been paralyzed by fear.

"And what do you think you will lose if you do not help us now, priest?" Étienne said, his deep voice sounding like a legion of angry demons.

Father Clarence's white face wavered as if he were about to be sick. He whispered prayers and called upon saints I hadn't even heard of, until finally his eyes rolled back in his head and he passed out.

As quickly as Étienne had transformed, he snapped back to his ethereally handsome self. I glared at him, hands on my hips. He winked at me.

"Well, aren't we just full of surprises? And where was *that* when we were fighting vampire thugs in an alley?" I sniffed.

He chuckled. "Parlor tricks, Duchess. But I do believe Father Clarence will help us now—just as soon as he comes to. In the meantime..." He shifted the limp priest over his shoulder. "I suggest we make him comfortable in your carriage and find our way to the bookshop. We're running short on time."

19

ÉTIENNE

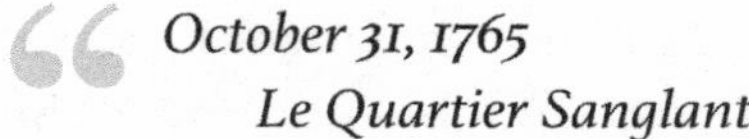

October 31, 1765
Le Quartier Sanglant

Father Clarence roused himself shortly after the carriage trundled off from the abbey. I'd considered tying him up, but Daphne would hear none of it.

"He is a priest, Étienne! That would be incredibly undignified. Besides, we need his cooperation and he's already bound to be cross with us for abducting him in the middle of the night."

"Cross and confused," Father Clarence said. He rubbed his head. When he saw me sitting across from him, he paled and thrust himself back in his seat. He held his rosary up in front of him and started reciting a litany of prayers. "Back, vile beast! Back to the depths of hell with you!"

I arched a brow and looked to Daphne.

"Monsieur, *please*. That is uncalled for. We didn't have time for introductions back at the abbey, but may I present to you Monsieur Étienne de Noailles, vampire emissary to His Majesty," Daphne said.

I inclined my head.

"A pleasure," I said smoothly.

Father Clarence looked even more horrified. Briefly, he appeared to consider his surroundings and his options—possibly to try and make an escape. Daphne seemed to read the same from him because she tutted and lifted her gown up to her thigh, drawing forth her flintlock pistol. She held it steadily, aiming at his knee. I found her threatening self-assurance incredibly erotic.

"Father Clarence," she said in a bored, aristocratic tone, "I really am sorry for the manner and insistence upon which you were brought with us this evening, but I'm afraid I've run out of time to do things with more decorum. You say you are confused, and I aim to alleviate that. I will also promise you that you will not come to harm while you are here with us. Unfortunately I cannot maintain that same assurance when we reach our destination. Humbly, I beg your patience while I explain everything to you."

She lowered her pistol and Father Clarence lowered his rosary. He nodded at her.

"My companion tonight has been wrongfully accused of the murder of Madame de Pompadour. We've been investigating the manner of her death for weeks and have been led to a particular establishment in le Quartier Sanglant. The last time we were there, we were attacked by an invisible force—a force with the voice of my husband. We found evidence of a summoning circle as well as a copy of the *Pseudomonarchia Daemonum*. We believe someone has called forth the demon Asmoday and he is somehow tied to either the body or the soul of my husband. We need someone to perform an exorcism and banish the demon back to hell."

"But, madame, what you ask is impossible," Father Clarence pleaded. "I cannot do it alone—and certainly not without permission from the Vatican. They require proof that these events are indeed demonic."

"I know," Daphne continued. "And under any other circumstances, we would petition the Vatican for help. But two of my friends have been taken tonight, and I fear the worst. I have no more time to waste in seeking permissions. My cousin's and her husband's lives depend on our urgency."

Father Clarence's features softened. "Madame, my heart goes out to you, but I simply do not think I am qualified to be able to hold an exorcism without—"

"What will it take?" Daphne interrupted, her manner brittle and nearing panic. "Money? Or perhaps you desire something else? A title? I am friends with the king, you know. Or—what else? A lover?"

Father Clarence's mouth dropped open, and he reddened in embarrassment.

Seizing her moment, Daphne leaned forward. "Is that it, monsieur? You wish for something discreet and carnal? I will take you to bed myself, if you want."

I could not control the growl of displeasure that escaped from my chest.

"Perhaps you prefer a male companion? Monsieur de Noailles is one of the most legendary lovers in all of Paris. Do you not find him handsome, Father Clarence?" Daphne pushed forward, kneeling before him. Desperation shone in her angelic face. I wanted to break something. Father Clarence would be a start.

"Madame, please." Father Clarence shied away from her kneeling form. "I have forgone such earthly pleasures. I do not carry a price."

The carriage shuddered to a stop, and I felt despair leech into Daphne. We'd arrived in le Quartier Sanglant. Cold and withdrawn, she sat back and opened a hidden drawer beneath her seat. She pulled out several small throwing knives, a handful of thin wooden stakes, and a small pouch of gunpowder and bullets. She started to unfasten some of her heavy petticoats and her panniers, slimming down to her silk gown. From a second hidden compartment inside the carriage, she brought forth a simple leather harness that buckled around her shoulders and beneath her breasts. In it, she stashed her throwing knives and her pistol, coolly detached from Father Clarence's and my astonishment. In her pared-down Artemis costume and armaments she no longer bothered to conceal, she looked like a goddess preparing for battle.

In one final moment of despondency, I snarled and seized Father Clarence by the throat.

"Fuck the Vatican," I raged. "If you don't agree to help us, I'll kill you now and distribute your body parts to the impoverished vampires nearby."

Father Clarence quaked at my violence, but Daphne laid a hand on my arm.

"No, Étienne. Leave him be. There doesn't need to be any more unnecessary killing. This is not his fight, *mon cher*. If he cannot help us, we must face it on our own. If only there was time to get a message to the Order—"

"Wait—but the Order does not have female members," Father Clarence choked through my grip. I loosened my hold.

"What do you know of the Order?" I demanded.

"Well, I know them by reputation, as any priest does. They do the work of God where we cannot! But surely, madame—" He eyed Daphne's leather harness full of weapons, and his fear melted away. "You *are* with the Order, aren't you, madame? Oh, I cannot believe it! You must tell me—what are they like? Since when do they allow women among their ranks? Never mind, never mind. That would be presumptuous of me to ask, and I am sure you took some sort of holy vow to protect the Order's secrets. Oh! I cannot believe I am meeting a member of The Holy Order!"

His face split into a wide grin, and he reached for her hand, presently curled around a small glass vial of what I guessed was holy water. Daphne cocked her brow, perplexed by his sudden change in demeanor.

"Madame, if I have offended in any way, I regretfully apologize. I will do whatever I can to aid you in your mission. I only ask that you speak well of me to your masters."

"You will help us?" I asked suspiciously. "Meaning you will perform an unsanctioned exorcism?"

He nodded vigorously, his eyes wide and sweat condensing on his forehead. "Yes, yes. If that is what you require. I am bound to do as you ask." Father Clarence felt about his pockets and produced a small, yellowed bible and his rosary. He gestured to the vial of holy water in Daphne's hand, and she tossed it to him.

"Very well, Father Clarence. I thank you for your change of heart. Étienne and I will do what we can to protect you, but understand that we face a cruel and extremely dangerous foe tonight."

Father Clarence nodded. "Asmoday."

Daphne shook her head. "I refer to my husband."

Vibrating with excitement and no small amount of fear, Father Clarence got out of the carriage. Daphne made to follow him, but I held her back.

"Are you certain about this?"

"Of course not. But we don't have a choice. I don't know what we're going to face in there, Étienne, but I would rather face it with a man of God than without," she said, frowning.

"You go in with a man of God and a beast from hell," I said, lightly touching her cheek. She smiled, and the sadness in it nearly undid me.

"You are no beast from hell. Trust me. I know the type." She leaned forward and pressed a small, chaste kiss to my lips.

With that, we left the safety of the carriage and began our march to the bookshop.

Father Clarence babbled incessantly to Daphne the entire way to the Rue des Oubliés, asking her question after question about the Order. I rolled my eyes in annoyance. If this priest failed us tonight, I would happily drain him. Now that he knew of Daphne's allegiance to the Order, he looked at her with something like boyhood admiration. I could understand it, but it needled my irrational jealousy.

For her part, Daphne was quiet in between her terse, one-word responses to Father Clarence. Her eyes darted around, and her muscles twitched with the slightest noises, though there weren't many. Curiously, and perhaps inauspiciously, the district was silent. There were none of the customary sounds of a lively neighborhood —no raucous groups loitering around late-night taverns or brothels. In fact, I couldn't see a single lit candle or the glow of a hearth anywhere. Le Quartier Sanglant appeared to be deserted once again.

A couple of streets away from the bookshop, Daphne hauled up. She beckoned to Father Clarence and me and motioned for us to be quiet.

"Étienne, can you detect anything?"

I took a deep breath and reached out with my senses. I heard rats scurrying around piles of refuse and wind whispering through broken windows. I heard the heartbeats of Daphne and Father Clarence, one steady and the other racing. I smelled the grit and damp of the streets—stale blood and old sweat, sour ale, and the offal of animals and vampires. Beneath it all, there was an almost undetectable thread—silk, rosewater, fresh blood, and sulfur.

"They are here. Charlotte is, at least. I am less familiar with Philippe's scent. I'm afraid I cannot tell if she is dead or alive. There is fresh blood in the air, though it could be from the broken glass we found at the palace. I'm certain the blood is from small wounds —if there were a greater quantity, it would be a much stronger odor and a greater draw for me."

Father Clarence grimaced and crossed himself.

"Save your prayers for the exorcism, priest," I grumbled.

Daphne let out a sigh of relief. "There is still hope, then."

Father Clarence patted her arm. "There is always hope, my child."

Checking the powder and shot in her pistol, Daphne nodded

and started forward again. Father Clarence followed closely behind her, now thankfully silent. I brought up the rear, pausing every few steps to listen for something—anything. As we neared the dilapidated storefront of the bookshop, the sulfur grew stronger—much stronger than it had been when we were here last. I took that to mean either Asmoday had been here more recently or he had grown stronger since then. Possibly both.

"Be on your guard," I warned. Daphne flashed me a look that said, *Well, obviously.* Father Clarence wiped the sweat from his brow.

The shop looked exactly as it had when we'd been here the last time. I wasn't surprised. I didn't think anyone would be so foolish as to come here—except for us, of course. I stepped through the doorway and held up my hand to stay the others. I closed my eyes and listened carefully—there it was, the faint fluttering of another heartbeat.

"Someone is here," I whispered to Daphne. "But I only hear one."

Her lips tightened in a firm line. We crept forward slowly, me leading the way, followed by Father Clarence, with Daphne bringing up the rear. This time, I picked up a small candle from a shelf and lit it, then passed it back to Father Clarence. I moved to the back room and the staircase beyond. Even with the wavering light of the candle, the darkness seemed to close in on us. Father Clarence's breaths came in shallow pants and the beads of his rosary clicked softly in his trembling hands.

The stairwell gaped before us, and we began our descent.

Halfway down, I could make out Charlotte's pale skin on the floor, directly atop the pentagram. She was breathing but showed no signs of consciousness. I frantically searched the rest of the room for another presence but saw nothing. We appeared to be alone.

I hurried down the remainder of the stairs. At the bottom,

Daphne caught sight of Charlotte and rushed forward, but I stopped her.

"Wait," I cautioned. "See where she lies. Remember what happened the last time."

"Charlotte!" Daphne hissed. "Charlotte, it's me, Daphne! Wake up, *chérie*."

Charlotte did not stir.

Father Clarence came forward and bent down, crossing himself again. He reached one hand out, but the moment his fingertips breached the summoning circle, the air in the cellar changed. Gusts of rank, rot-scented air swirled around us, carrying a languorous disembodied voice.

"Oh, I really wouldn't do that if I were you, Father."

I looked at Daphne, who had paled. Her features twisted in rage.

"*Henri!*" She snarled. "Or should I call you *Asmoday*?"

A deep, malicious laugh echoed off the walls. "Very good, *ma pute*. We're a little bit of both at this point."

Father Clarence swallowed a squeak and began reciting from his bible. The laughter grew louder, drowning out the priest's prayers to a litany of saints, until he called upon Archangel Michael. Suddenly, the laughter became a roar, and for a second, all was silent.

Daphne looked around wildly. She threw herself forward, reaching for Charlotte's limp arm. The moment she breached the circle, she was thrown backward with violent force.

"Daphne!" I ran to her. She was uninjured but dazed.

Father Clarence's eyes widened, but he did not cease his prayers. The small candle shook in his hand when another gust of foul wind blew through the room. Our only light now extinguished, Father Clarence cried out in fear. Without the ability to read the correct passages, he whimpered and resorted to a furious repetition of the Lord's Prayer.

"What did I say?" the voice bellowed. "You never listened to me

—never minded me. You dishonored our marriage vows then, just as you dishonor them now. Fucking that vampire! Oh yes, *ma pute*, you think I don't know? I know *everything.* I can smell him all over you, little whore. You hear that, priest? You think I am the worst of your troubles? Turn your prayers to this sinner, you fool."

Daphne shook with fury. Her pallor brightened to a flush of anger.

"*Monster,*" she spat. She fumbled in her pockets and produced another small candle and a flint. She struck at the flint unsuccessfully. The laughter resumed.

"Stupid woman. Must I do everything for you?"

At once, the room lit ablaze. Several torches along the walls glowed with a sickly, yellow light, casting the cellar in a polluted incandescence. As soon as my eyes adjusted to the brightness, I saw Daphne was paralyzed in revulsion.

Across the room stood a very solid—very real—man. He had once been attractive, I thought, but now his skin stretched and bunched over his sagging flesh in an unnatural way. His clothes were stylish and expensive and would have been impeccable if not for the splashes of blood that covered them. His face was unmarred except for the gaping black voids where his eyes should have been. He grinned cruelly at us, then adopted a tone of bored nonchalance.

"There now," the man said. "Is that better?"

"Henri." Daphne's voice broke through on a sob.

"In the flesh—well, sort of."

"What has happened to you?" Beneath Daphne's terror was a hint of pitied sadness.

"You did this to me!" Henri snarled at her. "If you'd only been a better wife, I would not have sought fulfillment elsewhere—all the way in Venice! If you'd just been compliant, I wouldn't have been driven into the arms of all those other women. I wouldn't have been there that night in Venice when *he* found me."

"When who found you?" I asked.

Henri ignored me, focusing on Daphne. "You did this to me, wife, but it's not half of what I'm going to do to you." Henri raised his hand in the air, and to my horror, Daphne choked a constricted scream. Her body lifted from the ground, and she clawed at her throat, losing her breath with every gasp. Henri cackled and watched her feet kick and twist midair.

Without thinking, I hurled myself at him, fangs extended, face already contorting into something monstrous. Henri saw my attack and sidestepped, but my shoulder caught him in the chest and we both went down. I heard Daphne fall to the ground and suck in air, and I knew I'd temporarily hit my mark. Henri growled and shoved me with the force of ten men, throwing me into the wooden crates in the corner. I staggered up just in time to see him lunging for Daphne. With supernatural speed, I threw myself at him again, driving him against the stone wall. He grunted with the impact but recovered quickly, wrapping his hand around my throat. His grip tightened, and I started to choke.

"Father Clarence!" Daphne shouted. "Help us bind the demon!"

Henri sliced his other hand through the air, and Daphne shrieked and staggered back as if she'd been backhanded. Darkness began to encroach on me as I lost the ability to breathe, but as my world began to slip away, I was dimly aware of another presence joining the fray. Another man stepped out from the top of the stairwell.

"Philippe!" Daphne called. "Oh, thank God. Philippe, the demon—he has Charlotte!"

Henri tipped his face up toward Philippe and grinned savagely. When he spoke his voice lost the low, aristocratic drawl and reverted to the raspy, guttural demon tone. "At last, you're here!" he hissed with glee. "*Master*."

20

DAPHNE

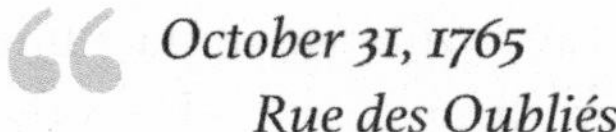

October 31, 1765
Rue des Oubliés

Master.

Henri had called Philippe *master.* Had I misheard him?

"Daphne! Are you all right?" Philippe bounded down the stairs, his eyes never leaving my face. He was still wearing his Apollo costume, minus the mask and lyre. His thin, blond hair had come out of its queue and hung limply about his face. *I must have misheard.* There was no way Philippe was...

He reached me and grasped my shoulders. This close, I saw lines of rough scratches across his face and a cut on his lip.

"Daphne, you're certain you're uninjured? He hasn't hurt you?"

"No, I'm fine," I started, confusion preventing the pieces from coming together. "What happened to your face? Was it Henri—Asmoday? What...what are you doing here, Philippe?"

He touched the red mark on my throat from Henri's earlier attack and frowned.

"This wasn't supposed to happen," Philippe murmured, but it wasn't directed at me. He whirled around, teeth bared at Henri, who still held Étienne by the throat. I could see his eyes rolling back in his head—he was about to black out. "She wasn't supposed to be harmed!"

A look of cold resolve crossed Henri's face. When he replied, it wasn't in Henri's voice—it was the hellish growl of Asmoday.

"She was uncooperative," he said.

Uncooperative? What the hell was going on? I looked around. Father Clarence was cowering behind the smashed wooden crates. I didn't think Philippe had even seen him.

"Daphne, my love, do not worry. We'll have this sorted out in no time." Philippe smiled at me, and I wondered if there was a touch of madness in it. *My love?*

"What shall I do with the vampire?" Henri asked. Étienne was clawing at his hand, leaving deep, bloody gashes all up his arm. Henri did not seem to notice.

"Well, I think that depends on our lovely Daphne over here," Philippe said in a light tone. *Definitely mad.* "What do you think, darling? Have you gotten him out of your system? Only I don't want to kill him now and have him become a martyr for your affections. But I worry that if I let him live, you'll just go on mooning after him, and we *cannot* have that."

My mind worked, but nothing was making sense.

"Philippe, what the fuck are you talking about?"

He sighed and nodded to Henri, who dropped Étienne to the ground in a pile of limbs. Étienne gasped and coughed, and Henri stepped lightly on his chest, ready to bring his foot down and crush Étienne's heart.

"This never would have happened if you'd just done what I wanted in the first place," Philippe said. He laid a gentle hand on my cheek, but there was something tightly controlled in his eyes.

"I don't understand."

"Oh, my Daphne, don't you see? You were *always* mine. You've always been meant for me—since you first came out to society and started coming to Versailles. Don't you remember? Well, perhaps not. You always were the belle of the ball, and I only ever watched from the fringes. Always there for you, my love, ready and waiting for you to notice me."

"Philippe, this cannot be. You don't know what you're saying. Has he gotten to you? Asmoday? Does he control you now, my friend?" Fear raced through my blood at these bizarre admissions. They simply couldn't be true. I would have known if Philippe had harbored feelings for me—wouldn't I?

"*My friend.* Yes, I'm afraid that's all I ever was to you. Even when you were supposed to marry me after Michel—well, I had to force your hand, didn't I? If you weren't under his protection anymore, you'd be forced to find a husband—to turn to me. I was there, Daphne! Right there. But you chose the wrong man—you chose this *thing* who abused and tortured you. For a time, I let him—you deserved it, you know, for choosing him over me—but then it just became too much."

My heart stopped at his words, and a pained cry escaped my lips. "No! You—you didn't. Oh, Philippe, tell me you didn't take my Michel from me."

He lifted a shoulder. "Well, *I* didn't kill him. I simply provided a few financial enticements to his lover to drink more than was necessary. Things just played out as they were meant to after that."

The room started to close in on me, and I fought for breath. Philippe looked at me with concern and shoved me toward one of the wooden crates. Father Clarence flinched at that, but Philippe took no notice of the priest, who was still clutching his tattered bible and rosary. As I grabbed the crate for balance, I felt the clammy hand of Father Clarence on my wrist. He slipped me the vial of holy water. I maintained eye contact with Philippe, trying not to give the priest away.

"You look so pale, darling, best sit down for a bit," Philippe said.

"I can't... I don't understand. You're married to Charlotte! You have one of the most enviable matches in the *tonne*! How can this be?" Tears sprung from my eyes as the weight of his words sank in.

"Yes, and she tried, the poor thing. But she just wasn't *you*, you know? She did allow me to remain close to you, which I'm grateful for." As if only just realizing she was in the room, Philippe tilted his head down at Charlotte's prone form. "And now she will serve an even greater purpose, bless her."

"What greater purpose?"

"She will die so that your love may live," he said triumphantly.

Unbidden, my gaze darted to Étienne. Philippe saw it and growled.

"No, Daphne. But that's a curious development." He frowned. "It used to eat me alive, you know, the fact that you didn't love me. I would lie awake at night wondering what I could do to earn your affection. After Michel, I had hoped you would turn to me, but when you didn't, I had to figure something else out. Then, along came Jeanne and her fascination with the occult! It didn't take much for me to convince her to let me into her private library—especially when she believed it was on behalf of the Order. *Mon dieu*, but that woman could be dense. It took me ages, but I finally found what I was looking for—a power strong enough to bend your will to my own: Asmoday! A demon who rules by lust. Everything just fell into place perfectly."

"But if Jeanne helped you, why did you murder her?"

Philippe shrugged again, unaffected by the destruction he'd wrought. "Well, the first time I summoned Asmoday was in her library. She walked in on me. Summonings require some sort of sacrifice, and I'm afraid Asmoday needed a bit more than blood in order to assent to help me."

Henri grinned, showing off monstrous rows of sharp teeth. Frighteningly, Philippe chuckled.

"Oh, the things he did to that poor woman before and after her death." He shook his head. "Then, of course, Asmoday informed me that he could sway your affections in my favor but that it would involve a handful of lives in order to work. What is it the English say? *In for a penny, in for a pound.* Naturally, I had to clear the way for you to become mine, so it made sense for me to remove your husband from the equation. I went all the way to Venice to track down Henri—you should truly thank me for that one. I walked in on him *in flagrante delicto*—sodomizing some unfortunate prostitute in the back room of a gaming hell. Asmoday rather liked your husband. It turns out he could withstand an abnormal amount of pain—it took him *hours* to die. Asmoday took possession of his body after that, and we returned to Paris."

"If you've been after Daphne's heart this whole time, why have you been trying to kill me?" Étienne bit out.

"Truthfully, the Order did think you were Jeanne's murderer. I needed a scapegoat, and you were convenient. They were more than happy to sign the death order. I'm afraid your rather liberal political views have put a target on your back. It would have been much easier if Daphne had done what the Order asked and killed you without issue. Unfortunately, you stuck around and the two of you started to become *close*. What was left for me but to deal with you as well?"

"Asmoday never came for me," Étienne said.

"No. I didn't know how a vampire would fare against a demon. I certainly couldn't take the chance that you would win. Still, it should have been easy enough. Everyone knew your weakness for women, and I knew that quicksilver would poison a vampire. I sent Brigitte into your sister's brothel with a handsome payment and specific instructions. When she returned to me having failed her task, it was right that she would pay with her life. It was only fair."

"Philippe," I tried. "This is madness. You must know that Asmoday is using you. He will never give you what you want. He is a demon—full of lies."

Henri hissed at me. Philippe glared.

"No, darling, he *will*. Once I finish with Charlotte, I'll give him Noailles and then he'll work his magic. You *will* love me, Daphne, and we *will* be together." He shook with manic energy—his eyes bright with hysteria. I clasped the vial of holy water in one hand

and frantically sought an exit. My flintlock was in my chest harness, but I didn't think I could reach it without Philippe noticing. I needed a distraction. I darted a gaze at Étienne, who watched us from beneath Henri's foot.

"Philippe, I had no idea you felt this way. Why did you never come to me yourself? Perhaps if you'd just told me of your feelings, things would have turned out differently. If only you'd spoken to me. I would certainly have chosen you instead of Henri," I said in a soothing voice. I stood and edged forward, deftly unstopping the vial in my hand.

"Hey!" Henri shouted. I froze in place. *Had he seen?* "Henri may be dead, but I still have access to his memories. That's rather unkind, Daphne."

"Silence!" Philippe yelled at him. "Do you really mean it, darling?"

I swallowed and nodded, then took another step forward. I was right in front of him.

"And what of Noailles?" Philippe asked.

I tried for casual. "He is a vampire."

Philippe's eyes narrowed, and he slowly shook his head. "You must think I'm a damned fool."

Henri hissed a laugh. Dread gathered in my gut.

"It's not that easy, Daphne, but it doesn't matter anyway. I will sacrifice Charlotte, and then when you say those words, you *will* mean them, and I *will* believe you. There's no turning back now." Philippe started to turn to Charlotte, and panic propelled me forward.

I flung the holy water at Henri, praying the Order's teachings were right. It splashed across his face, and he shrieked—an unholy, ear-splitting sound. Angry burns erupted on his ill-fitting skin. Étienne seized his moment and snatched at Henri's foot, wrenching it to the side with a sickening crack. Philippe turned to the noise, and I reached for my pistol. *Too late.*

He whirled back to me, betrayal and rage written across his

face. He backhanded me, knocking me off balance, and I lost my grip on the pistol. I tripped over the wooden crates and fell backward next to Father Clarence.

"Finish the exorcism!" I hissed. "We will keep them busy."

He nodded, his terrified eyes wide, and began shouting passages from his bible. I looked back over the crate. Henri was limping, the wounds on his face smoking, but he had otherwise recovered. He and Étienne were throwing punches and kicks in a blur of motion—his demonic strength against Étienne's vampire speed. I didn't have much time to watch though. Philippe came for me and pulled me up by my hair. Tears stung and pain seared my scalp.

"I'm going to have you, Daphne, one way or another." He wrapped his hand around my neck and pushed me back against the wall. Holding me by my throat, he fumbled for the buttons of his breeches.

Blind rage ignited in me, and I kicked at him, connecting with his shin. He swore but stayed his course, reaching for the hem of my skirts. I beat against his arms, which were surprisingly strong despite his wiry frame.

I heard a roar from the other side of the room and saw Henri stumble. Between Étienne's assault and Father Clarence's prayers, the demon was suffering. Étienne saw his opening and hurled Henri against a wall. Henri grunted with the impact and slid to the ground. Étienne leaped over him and seized his throat, fangs bared.

Philippe, still struggling with my dress, swore in a high-pitched cry of despair. His eyes lifted to mine, and I saw the full measure of his emotions. *Hate, sadness, regret, shame.* Suddenly his head jerked forward with a loud crack. He fell, slumped over. I coughed and wheezed a ragged breath, then look up into the apoplectic visage of Charlotte. She held a large board wrested from one of the broken crates.

"Oh, Daphne!" Charlotte threw her arms around me and sobbed. "Are you okay?"

Philippe groaned at her feet.

"One moment, *chérie*," she said. She raised the board overhead and brought it down on Philippe with another violent *whump*.

"That's for hitting me and ruining the ball!" She kicked him in the stomach. "That's for murdering all those poor people!" She kicked him in the groin. "And that's for using me to get to Daphne!"

Eventually, Philippe floated away into unconsciousness. Charlotte continued to kick him, laying out sin after sin. I touched her arm, and she collapsed into me, sobbing hysterically. I pulled her back to sit on the crates next to Father Clarence.

"Charlotte, if you have any God left in you, you will help Father Clarence pray," I said. I retrieved my pistol from the floor and gave it to her. "If he wakes, shoot him in the knee."

"What about the head?"

"No, *ma petite amie*. We need him alive to exonerate Étienne to the Order," I said.

Her eyes narrowed. "That's not the head I was talking about."

I managed a wry smile and made my way over to Étienne, who was covered in a thick, black liquid. Henri sputtered beneath his hands, his voice vacillating between Asmoday's and his former human voice. There was a loose mass of flesh where his throat should have been.

"You bitch," the creature chuckled at me. "You weren't worth the blood I spilled. I'll be back on Earth before you know it. This world is filled with desperate, greedy men."

Étienne squeezed the creature's throat, and a choking, gurgling sound spewed out.

"If you harm so much as one hair on her head, I swear on Lucifer himself that I will follow you into hell and torment you all over again." Étienne's eyes were black as pitch, and the threat in his voice frightened even me.

The creature turned its dead, empty eyes on him and laughed louder.

"Witless fool," it snarled. "She will never love you. Not in the way that you love and long for her. You will pine for her every day, just as Philippe did, except you have an eternity of misery to face without her, vampire."

A look of gut-wrenching sadness crossed Étienne's face, and I knew the creature's words had struck true. *Is Étienne in love with me?* Then his face changed, the sadness replaced with cold anger. He lifted Henri's head from the ground, then smashed it back down. More black liquid sprayed forth—from the sound of the smack, I suspected Henri's skull had fractured.

Étienne glanced back at Father Clarence, who had fainted in the corner. Charlotte attempted to rouse him, but it was no use.

"How about we send this vile thing back to hell?" Étienne said, grabbing the bible and rosary from the prone priest's hands.

I found the passage Father Clarence had been reading, whispered a silent prayer that this would work, and shouted at the top of my lungs.

"Depart, then, impious one, depart, accursed one, depart with all your deceits, for God has willed that man should be His temple!"

Henri's body lifted from the ground, and a deafening roar filled the room. Just as suddenly, the body slammed back down to the ground and started to dissolve into the same viscous black liquid. The torches on the walls blew out in a rotten gust of wind, and the room plunged into silent darkness.

21

ÉTIENNE

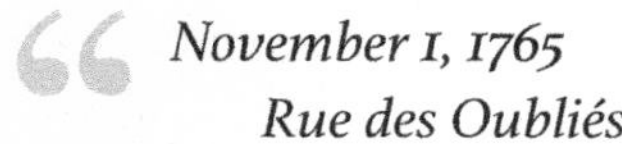

November 1, 1765
Rue des Oubliés

"Is everyone okay?" Daphne asked.

Murmured assent came from all except Philippe, who remained unconscious on the floor with several bleeding head wounds. I made my way to him and tore several strips of fabric from his absurd gold waistcoat, then used the ties to bind his hands and feet behind him.

With perfect timing, Father Clarence roused himself from the floor.

"Oh! Is it done? Is it over? Is the demon gone?" the priest queried.

"No thanks to you," I growled.

Daphne interceded before I could wring the scrawny priest's neck. "Father, if you would be so kind, please take the *comtesse de Brionne* upstairs and back to my carriage. I need you to bring it here so we can move Philippe discreetly. Besides, I'm not sure how long we've been down here, and I can't chance us not making it to the carriage before dawn."

"I'm certainly not leaving you alone with *him*," Charlotte mumbled. "I cannot believe I married this monster."

"I will be fine, Charlotte. Étienne is here with me. Hurry now! I don't want to remain here a moment longer than we have to."

"Allow me," I offered, escorting Charlotte and Father Clarence up the stairs. They both clung to my arms as I navigated my way through the blackness. From the top of the landing, I could see a worrying pink blush through the open front window. A new day was upon us.

I rejoined Daphne in the cellar, and we hauled Philippe upstairs together. We sat in the bookshop, nervously aware of the uncomfortable silence that stretched between us. Finally, I could stand it no longer.

"Daphne, are you all right?"

She turned to me, but I doubted she could see much in the gloom of the shop. I, on the other hand, could see her as perfectly as in the light of day.

Her hair had tumbled out of the elaborate coiffure, and her pale gown was stained with blood and filth. Her body sagged with exhaustion, and her eyes glittered with unshed tears. She was staring out the window at the lightening sky, chewing on her bottom lip.

"How can I live with this?" Her voice was a whisper. "Everything that happened...all of these horrors...they were all my fault. People are dead because of me, Étienne. Charlotte's marriage is over, and her future is... I don't know if she can bear the scandal. Asmoday is gone and Philippe's capture will prove your innocence to the Order, but how much of a difference did it all make? Paris is still rife with plague, and I fear for the people. If a solution isn't found—if the king doesn't do something, I believe your uprising will indeed come to pass."

I walked over and reached for her, then thought better of it and dropped my hand. Asmoday's cruel words rang through my head. She didn't need yet another man pining for her, especially after everything she'd been through. Unsure of myself, I cleared my throat.

"When I was turned, it was not by my choice," I began. "I was staying with a friend in Budapest, and we went out one night—drinking, gambling, carousing. There was a beautiful woman who caught my eye, and I followed her back to her home. She attacked me—bit my throat and nearly drained me. As I lay dying on the floor of her cottage, she offered me the choice: die there and face my eternal judgment, or drink from her and live forever. I could not speak. I was too weak to tell her, but I wished for death. I knew I would face demons eventually, and it didn't matter that I would face them that night or a thousand nights hence. She took pity on me though, believing someone of my roguish nature would consider an eternity of sin a blessing. She forced me to drink her blood, and I became a vampire."

Daphne's tears spilled down her cheeks, but I did not reach to brush them away. I did not trust myself to touch her, fearing I would never be able to let her go.

"When I returned to Paris some time later, I'd become accustomed to my abilities, but I feared the judgment of my family and friends. I was in Paris when my father died—not abroad, as Josephine believes. I'd come home but was too afraid to return to my old life. My father died alone while I hid myself in a basement eight blocks away. Not a day has passed that I don't regret my cowardice."

Daphne touched my arm, and I stiffened. Immediately, she pulled away.

"I'm sorry," she said.

I sighed. "I tell you these things because I carried on. The things that haunt us never simply go away, Daphne, but we are made stronger as we learn to bear them. Philippe's actions are not your fault, but you will have to live with them. Lives may have been lost in the balance, but think of all the lives you saved in your fight for truth—mine, Charlotte's. Hell, even Father Clarence's. The countless others who would have fallen prey to a weak man with a powerful weapon. Let that knowledge be your strength."

She considered my words, and we watched the sky soften through the window.

"Étienne, what Asmoday said down there about you —about us..."

"Lies designed to provoke. Nothing more," I said, cutting her off. She nodded, but I could have sworn I saw a flash of something like disappointment in her eyes. It was gone in an instant. My heart clenched.

"I will ensure that your name is cleared of any charges within the Order," she said brusquely.

"You think they'll believe you?"

She shrugged. "I will present my case to them and request another assignment. I only hope that I can use my position to do what's right for Paris. I believe I have the power to affect some change for the better, even if it is small."

"Eradicating the vampire menace?" I said, a smile breaking through my melancholy.

She laughed. "More like...rethinking where the threats lie, seeking truth before administering justice, finding a cure for the plague and the grain blight, convincing the king to cease alienating the vampires and the bourgeoisie."

"Careful, Duchess, lest the aristocracy hear your liberal words," I teased.

She beamed at me, eyes darting to my lips, and I would have faced a thousand demons to kiss her then. A muffled groan came from the bundle that was Philippe, and I growled and kicked him. A low rumble echoed in the alley before us, heralding the arrival of the carriage. I hauled him up and slung him over my shoulder, then made a mad dash for the safety of its dark interior.

I threw Philippe on the floor and sat across from Father Clarence. Charlotte took the seat to my left, and Daphne climbed in last.

"So," Charlotte said brightly, "are we all going to recover at Château de Champs-sur-Marne?"

Daphne blushed. "Certainly, you are all most welcome if you wish to stay with me."

Father Clarence inclined his head. "Thank you, madame, but I must decline. I have a congregation to attend to and a mass to prepare for. If you'd be so kind as to convey me back to the Basilique Saint-Denis, I would be most grateful."

Charlotte's piercing gaze bored into me.

I shifted uncomfortably. "Thank you, but I must also decline. My home is better suited to my uncommon needs."

"But the bed in the wine cellar!" Charlotte protested.

Daphne elbowed her and glared. "Hush, Charlotte!"

I cocked a brow. "You've kept the bed in the wine cellar?"

"I haven't had time to move it," Daphne defended. "I'll get around to it eventually."

My resolution to give her up wavered slightly. *Is there a reason she hasn't moved the bed?* I watched her cautiously, warming at the stubborn blush that stained her cheeks. She studiously avoided looking at me.

Quiet descended on the carriage until we reached the abbey. Father Clarence made the sign of the cross over Charlotte and Daphne and kissed their hands. He eyed me warily, then smiled and shook my hand.

"May the Lord bless and keep you," he said as he stepped out. "Do remember me to the Order, madame!"

Daphne promised to do so, and the carriage trundled on in silence, Daphne refusing to meet my gaze and Charlotte staring at me like a bug in a bell jar.

When we neared my château, I coughed awkwardly. "I dread the thought of leaving Philippe in your hands, Duchess, as capable as they are. Would you permit me to hold him in custody at my own home until the Order can be informed? I assure you he will come to no other harm in my care."

Daphne's brow furrowed. "But in the daylight..."

"I have a very secure room and a number of able servants to stand guard. I would feel much better if you ladies were allowed to rest knowing that he was not under the same roof, at least until he stands before the Order."

Charlotte frowned at the unconscious man tied before us. Then, she hauled off and kicked him in the stomach again.

Seeing this, Daphne winced. "Yes, you're right, Étienne. He'd probably be safer in your care anyway."

The carriage came to a full stop outside my home. A footman and my butler came out and helped me carry Philippe inside, taking care to avoid the early morning sunlight. As desperate as I was for Daphne, I did not spare a backward glance when I entered the hall.

I locked Philippe in a small, empty storage room in the lower level of the house. To ensure his confinement, I hefted a large bookcase in front of the door and instructed three men to stand guard at all times.

Finally able to be alone with my thoughts, I went to my room, stripped naked, and fell into a heavy, dreamless sleep.

When I awoke the next evening, it was to an exaggerated pounding on my door.

"Yes, yes—I'm awake, damn you!" I tripped out of bed and grabbed my dressing gown just as the door burst open.

My butler, Robert, stumbled in on the heels of Dr. Van Helsing, who pushed her way inside my bedchamber as if she'd been in my home a thousand times. I eyed the curvy, enigmatic doctor warily.

"Good evening, *Monsieur l'Émissaire*," she said with a polite curtsy.

"My apologies, monsieur," Robert said. "The lady was most insistent that she see you immediately. She would not be detained."

I nodded and dismissed the suffering man. "Thank you, Robert. All is well. You may return to your duties."

"I am sorry to be so forceful, monsieur, but I do have other patients to attend to." Van Helsing bustled over to my bureau and started removing a series of instruments from her reticule.

"There must be a misunderstanding, Doctor. I did not send for your services. As you can see, I'm perfectly healthy. I'm sure you are aware, but I'm able to heal from most injuries with rest and blood." I went to the wash basin and splashed some water on my face.

"Nevertheless, I have been retained with the express purpose of ensuring your physical health," Van Helsing said. "I aim to do my job to the best of my abilities."

"I don't recall offering you employ—"

She snorted a little laugh. "No, no, of course you did not! You wouldn't, would you? Now, hold out your arm, please. I need to examine your blood."

"Doctor, please. I've had a very taxing few weeks, and I'm in no mood to play games. Who hired you to look after me, and to what end?" I held out my arm anyway. Van Helsing took it and began turning it this way and that, finding a good place to draw blood.

She regarded me with an expression of pity. "Why, Madame de Duras, of course. As to what end, I'm sure I cannot say. I can only guess that she cares for you and wishes to ensure that you remain in rude health, and since I am the very best vampire doctor in all of Europe, she paid me a full year's wages to periodically drop in on you every month or so—just to check in."

"That is unnecessary," I said. "I don't need a nursemaid."

Van Helsing tutted. She poked and prodded me in what was a very thorough—and thoroughly embarrassing—examination. Unsurprisingly, she proclaimed me fit and packed up her bag with haste. As she made to leave, she handed me a vial of virgin blood.

"Just in case," he said.

"Wait. You...you said that she cares for me?" The supposition flustered me, but I didn't know why. *Of course she does.* She was a good person, and we'd become friends—of a sort. Forced proximity often had that effect on people. I knew she cared for me, but, ever the narcissist, I wanted to hear Van Helsing admit it aloud.

"A great deal, I should think. My services do not come cheap, monsieur, and she did not bat an eye at the continued cost of maintaining your well-being." She looked at me like I'd gone soft in the head. "Surely you knew all that, right?"

"Well, the duchess is a wealthy woman. Such sums are probably trivial to her," I reasoned.

Van Helsing laughed again, her gaze perceptive. "My, my! What a fool love has made you, monsieur."

"It is not love," I said reflexively. "Merely infatuation. Or, at best, a friendship united by shared trauma."

"I did not examine your eyesight, monsieur, but perhaps I should have. I did not think you were blind." Van Helsing inclined her head with a grin and promptly hurried from the room, leaving me alone with my astonishment.

22

DAPHNE

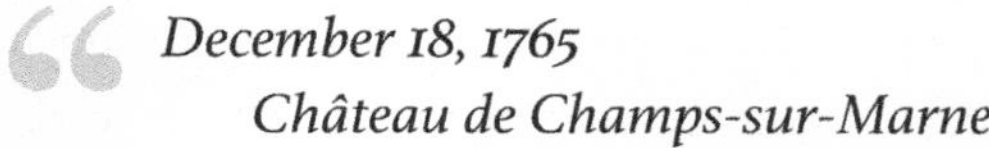

December 18, 1765
Château de Champs-sur-Marne

"*MON DIEU*, ARE YOU REALLY WEARING THAT?" CHARLOTTE GASPED, referring to my plain dress. In the days since the affair in the bookshop cellar, I'd taken to wearing much more...simple attire. It wasn't that I was avoiding society at Versailles, per se, but ever since Étienne had come into my life, I found myself less and less thrilled by the glitter of the palace.

Most days I spent at home working for the Order again. Étienne's exoneration had been my first priority, and after that had been secured, I took advantage of their good favor to petition for some changes of my own. The Order had readily agreed...partly, I think, because of their embarrassment at being blind to Philippe's true motives. I'd forced my way into a leadership position—organizing missions and investigations, managing my own network of informants, occasionally donning a disguise to enjoy a little espionage on my own.

This style of dress made it so much easier and more comfortable to get around, especially without panniers. The gown was a deep-emerald-green velvet, reminiscent of the color of Étienne's jacket at the garden party months ago. The memory of our first meeting sent a wave of sadness through me.

"I'm not going to court, Charlotte."

"Well, no, but don't you want to wear something with a bit more...you know..." She gestured expansively at my bodice.

"Elegance?" I finished for her.

"Cleavage," she replied.

I laughed. Despite everything that had happened, Charlotte's spirits had not suffered more than an occasional dip. Philippe had been carted off for a secret trial within the Order where the agents and other members had vehemently condemned his actions and, while unwilling to sentence an aristocrat to death, stuck him in the worst of all possible places—a filthy oubliette in the island prison le Château d'If. To avoid further embarrassment, the Order offered Charlotte a falsified death record for him (as well as for Henri, who was *allegedly* killed over some unpaid gambling debts in Venice.) The falsified death record allowed Charlotte to maintain her wealth, title, and property as well as her reputation—and she was free to pursue any number of courtly love affairs. Most of the time, however, she could be found at my château, assisting me with my work for the Order. Once they realized what a valuable asset she could be, they had eagerly requested her participation. We'd been devising plans for a separate branch of women agents, Les Dames Dangereuses, or DD for short. Charlotte had proven herself an extremely capable coconspirator.

So, now she was here in my bedchamber, helping me dress and get ready for one of the most nerve-wracking errands of my life.

"Are you going to invite him to your Christmas party?"

"I have an invitation ready, just in case. If it doesn't go well, he might not want to come. He might be cross with me for some reason." I chewed on my bottom lip.

"I'm sure it'll go well," she encouraged. "Unless he was offended that you sent Doctor Van Helsing to him to spy on him for the rest of the year."

"Not to spy!" I defended. "Just to, you know, look after him, make sure he's all right. Van Helsing doesn't report to me, Charlotte. I just wanted him to be safe."

"He's a vampire, Daphne. He doesn't need you mothering him," she said, rolling her eyes.

"Well, how else was I supposed to be able to sleep at night? Worrying about him constantly—always thinking about him. It's maddening! I had to give myself some peace of mind. Van Helsing's support allowed me to do just that." I fastened a strand of pearls around my neck.

Her brows lifted. "Has it? You are such a horrible liar, Daphne. The whole time since the cellar you've been moping around your château, anxiously checking for letters from him every morning, tying yourself up in knots, and consequently forcing your attentions on work. If that's peace of mind, *mon dieu*, I'd hate to see what you're like when you're distraught."

Peevishness crept into my tone. "Just what are you implying, Charlotte?"

"Implying? Nothing. Stating outright? That you're in love with the man and you're too much of a twit to go after him and tell him so."

I *tsked.* "Don't be ridiculous. I am *not* in love with him. And even if I were, it wouldn't matter because he told me himself that he does not love me."

"He did not! When was this?" She came to stand behind me, helping me with my hair.

I felt the pressure of tears behind my eyes. I squeezed them shut and swallowed. "Back at the bookshop. Asmoday—before he was exorcised—told Étienne that I would never be able love him in the way that he wanted. I asked him about it afterward, but he brushed it off. Said it was a lie meant to provoke him."

Charlotte's eyes widened, then she broke into a fit of giggles.

Irritated, I scowled at her. "It's really not funny."

"No, no, you're right, darling. It's just—you're so oblivious! And you're the best intelligence agent in the country. It's not often you miss things, but when you do—*mon dieu*—you really miss them!"

Anger surpassed my annoyance.

"What the hell are you on about?" I balled my fists at my sides. Charlotte continued to cackle, until she was wiping tears from her eyes and gulping down air.

"I'm sorry, *chérie*," she sighed. "I just don't understand how you couldn't put it all together. Étienne is obviously in love with you, otherwise Asmoday would have offered up some other insult. He went for what he knew would hurt most."

"But he denied it!"

"Of course he did. We'd just battled your dead husband, a demon, and my own idiot husband who'd been murdering people across Europe to try and win your affections. I can't imagine he would have thought *then* was a good time to profess his undying love for you."

The realization slammed into me. and I staggered back.

"You think—Charlotte, do you really think he loves me?"

She threw me a pitying look and poured herself a large brandy from the decanter nearby. "Please don't be dense with me, Daphne. You know he does. I suspect you've always known, you're just too stubborn to admit that you rather like the idea."

For the first time in weeks, I felt a sense of lightness. *Is it true?* If he had loved me before—did he still love me now? Had he moved on with other women? How did I truly feel about him? *Stupid question, Daphne.* The truth of it burned through me. *I am in love with him.*

Charlotte handed me her glass of brandy. "Fortification? You appear to need something steadying."

I took the glass and downed it in one.

"So? What are you going to do about it?" she prodded. "He's still a vampire, after all."

I considered the question. It had taken me some time to accept that Michel's death was on Philippe's hands—to let go of my hatred of vampirekind that had sustained me through my grief and despair. But as my work with the Order had taken me out around the city more and more these days, I'd begun to see that Étienne had been right all along. Certainly, there were still vampires who deserved a stake through the heart, just as there were human aristocrats who deserved the same—or more, in some cases. I could no longer lay the blame at the feet of the blood plague. Evil needed to be rooted out, wherever and however it lay.

Reading my thoughts, Charlotte took the brandy glass from my trembling hands. "Would you give it up, do you think? To be with him forever?"

The tough question. Would I—could I—give up my humanity for him? A lifetime of sunrises? The pleasures of a mortal life?

I would.

"Yes," I breathed. "Yes, Charlotte, I think I would sacrifice just about anything to be with him."

She nodded sagely. "Great love demands great sacrifice."

I blinked back the tears that welled in my eyes.

"Besides," she continued, refilling the brandy glass and sipping at it herself, "think how much better of an agent you'll be with all those supernatural gifts!"

Would he accept me? I wasn't certain. Regardless, I had to tell him. I *would* tell him—as soon as I'd delivered my message to him from the Order. I kissed Charlotte's cheeks and ran out my bedroom door, straight into Gaston. We both crashed to the ground.

"Madame! Are you all right?" he said, helping me to my feet.

"Yes, yes. I'm sorry, Gaston. I was distracted. Were you coming to find me?"

"*Oui*, madame. You have a visitor." He handed me a calling card. "He is waiting for you in the drawing room."

Étienne.

He is here? But I was on my way to see him! My stomach twisted. I inhaled shakily and straightened my dress.

"Thank you, Gaston."

I went downstairs and entered the drawing room. He stood at the fireplace, staring down into the flames. I hadn't seen him since All Hallows Eve, and my heart leaped at the sight. He was as uncommonly beautiful as I remembered—wavy black hair tied back; chiseled features; lean, muscular body wrapped in gilt-embroidered navy wool. His full lips were curved in a private smile that vanished when he saw me.

"Duchess." He bowed formally, and my chest tightened. His manner had me rattled.

I inclined my head. "I was on my way to you with a message from the Order, but I see you beat me to the punch. To what do I owe the pleasure of your visit, monsieur?"

He coughed and fidgeted with his cuff. It comforted me that he, too, appeared to be nervous.

"Shall I call for some tea?" I offered. "Or perhaps something stronger?" I gestured to the sideboard with crystal decanters of brandy, sherry, and whisky.

"No, thank you. I...I came to call on you to...thank you for Doctor Van Helsing's care. And to, you know, see how you fared."

"Of course," I said. "I hope I didn't overstep. I mean, I'm sure I did, but I was worried about you and I wanted to ensure that you had access to the best possible care. I...I'm sorry. Thinking on it, it was probably quite overbearing. I should have asked." *Stop babbling, Daphne!* Awash with anxiety, I sat on the small couch across from the fireplace. I pulled a cushion onto my lap and toyed with the tassels.

"No, it was kind of you, really." He gestured to the empty space next to me, and I nodded. He sat, maintaining an even distance from me.

"And how do you fare, monsieur? Are you well?"

"Yes, of course, quite well. I saw Josephine recently. She sends her regards."

Warmth filled me at the thought of his resourceful, plucky sister. I smiled. "Ah. Yes. I hope she's well too."

He nodded. An awkward silence settled between us.

This is interminable.

"I have been working with the Order quite a bit," I blurted suddenly—and a touch loudly. I winced but carried on. "That's why I was coming to see you. I'm trying to get a group together to work with the vampires—looking for a cure, discussing their rights and grievances...trying to prevent that revolution you're always on about. So far, the Order isn't entirely on board—neither are the nobility, for that matter. I could use your help."

"My help?" he repeated, looking stunned. "Yes, of course. You've taken up my cause?"

I nodded. "Oh, and Charlotte has joined as well. We have been designing missions for other members. We're forming a group of primarily women agents. It's been quite thrilling."

"How is Charlotte? Well, I hope?" A pained smile crossed his face.

"Yes, quite well, now that everything's settled with her estate."

"Good. Good."

"Yes, it is good, isn't it?"

The clock on the mantle chimed nine o'clock. The fire crackled in the hearth. I was going to die of discomfort. *Tell him, Daphne. Tell him you're in love with him. Tell him you want to be his forever.*

Étienne studied me, his hazel eyes glittering like gold coins. He seemed to relax a fraction, then offered me the first genuine smile I'd seen all evening. The smile broke into a warm chuckle that turned into a full-throated laugh. I giggled along with him.

"It's bad, isn't it?" I sighed. "The tension between us."

"Yes," he smiled. "But I don't know why it should be." He took my hand in his, and our eyes met. "I miss you, Daphne."

"You do?" I said somewhat breathlessly. "Why have you stayed away so long?" *Have you found another woman?*

"I wanted to give you a respectful distance after everything. For a time, I convinced myself that you would want to be rid of me—that there was nothing left for us. Our conversation at Versailles that night felt so final, I convinced myself that I'd have to let you go. That you deserve a long, happy, mortal life—a life without me. If you say so, Daphne, I swear I'll leave you alone and never darken your doorstep again. But if there's hope—if you feel differently… I came here tonight to…to…"

"To find out?"

He nodded, his handsome face a study in angst. Desire gathered in me. *He is mine.*

"Shall we see, then?" I breathed. I didn't wait for him to respond or for the confusion to fall from his face. I leaned forward and set my lips to his.

He melted into me immediately, returning the kiss with the full force of his passion. He brought his hands up to my head, lacing his fingers into my hair as he had before. Pins scattered across the couch and the floor. He sucked my lower lip into his mouth and stroked it with his tongue. Lust stormed through me, setting my skin ablaze, tightening my nipples, and heating my core. I bent over him, pushing him back against the cushions. He moaned against me at the feel of our bodies pressing against each other.

"God, Daphne," he growled, breaking away to drop tiny kisses along my jaw. "How I've missed you. You don't know how much. You're all I can think about. It makes every day without you feel like a hundred years." His fingers found the buttons of my bodice, and he frantically tried to undo them, seeking the feel of my bare skin.

"Why the hell do all your gowns have so many damn buttons?" On an oath, he wrenched the fabric in two, sending buttons flying in all directions.

"Étienne! I liked that dress," I protested. He dropped his head to tug one of my nipples into his mouth, and the dress was forgotten. I ground my hips against him, loving the feel of his arousal beneath my legs. He sucked in a breath.

"I missed you, Étienne. I was so worried that you didn't care for me or that you'd found another lover since we— *Oh yes, right there!* I cannot go back to my life the way it was, the way *I* was before you. You were right about me—about everything. I don't want to be without you, Étienne." I fumbled with the buttons on his breeches, and he reached for the hem of my skirts, lifting them up to my thighs. When he pushed them up to bare my sex, he bit back a groan.

"Perfection," he breathed, sliding a finger through my damp heat. He circled the bud of my pleasure, and I cried out. "You're so wet—so ready for me. So responsive to my touch. It's one of the things I love most about you, darling. I'm afraid this won't last as long as I'd like. It's been a while since—"

I grasped his hard length, and he huffed in torment.

"Drink from me," I murmured.

"What?" he gasped, growing harder in my hand. "Darling, no. I will not just use you for blood."

"I want to be yours, Étienne, completely. I want to be yours forever."

His eyes snapped open and found mine in the firelight.

"Daphne," he said, placing a hand on me to stop my explorations of his body. "You don't mean that. I can't ask you to give up your mortality, not for me. I don't deserve such a sacrifice."

"I'm in love with you," I blurted.

For a moment, we remained frozen. He stared at me, eyes wide. Panic started to build while I waited for him to respond.

"Étienne?"

His lips broke into a wide, beautiful smile, and his eyes shimmered with emotion. "Daphne, I've loved you since the very moment you tried to kill me, and I'm going to love you until one or both of us is dust."

I bent to kiss him, shutting my eyes against the threatening tears. I slid my tongue into his mouth, gently testing the sharpness of his fangs. He slid his hands up my thighs, and I sighed into him, stroking his hardness until he threw his head back with a guttural curse.

"Putain de merde, Daphne, that feels—"

I stroked him again, firmer this time. His eyes squeezed shut again, and he whimpered.

"Daphne, please, you're killing me. I'm going to—"

I straddled him, shifting slightly to position him just at my entrance.

"Tell me again," I demanded. Once more, his gaze flew to mine. That devastating smile again. He let out a breath so deep, it seemed he had been holding it since he first arrived.

"I love you, Duchess. In fact, I'm really quite mad for you."

I laughed and slid him inside me. He cursed a litany of smut that rushed through me. He pushed me back down on the couch, driving into me with fire. My pleasure built to its breaking point, and Étienne sensed it. He reached between us and pressed his fingertip against my bud.

He pulled out and ducked between my legs, setting his tongue and fingers to work. In moments, I began to see stars. When I came apart, I felt his teeth on my thigh—a momentary prick of pain, and then another tidal wave of pleasure, unlike anything I'd ever experienced before. He moaned helplessly against my thigh, gently sucking while I twined my fingers in his hair. He looked up at me, his eyes black pools of lust, need, and love, and then groaned and shuddered, spilling between us. Too soon, he pulled his mouth from my thigh, and I mourned the loss of his warm, wet lips.

"You are, without a doubt, the most delicious thing I've ever had," he grinned.

He collapsed above me and rolled off the couch, bringing me down to the floor with him. He wrapped his arms around me and nuzzled my neck.

"My love," he said again. His smile would have made angels weep.

We lay there for a few moments, temporarily sated.

"So," I hedged, breaking the silence, "is that the only reason you came here tonight?"

Étienne kissed my temple and adjusted his clothing. He reached into his pocket and produced a small box. I gasped.

"It's not what you think," he said hurriedly. "That is—I visited Georges the jeweler after we questioned him. He didn't have any real information for me about the murders. He could not find Jeanne's ring, for obvious reasons." He chuckled. "He was incredibly worried about how you'd respond to his failure. I told him you'd changed your mind and that I was there to acquire something else on your behalf."

I opened the box to find an exquisite amethyst-and-diamond choker. It sparkled in the glow of the fire, and I blinked back tears.

"Étienne, it's beautiful. You didn't have to— I don't deserve—"

He silenced me with a kiss. "Yes, you do. I came here tonight to ask for your forgiveness—to tell you that I can't help myself. You're worth someone ten times the man that I am, but I'm too selfish to let that man come along and take you from me. If you let me, Daphne, I swear I'll endeavor every single day to deserve you."

Tears rolled down my cheeks, and I kissed him again—this time slower and more gently.

"No, Étienne. I was wrong about so many things. I thought the world was divided into light and dark, but then you came along and showed me otherwise. If anything, I should be the one proving myself to you."

Étienne tightened his hold on me. "You have nothing to prove to me, but I'd be lying if I said I didn't want to hear it again."

I sat up and tugged at the rest of his clothes, eager to have his sculpted, naked body beneath me again.

"I could *tell* you," I teased. "But perhaps I should just *show* you instead."

He laughed, low and seductive. "Nymph and goddess no longer," he said.

"No?" I slipped out of my skirts and chemise, baring myself to him. "Then what am I now?"

A heady possessiveness that heated me all over again flashed in his gaze, and he smiled.

"*Mine.*"

EPILOGUE

CHARLOTTE

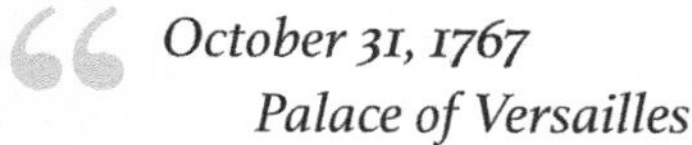

October 31, 1767
Palace of Versailles

I WATCHED DAPHNE AND ÉTIENNE TWIRL AROUND THE BALLROOM, their eyes never straying from each other. Daphne—recently turned vampire and soon to be the *duchesse de Noailles*, thanks to Étienne's newly bestowed title—was still the main topic of courtly conversation tonight. As the first titled woman to willingly succumb to the blood plague, she had shocked the court to a dangerous degree but had weathered their disapproval with grace and aplomb. While her decision to ally herself with the supernatural set pushed her firmly to the fringes of the *tonne*, she didn't seem to mind in the least. I wondered if Daphne had even *noticed*, honestly, considering how starry eyed and in love my cousin seemed to be.

To both Daphne's and my surprise, the Order had handled the news of her turning with eager anticipation. As I'd suspected, her increased stealth, strength, and speed were extremely beneficial for her work with the organization, and Daphne's progressive influence on the attitudes of the upper circle had started to turn a few minds to her new vampire rights cause—gradually, but with conviction. The Order seemed to be undergoing a change of nature as well, or so I hoped.

The allemande ended, and the band struck up a lively minuet. All the couples on the dance floor—save for Daphne and Étienne —changed partners and began anew. Unsurprisingly, they had enjoyed a scandalous courtship, even by Versailles standards, and they'd eschewed propriety yet again by attending this year's All Hallows Eve masquerade in matching Persephone and Hades costumes.

Really, I thought with a smile. *Can't they keep their affections to themselves for an evening?*

The dance ended, and I watched them kiss, oblivious to the whispers around them.

I didn't bother to hide my grimace. I was happy for them, truly, especially after everything they'd been through, but it didn't stop the pang of envy that shot through me. I'd thought I'd had love once. Well, not love, really, but at least affection. The lovers I'd had after Philippe's imprisonment had all been temporarily satisfactory but had proved wanting in the end. Observing Daphne and Étienne on the dance floor now made me realize that the thing I'd been missing—the thing I'd been longing for—was a love of my own. A love like Daphne and Étienne's, a love that would defy the laws of nature and humanity and...well, any other laws.

Sadly, as I looked around the luminous ballroom, I reasoned I wasn't likely to find a love like that within the walls of Versailles. That was fine. Really, it was. I had my duties to the DD to occupy my mind and my time.

Speaking of which, I should really get back to work. My target tonight made Philippe's crimes look like child's play, and I was determined to see him brought to justice. Multiple counts of rape and abuse—including children—had been levied against him, and the DD had gathered enough evidence to warrant action from the

Order. I was that action. I saw Daphne flick her fan twice in my direction—the signal that my target had arrived.

I climbed down from the perch in the beech tree from which I'd been surveying the ball, grateful for the freedom that my costume allowed. I certainly didn't enjoy donning men's attire as often as Daphne did, but one had to admit, breeches did make it easier to skulk around in the dark. Initially, I was disappointed that I wouldn't get to attend the masquerade in an outrageously expensive gown, but once I'd received the details of my assignment, I'd sort of come around to my Cupid costume.

I brushed the dirt from my toga, adjusted my mask and wig, and sauntered into the hall through the open glass doors. It didn't take me long to find my target in the crush of people—the *marquis de Sade* stood out like a sore thumb. I wound my way around the edges of the ballroom, making my way to the vile man. He was dressed as a wolf—something that felt uniquely perverse to me, given all the innocents he'd preyed upon. I approached him with a glass of champagne in hand.

"Monsieur," I said, lowering her voice in what I hoped was a masculine timbre, "you look like you could use a drink."

The marquis eyed me appreciatively. "Most gracious of you, dear boy. Have we been introduced?"

I smiled shyly. "No, monsieur. But I am most anxious to remedy that. My name is Latour."

"Latour. I am Donatien." Sade's eyelids began to droop—a sure sign that the sedative I'd slipped him was already beginning to take effect.

"Donatien," I said, taking his arm. "Might we find a quiet place to better get acquainted? I find these ballrooms can be *most* stifling, don't you?"

Sade blinked slowly and murmured his assent, allowing me to steer him outside toward the hedge maze. Out of nowhere, Daphne intercepted me, shoving a square of parchment into my hand. As quickly as she'd been there, Daphne melted away into the crowd. I pulled the marquis hurriedly through the garden and darted a look at the note.

Someone else has been watching the target. Étienne spotted him and is on his trail. Guard yourself well!

"*Merde,*" I swore.

"What's that, Latour?" Sade tripped over his feet, and I almost fell. "*Mon dieu*, I *do* feel peculiar… Where are we going, my friend?"

I reached the hedge maze and thrust him forward. "How about a little game, monsieur? I'm sure you'd enjoy that. I know how fond you are of games."

Sade chuckled and mumbled something unintelligible. I made a left, a right, then two more lefts inside the labyrinth until I was absolutely certain we were alone.

"All out here on our own, are we?" Sade slurred. He began to pluck at the falls of his breeches, unsuccessfully attempting to remove them. "Come on, then, boy, let's play that game of yours…"

I unclasped the thick black cord from my neck that would serve as my garrote, but before I could pounce on the man, I heard a high-pitched whistling, followed by a soft thump, and then a groaning wheeze. Sade collapsed forward on top of me, and we crashed to the ground. I shoved the marquis off me and swallowed a scream—protruding from his chest was a long, thin arrow shaft. Blood seeped out from the wound, staining his brown velvet waistcoat.

Panicked, I ducked down behind one of the bushes and cast my gaze around wildly. *Where did the arrow come from? Who else is here? Who else wants Sade dead?*

I waited long minutes for any other sound but heard nothing. Satisfied that I probably wasn't in any danger—the arrow could have hit us both, but it hadn't—I crawled forward to check Sade's pulse. The arrow, it seemed, had pierced his heart. *He is dead.*

Suddenly, I heard a crashing noise behind me. Before I could escape, a man tumbled out of the bushes and stood over me, a crossbow raised to my chest. A long, black cloak obscured his face and his form, giving him an air of menace.

"Do not move, boy," came a voice from beneath the hood. "Or I shall kill you as well."

Irrational anger replaced my fear. I stood, throwing my shoulders back and finding my haughtiest aristocratic tone.

"Who the hell do you think you are?" I snarled. "Do you realize what you've just done?"

The man threw back his hood and glared at me. My jaw dropped open. He was the most beautiful man I'd ever seen. He didn't have the dark, seductive beauty of Étienne but rather a rugged self-possession that bordered on dangerous. Waves of chestnut hair fell across his face, mussed from wearing his hood. Dark slashes of brows and long, gossamer lashes set off vibrant green eyes. His strong jaw hadn't seen a shave in several days, his nose had been broken and reset at least once, and he carried a thin, crescent-shaped scar from his brow to his cheek. I felt my knees wobble a bit when the man sneered at me, his full lips drawing back to reveal a set of perfect white teeth.

"Ungrateful fop," he hissed. "I just saved your life. Don't you know who this man is? He eats young lads like you for breakfast."

Finally coming to my senses, I remembered my disguise and pitched my voice low again, growling at him in fury. "He was *mine*. You have no idea what you've done."

Disgust twisted the man's face. "Yours? Well, I'm certain you'll be able to find another demon to entertain your desires. Now, if you'll excuse me, I'll be off. I don't want to be around when the guards find his body."

I couldn't help it. I snickered at the man's choice of words—a demon to entertain—*oh, if he only knew*. My irritation returned, however, when the man turned to leave out the back gate.

"So, you're just going to leave me here to clean up your mess? I don't think so! I had my own plans for dispensing with the body, but if you were so insistent that he be *your* kill, you deal with it."

The man cocked his head in confusion. "Dispensing with the body? Wait—are you... You were not his lover?"

I threw my head back and laughed. "Certainly not! I was here to see that he pays for his crimes. I had everything worked out until *you* arrived and mucked it all up. How am I supposed to explain an arrow to the chest, then? I can't, you idiot! If only you'd let me finish my job and strangle him properly, it would have been easily made to look like an accident. But no! Typical man, running into a situation without thinking it through and then leaving me to clean up. Well, not this time, monsieur!"

"Wait—your job? 'Made to look like an accident'? What are you talking about, boy? Are you well?" He looked at me like I was mad.

"Yes, yes, and yes. Don't you know? He was particularly fond of throttling during sex. We have numerous statements testifying to that. One small slip and, oops! *Quel terrible accident!* No one would be the wiser."

I glared at the man, beyond irritated that he'd ruined my assignment and my evening, and had so unsettled me that I'd muttered on about my plot to kill the marquis. *Hopefully he's too thick-headed to pay much attention to me. Still, it's probably best to make use of this disguise and let him think I'm some mad dandy.*

I took in the man's impressive stature and form—purely to see what I was dealing with, of course, and not because I enjoyed looking at him—and reasoned he must've been the man that Daphne and Étienne had gotten wind of, but that begged a much bigger question.

Who was he?

THE MAN

I continued to stare, trying to make sense of the lad's mutterings. Who was this fop? In the gloom of the hedge maze, all I could see was a small, lean figure clad in some kind of ridiculous Roman costume—a pleated silk toga; small, feathered wings; and a bow with a quiver of arrows. A wreath of golden flowers and hearts sat atop a queue of short brown hair. The lad had a sweet enough face—big brown eyes, mink-like lashes, rosy cheeks, and a cupid's bow smile—but that could have been the beauty of youth. Was he a bit off in the head? What was he doing out here? Was the boy a guest of the masquerade? Was he one of Sade's men?

I shuddered at the thought. If he was with Sade, he would need protection. I started to say so when we heard the crunch of footsteps along the gravel path.

Someone else is coming!

We could not be discovered here with the dead marquis—especially with the young man and his quiver of arrows. I swallowed an oath. I should have been more careful. If I didn't act now, the boy would likely be blamed for the marquis's death. *I cannot have another death on my hands.* I did the only thing I could think to do. I whacked the boy on the back of the head with my crossbow, knocking him out. I slung the boy's body over my shoulder—quite a sturdy young thing—and snuck back through the bushes to the drainage grate in the wall. Once I was through the wall, I picked up my pace, not bothering to stop when I heard the pair of voices discover the body of the dead marquis.

"Mon dieu, *Étienne!* An arrow? It's not one of hers, is it? Where is she? What do you think happened?"

"I don't know, Daphne, but I smell someone else here. I think—I think she's been taken."

Thank you for reading! Did you enjoy? Please add your review because nothing helps an author more and encourages readers to take a chance on a book than a review.

And don't miss THE AGENT AND THE OUTLAW, book two of the *Les Dames Dangereuses* series, by Lily Riley, coming soon!

Until then, find more Mystic Owl books with FOREVER AFTER by Ashley R. King. Turn the page for a sneak peek!

You can also sign up for the City Owl Press newsletter to receive notice of all book releases!

SNEAK PEEK OF FOREVER AFTER

BY ASHLEY R. KING

AUTUMN

Darkness snaked through the narrow streets of Covey Crossing's downtown, a few pale orange streetlights shedding little light on the pavement. Having just finished her shift at the library, Autumn snagged a caramel frappe from her favorite local coffee shop just down the block, Jitter Beans, before heading to her car. Her cardigan fluttered about her in the fall breeze, a slight chill skating up her spine.

Fall had just begun in Georgia, a little nippy in the mornings and evenings, but the in-between times could still fry a person like an omelet. Every once in a while, southern Georgia would experience a cold snap like the one they were having right now. She loved it and contemplated moving somewhere that had fall weather year-round. Then she'd have to leave her father, and well, could she ever bring herself to do that? Another shiver raced through her, and this time it wasn't from the cold.

She hustled down the sidewalk toward her beat-up car in the distance. Even though Covey Crossing was one of the safest places on the planet, her father, ever paranoid, still taught her to keep her wits about her. She scanned as she hustled, frappe proudly brandished in front of her body, several books tucked into the large cat print tote slung over her shoulder.

She couldn't wait to scoop the whipped cream and caramel off the top of her drink as soon as she got home. She could practically taste the sweetness on her tongue, her mouth watering at the thought. And then she'd curl up in her favorite reading spot—nearly disappearing into the plush, oversized cushions of her favorite blue chair. She'd be wrapped in a fuzzy blanket, her Halloween lights draped across the mantle flickering and playing off the lamplight—and dive into the pile of new romance releases she'd gotten from work.

Movement across the street caught her attention, shadows dancing across the sidewalk, but nothing was there. Awareness pricked at the back of her neck, causing her steps to hurry. She kept glancing over to the other side of the street, her stomach churning as the shadows grew larger, imposing, and then disappeared as if it'd been a trick of the eyes. The lamplights were barely doing their job, and she cursed her need for caffeine when suddenly a pale man appeared where she'd been staring. Flickers of orange splashed across his mulberry red...frock coat? Was that a Victorian-era frock coat over a vest, topped off by a black ascot? She squinted and noticed the rest of his outfit was more structured than the jeans or jorts she was used to seeing. Charcoal pants tapered over black Victorian lace-up boots. And yep, that totally was a frock coat. Autumn knew her Regency and Victorian English era clothing exceedingly well thanks to the steamy historical romances she adored.

What in the world? This guy was dressed for the wrong century *and* geographical location. Besides, he was definitely too pretty to be in Covey Crossing, or well, anywhere for that matter, Hollywood included. He looked ethereal and sophisticated. He even walked with an air of royalty, shoulders back and not slouched like Autumn. When he froze under the spotlight of one of the lamps, the sudden movement looked like a tremor went through his body.

Autumn held her breath, her hand flying to her chest as she hid in the shadows, coffee gripped tightly as if that would make her disappear. His head turned slowly, his eyes zeroing in on her even in the darkness. His stare felt like the barest hint of a caress, the backs of fingertips sweeping across her cheekbones. But there was no way...unless... She shook her head. *Forever After*, the reality show she'd signed up to be a contestant on was filming there, and she was due on set tomorrow. Could she be catching her first glimpse of the star?

Forever After was a dating show with a twist. Instead of having the usual warm-blooded bachelor, this one planned to feature a vampire, and the vampire they picked was rumored to be gorgeous —*But aren't they all?*—and she knew for a fact that he was English, a duke to be exact. There were no photos of him online that she could find. She had to guess it was since he wasn't as popular as most of the other vampires in the world. The majority were either rock stars, or actors, or were simply treated as such. So, of course, Autumn couldn't be sure it was him but either way, this guy was exceedingly striking—even with the artificial lights upon him. Those rarely did any favors for anyone.

Before she had a chance to categorize his features, he disappeared. Poof. Not a trace to be found or heard.

Her breath expelled in a loud whoosh, and she blinked furiously. Autumn's heart thudded wildly, her blood throbbing through it. Of course, her first reaction was to get the hell out of there because, well, it was a *vampire*. Despite how common they were in the world now, they weren't common to her, and they were predators for crying out loud. Yet...she felt another instinct pulsing beneath that need to disappear, this one baser, primal even. Lust licked at her veins as she recalled a face cut from the finest marble. Conflict twisted and vined its way through her—to leave or to stay? Pretty faces could mask a lot of ugliness. Even so, a tug tightened her chest, an invisible tether that beckoned her closer almost as if she'd been held in thrall although she was pretty sure she hadn't. The latest research proved that vampires couldn't do that anyway. Regardless, she couldn't get the image of those burning eyes out of her mind. She had never seen anything so intense.

She hoisted her tote higher on her shoulder, multiple volumes within jostling around, her coffee gripped slightly tighter as she headed toward her car. Not much farther. Still, she couldn't shake the feeling of disappointment, of missing out. It lingered about like stale perfume, putrid and forlorn. If the man was *the* Oliver Gray, the very vampire who's heart she would be trying to win on the show, then she'd see him again in mere hours. But still. This felt important. And so few very things in her life had ever felt that way.

Heaving a sigh, she picked up the pace, the worn soles of her cheap ballet flats slapping against the pavement. Just as she neared her car, a blur caused her to stumble as it whizzed past. It stopped just far enough away to not be scary, but still close enough that she could spill her coffee all over the thing, which she did. It materialized into the gorgeous man she'd seen across the street. He currently wore the whipped cream and caramel from her coffee all over his coat and pants.

Damn it—the best part.

Her bag had fallen from her shoulder, books splayed all across the concrete. She bit back a curse, trying her hardest not to cuss like a sailor, knowing she should probably just let it go. Her mother, God rest her soul, once told her that if Autumn could have a motto, the one most appropriate would be "Do no harm, take no shit."

But as she watched the vampire in front of her take stock of his ruined clothes, and then cut to the mess of books, she found that she could *not* just let it go. After all, she'd dreamed of that coffee *all* day, especially when her feet hurt from standing, especially when she had to listen to a patron spoil a book she'd been anxiously waiting to read, and especially when she saw the slight smile on the freaking vampire's lips.

"What is your problem? Do you get off on scaring women in the dark because let me tell ya, you picked the wrong one today." Normally she was meek in front of others, despite that not being her true nature, but something about this guy made her unable to hold back.

Mr. Gorgeous Vampire's lips curved the slightest fraction as his attention moved from his coffee-stained clothing to her face. "Is that so?" A deep rumbling English accent graced the air causing Autumn to pause momentarily.

Everyone had a weakness. Superman and his Kryptonite, Elizabeth Bennet and her ability to jump to conclusions, and Autumn? Well, hers was an English accent on a handsome man. It was made a little worse because he was totally decked out in Victorian clothing that made her heart flutter, but that era wasn't her favorite. No, she needed a man in Regency era clothing, walking across a foggy field, morning coat just a flapping, chest hair on display, eyes hooded with determination and love, but this was...well, it was still thrilling. Autumn could do with some thrilling, which was why she signed up for the show in the first place.

"Uh-uh, don't smirk at me, sir. You're not Damon Salvatore with piercing blue eyes." Okay, yes, he had the piercing eyes, which up close were a sight to behold, but she couldn't let him know that.

"I just...here, let me help you," thicker English accent goodness commenced as he bent down, scooping her books up quicker than she ever could. He didn't hand them back right away. Instead, he scrutinized each text, a little furrow popping between his brow.

While he chose to be nosy, Autumn had an opportunity to further study his otherworldly beauty. She'd heard vampires were beautiful and had an air about them that enticed humans, part of the predator and prey thing, but she'd never seen one in person. Her pulse spiked, and she thought to just leave the books behind and run, but he *had* to be the bachelor on *Forever After*. He wouldn't just...eat her the night before the show? *Right*? *Right. Ha*. She'd like to see him try. She'd kick him in the balls. Tethered by that thought, she stood tall, daring him to mess with her. And while doing so, she decided, hell, might as well outright ogle him.

Of course, his face boasted a sharp jaw. It was the sort of definition that she imagined would twitch and pop when he talked, or when he found himself in deep thought or angry. Sulky, full lips rested in a pout. Perfectly shaped, thick brows curtained luminous blue eyes flecked with silver, set above his aquiline nose. Light scruff dotted the angles of his face, and his side swept honey brown hair minus a few rebel curls, tapered down the back with short sides.

"I enjoy reading romance novels as well," the vampire finally spoke, clearing his throat and then holding one book up in the air. "But I will say that I'm not a fan of this one in particular."

Autumn's stomach kicked over itself at his admission because she adored the genre. With a steadying breath, she squinted in the dark to make out the cover—*Pride and Prejudice*. *Oh*. Oh, that was her favorite novel of all time.

"You're not a fan of Jane Austen?" Her words were a growl.

The vampire shook his head. "Not particularly."

Autumn stepped forward and snatched the book from his hand. "Then, don't touch it. Don't sully it with that kind of talk." She cradled it to her chest like a baby, her hands petting the well-worn cover. She deposited it into her tote, tugging the rest of the books from his long-fingered hands.

"And why are you here anyway, stalking me? What, are you going to drink my blood?"

His eyes flashed, his jaw popped at those words, and she shrunk back a step. Too much? Most definitely. Best not taunt a vampire, especially seeing as how humans were walking snack packs.

"No. I was curious as to why they were so hellbent on you. I needed to see for myself and I'm still unsure." He cast her another glance as he canted his head. "Be careful out here alone. You never know who you'll run into." Without another word, he transformed into a bat, an honest to goodness bat, and flew off into the night.

Autumn's mouth fell open as she watched his silhouette flash across the moon. Bats had been her favorite animal since elementary school. She loved sitting outside at dusk watching them flit about the sky. Now...now she wondered how many of those were vampires.

"*Ass*," she spat. She shook her head, trying to focus on everything else that just transpired. His words were cryptic, but her thoughts snagged on "they." The show? Someone had been hell-bent on her being on there? She had to admit she was shocked that she'd been accepted and figured it was down to the fact that the show was filming in Covey Crossing. Surely they needed a hometown girl to add in some sort of storyline.

A poof startled her, feet knocking into the books she knelt to gather. Oliver materialized before her, human—or vampire, rather—once again. "Did you call me an ass?" Disbelief engraved deep into his lovely features.

Autumn's eyes widened at his sudden reappearance, but she soon found her backbone. She straightened from the haphazard book pile, popping her free hand on her hip. "I did. And what of it?"

"That was rude."

"And you weren't? You were kind of an asshole there, mister. Making it sound like I'm not good enough."

And maybe that was the insecurity she battled with because as soon as the words came out she felt them curl up inside her chest like cat ready to nap on a rainy day.

Oliver placed his hand over his heart, looking genuinely offended. "I said nothing of the sort. I only meant I'm unsure because you don't seem like the typical person to do a reality show."

Autumn cocked a brow. "What do you mean by that?" She sneered as she stalked closer, the tips of their shoes touching.

The vampire's eyes glittered, his lips forming a smirk. "You know, cheery? Eager?" He shrugged.

"Oh, I can be cheery." Her tone was harsh, each word bitten off between her teeth like jerky.

A snort fell from Oliver's lips. "Indeed. I can see that."

The audacity of this guy. Autumn's nose flared, as she wondered how she was going to get through filming with him before staking him. *Kidding, sort of*. He wanted cheery and eager? She fought down a snicker. Her hands came to the sides of her face, her eyes wide and doe-like as she fluttered her lashes. "Oh my stars, you handsome thing, you're a vampire? Maybe you can suck my blood, and later I can sleep in your coffin." She pitched her voice ridiculously high and silly, her southern twang a little overstated, but she sounded cheery, that was for damn sure.

Oliver stared at her as if she'd sprouted a second head, but she didn't care. She harrumphed and set to picking up her books again, shoving them in her bag.

"You think me handsome?" That English accent was lilting and melodious. Autumn cursed her years of obsessively watching BBC period pieces.

She rolled her eyes. "Don't tell me you *don't* know. That you don't look in the mirror." A pause and then she went in for the kill. "Oh wait. You can't. Now if you'll excuse me. I have things to do."

Autumn couldn't quite put her finger on it, but something about the vampire rankled her, bringing out her snarky side. She was never this sassy with people she barely knew. Guilt threatened to seep into her pores, but she refused to allow that. *What's done is done and all that.*

Oliver reared back as if he'd been struck, his eyes wide. The silver flecks in them had multiplied. And were those the tips of his fangs that she saw peeking out from his sulky lips? He sniffed, ego clearly hit. "Many women were rather excited for the chance. Just because you were their pick doesn't mean you won't go home on the first day." He turned from her dramatically. "Good day madam!" and with a flick of his coat, he was off again flying across the inky sky.

Now she knew that Oliver Gray was as gorgeous as he was arrogant, and she hated him instantly. Paper crinkled beneath her foot —it must've fallen out of her tote. It was the ad for *Forever After*, the one she carried around to remind herself she was capable of change, of sluggishly crawling outside the box that had become the four walls of her life. Her father, Henry, had been the one to suggest it, which was a wild ride itself. He'd come over to her house, jumped out of his pickup truck, and rushed up to her with the ad haphazardly cut out of the Covey Crossing Journal, wielding the thing like a proud kid giving their parent their best artwork for the fridge.

Her strong father with his gray hair and salt and pepper beard, who came only to her shoulder, had been excited, his chest all puffed out. He'd thought this opportunity was perfect for her—his exact words had been "it says here he's a duke, there are moors, and he's romantic and broody. You love romantic and broody!" Remembering the moment now made her chest ache. Ever since her mother's death during her sophomore year of high school, she worried about him constantly.

Autumn had agreed to the show that very day, sending in her casting tape and references. She had been more than surprised to get a callback, and then absolutely astounded when she learned she'd made it to the final fifteen women who would have the chance to melt Oliver Gray's 'dark heart' as they'd dramatically put it.

And now here she was feeling like she'd rather ram a stake through it. But she'd promised her father she'd do this and better yet, she'd made a promise to herself that she'd step outside her comfort zone. This was the opportunity she so desperately needed. Of course, the money from the show would be nice, but she wasn't in dire straits to the point where she needed to stay on the show for that reason alone.

She flexed caramel covered fingers, her other hand fishing out hand sanitizer from her bag. That was fine. She'd go on the show, and she'd be sure to make Oliver Gray's existence living hell.

Don't stop now. Keep reading f Mystic Owl books with your copy of FOREVER AFTER by Ashley R. King.

And don't miss THE AGENT AND THE OUTLAW, book two of the *Les Dames Dangereuses* series, by Lily Riley, coming soon!

Don't miss THE AGENT AND THE OUTLAW, book two of the *Les Dames Dangereuses* series, coming soon, and find more from Lily Riley at www.authorlilyriley.com

Until then, find more Mystic Owl books with FOREVER AFTER by Ashley R. King.

On the Vampire Reality Show, Forever After, unexpected love isn't the only plot twist.

Autumn Reid is in a rut. At nearly thirty, she hasn't ventured outside her sleepy Georgia town, Covey Crossing. Spotting an ad for a new dating show, Forever After, she jumps on the chance. It's a dating show with a twist—a vampire bachelor. Sure, the winner gets either cash or immortality, but Autumn doesn't expect to make it that far. She just needs a shakeup in her dull life. What she doesn't expect is the infuriatingly handsome vampire duke.

Impoverished duke Oliver Gray desperately needs money to save his estate. When he's offered the bachelor spot on Forever After, he has no choice but to accept. But there's a catch—he must wear Victorian clothing and pretend to have been hibernating for the last one hundred years. Fine. He can pretend to be clueless and don a top hat. What he truly struggles to figure out is the alluring human with a smart mouth. He can't seem to send her home, not when something deep inside insists she may be his one true mate.

But a love-hate relationships is the least of Autumn and Oliver's problems. Contestants are being murdered one by one, and a vampire appears to be to blame. But the show must go on, and the director is convinced a relocation to their finale in England will solve all their problems. But Oliver and Autumn's dreams of forever after may be cut short when the killer follows them across the pond and decides Autumn is next.

Please sign up for the City Owl Press newsletter for chances to win special subscriber-only contests and giveaways as well as receiving information on upcoming releases and special excerpts.

All reviews are **welcome** and **appreciated.** Please consider leaving one on your favorite social media and book buying sites.

Escape Your World. Get Lost in Ours! City Owl Press at www.cityowlpress.com.

ACKNOWLEDGMENTS

As women, we're often taught to be quiet, not to take up space, and minimize ourselves and our accomplishments. So, before I get into all the incredible people who helped me make this happen, I want to take a moment to acknowledge my own effort.

I did it.

That being said, I would not have been able to do it without a team of family and friends supporting me, cheering me on, giving me thoughtful feedback, and lifting me up when I felt low.

This book is for all of you.

Finn, for giving me the kind of love to write about. Zoe, for just existing. Michelle, who has championed my stories from the beginning. Dad, who is proud of me no matter what. Cassie, the best brainstormer and cheerleader. Alisa, who would love me even if the book was bad. Brian, for fearlessly and thoughtfully editing my precious smut. Melissa, for such wonderful notes on my early, ugly drafts. Sarah, my favorite romance author, whose meticulous feedback and encouragement gave me the confidence to keep going. Heather, Tina, Yelena, and the rockstars at Mystic Owl and City Owl Press, for taking a chance on a debut author and spending your time and energy polishing my words to their final sparkling form. Last but certainly not least, for my friends and family members who have shown me love while I've been on this wild ride, thank you.

Thank you.

ABOUT THE AUTHOR

LILY RILEY is a romance novelist currently focused on historical paranormal books that feature a little bit of cheek and a lot of steam. *The Assassin and the Libertine* is the first of what will surely be several books. When Lily isn't writing about dreamy supernatural beings in 18th century France, she enjoys sipping wine, eating cake, and dancing naked by the light of the full moon.

Photo by Kara Brodgesell

www.authorlilyriley.com

facebook.com/authorlilyriley
twitter.com/authorlilyriley
instagram.com/authorlilyriley

ABOUT THE PUBLISHER

City Owl Press is a cutting edge indie publishing company, bringing the world of romance and speculative fiction to discerning readers.

Escape Your World. Get Lost in Ours!

www.cityowlpress.com

facebook.com/YourCityOwlPress
twitter.com/cityowlpress
instagram.com/cityowlbooks
pinterest.com/cityowlpress

Made in the USA
Coppell, TX
14 October 2021

64054240R00142